ALL THAT MATTERS

Denise Robins

CHIVERS
THORNDIKE

This Large Print book is published by BBC Audiobooks Ltd, Bath, England and by Thorndike Press®, Waterville, Maine, USA.

Published in 2005 in the U.K. by arrangement with the Author's Estate.

Published in 2005 in the U.S. by arrangement with Claire Lorrimer.

U.K. Hardcover   ISBN 1–4056–3340–9 (Chivers Large Print)
U.K. Softcover   ISBN 1–4056–3341–7 (Camden Large Print)
U.S. Softcover   ISBN 0–7862–7572–3 (Buckinghams)

The text of this Large Print edition is unabridged.
Other aspects of the book may vary from the original edition.

Set in 16 pt. New Times Roman.

Printed in Great Britain on acid-free paper.

British Library Cataloguing in Publication Data available

Library of Congress Cataloging-in-Publication Data

Robins, Denise, 1897–
    All that matters / by Denise Robins.
      p.   cm.
    ISBN 0–7862–7572–3 (lg. print : sc : alk. paper)
    1. Physicians—Fiction. 2. Rich people—Fiction. 3. Social classes—Fiction. 4. Large type books. I. Title.
    PR6035.O554A79 2005
    823'.912—dc22   2005002607

Dedication for:

Dr. and Mrs. PHILIP HOPKINS

CHAPTER ONE

It was the big night of the year at St. Martha's Hospital—the night of the annual dance.

Glynis had attended three so far in her young life, and had thoroughly enjoyed them. Tonight's dance she did not enjoy—she felt too unsettled and worried.

While she was dancing with the grey-haired lung specialist, Popham Gray, he said:

'You look extremely pretty tonight, my dear, if a man old enough to be your grandfather may say so, but depressed. What's wrong?'

Her reply had been the classic one when a girl didn't want a man to think she was thinking about a man.

'Nothing.'

To cover her confusion and an innate shyness which was painfully acute and almost ineradicable, she then tried to add the explanation that she was just a bit 'tired'. Then he laughed and said:

'Steve working you too hard, eh?'

That had reduced her to silence. She always *felt* silent at the thought of her employer. The famous, the wonderful, the handsome and wholly successful Steven Grant-Tally, M.D., F.R.C.S. Glynis was his receptionist and personal secretary.

She thought, as she stood alone by the

palms behind which a hired band was playing, that the fact that all women 'fell' so easily for Steve was frightening. Instead of making him seem more attractive, which was, perhaps, the normal reaction, it scared her. And having closely worked with him now for twelve months—getting to know him so well she was even more frightened of falling in love with him.

There was little guile in Glynis. Hers was a frank and simple character with only one complexity—that queer alarm which very clever successful people aroused in her. While she admired them from afar, she doubted their sincerity—their ability to live as ordinary people. And, above all, Glynis, herself, believed in ordinary people, and the simple lives they led. Immense glamour was in her opinion something to be seen in a film or be read about in a book but to be avoided in everyday existence.

Yet the goddess Glamour held a stubborn halo over her head. She had very real beauty. And it was a natural beauty that made men draw in their breath and women long to possess that exquisite skin, that slim supple figure, those eyes that were more green than hazel under the longest of sweeping lashes. Her close-cut hair had the burnt gold colour of sun on corn. Despite the 'gamine' cut, it waved thickly, and one lock had a habit of falling charmingly across her brow. She kept pushing it back with slim nervous fingers.

She saw a tall, red-headed young man striding across the dance floor in her direction and made a hasty exit. She was very fond of Robin Gellow. He was a house doctor here. He had fallen very considerably in love with Glynis when she first came to St. Martha's as a probationer three years ago. He seemed to offer what she needed in a man. Nice looks and common sense. Robin was steady-going as a rock. Why then hadn't she fallen in love with *him*? There was only one answer: *that he wasn't her man.* Life was a real enigma, madly irritating, and love was very illogical, Glynis soliloquized, as she rather heartlessly avoided Robin.

In the refreshment room she found her employer munching a sandwich, holding a mug of his favourite lager in one hand. He was talking to a stout lady with grey hair, wearing magnificent diamonds. Glynis recognized her as Lady Cookson-Reece, one of the wealthiest of Steve's private patients who had first come under his wing when brought to St. Martha's after a car accident. Since then she had patronized the hospital, endowed beds and treated them royally.

But the very sight of Steve with the fabulous old Countess (American-born and left with a fortune by a Chicago pork-canning father) depressed Glynis. Just another facet of Steve's character, she thought; the way he pandered to the rich and manoeuvred himself into the homes and hearts of his other well-to-do patients. His egotism. His superb belief in himself and that what he did was always right. His ambition to go up—up, up the ladder of fame. It seemed to suit him. He looked ridiculously young and happy for so brilliant a surgeon.

He had performed some of the most wonderful operations seen in St. Martha's since his uncle's time. The senior men here all said that young Steve Grant-Tally was 'Sir Campion all over again'.

And he was so devastatingly handsome—she had to admit it as she looked at him now. He had seen her and beckoned to her before she could turn and fly again.

Tall and debonair in his well-cut tails. A carnation in his buttonhole. Collar stiffly white against a brown skin—Steve had just come back from a fortnight's holiday in the Bahamas. (Spent in the villa of a rich American, full of gratitude because his small daughter had recently benefited from Steve's skilled surgery. Her hearing, endangered by serious mastoid trouble, had been saved.) Oh, Steve was strong-looking and fascinating, as well as clever, Glynis thought. Who should know better than she what vigour he put into his work; his tireless energy, his enthusiasm for his profession, was one of the nicest things about him. But she did wish he would concentrate more on the poor. The rich man's specialist; the handsome, luxurious Weymouth Street consulting rooms appealed less to Glynis than that other side to his life. There were only occasional days spent here when he worked without pay. His *charity* work, as she called it. Steve was one of the smart and lucky ones. He didn't need, like most young, rising doctors, to make money. He already had it. Sir Campion had bequeathed a fortune to him— cunningly made over most of it to his nephew before the death duties sucked the Grant-Tally estate quite dry. That was what maddened Glynis. Steve had everything. She was terrified of his glittering triumphs and the way things fell into his lap. It wasn't, of course, fair to hold it against him. Especially as he was such a hard worker. But somehow it seemed an insuperable barrier between him and the young girl with her quiet backwater nature and her sincere love of the 'under-dog'. Steven was the reverse of all her ideals. And yet . . . *he was her ideal.* Could any-thing be more maddening and more complicated? she asked herself tonight as she walked unwillingly towards him and Lady Cookson-Reece.

'You two young things should dance,' said her ladyship in her gushing, throaty voice. 'Go along, dear boy,' and she tapped Mr. Grant-Tally on the arm, smiled benevolently at Glynis, and having just spoken to her, thought, *'Such beauty, but no brains, I'm sure,'* and

5

sailed majestically on.

'What about it—most estimable steno-grapher? Will you trip the light fantastic with me?' Steven grinned at the girl who had become his right hand. It always seemed to him incredible that this 'child'—a mere twenty-four, and so pretty—should be dependable. She was such a relief after Miss Packing, who, although a loss to him when she left, had *looked* so unattractive. A busy man needed the joy of such beauty and grace as little Miss Glynis Thorne shed around her. He had marked her out when she was a 'pro' here, as being the best-looker of the nurses. She had a small but valuable amount of nursing experience to add to the qualities of a good secretary.

'Enjoyed your evening? You're looking depressed,' he said, as Pop had done. 'What's wrong?'

She made the same negative reply rather crossly.

'Nothing . . .'

The band struck up a samba. Steven, who danced well and lightly, quickened his pace.

He had what Glynis called his 'schoolboy' look which belied the keen mature brain behind it.

'Can you manage it, Goldilocks?'

She set her teeth and strove to conquer that furious blush that would stain cheeks and throat.

'You know that I hate being called Goldilocks.'

He laughed. Glynis amused him when she showed a spurt of temper. She was as a rule so cool and self-contained.

Dancing with her in the gay laughing crowd of nurses, doctors and their friends on the cold, frosty Boxing Night, Steven, not for the first time, wondered what lay behind the mask. He certainly had seen her eyes when she was dealing with a patient who suffered; watched them grow darker, soft with compassion under the black silk fringe of lashes. Sometimes, when he saw the rich corn-coloured head bent over writing-pad or typewriter, he had a crazy wish to stroke it. And lately, busy though he was, he had found his thoughts being distracted and his senses swimming with sudden violent longing to pull the lovely girl into his arms and kiss her awake. *Make* her respond to his passion. *Break* through the cool barrier, the stiff shyness, until she melted into his embrace.

Strange feelings, not common to Steve Grant-Tally. So far in his thirty years he had only known one love. The 'calf love' of a medical student for a nursing sister ten years his senior. He had thought his life ended when she, wiser than he, and self-sacrificing (for she had loved him), sent him about his business and quietly resigned from the hospital in which they both worked. But he had soon found how

7

right she was, and, turning from the love of women, engrossed himself in the passion for his work. Soon it had become his life. That and the ambition to get to the top of the tree as his uncle had done.

Before he was twenty-four Steven had done his National Service in the Navy, and returned to St. Martha's as Registrar. Then he got his M.B. and B.S. and later his Master of Surgery. By the time he had added F.R.C.S. to his name he had inherited his uncle's money, and stepped into his place as an ear, nose and throat specialist. So far he had succeeded. He had no time for marriage; although the one member of his family still left—his elder sister, Kitty, now Lady Barley, who had a baronet for a husband, and a beautiful Georgian house in Thurloe Street—laid innumerable traps for him. But Steven had eluded the débutantes she produced—the smart, good-looking Society types like Kitty herself, who would gladly have become the wife of Mr. Grant-Tally of Weymouth Street.

Steve did not want to be tied down—yet. He knew perfectly well the day must come (and soon) when he would want a wife and have to slow up a bit. Also that he was working and playing at too feverish a pace to last—his superb health, which was a legacy of youth, could not last either.

He shrank from the matrimonial tie. Yet this very moment he was remembering how a week before Christmas he kissed Glynis under the mistletoe which a romantically-minded housekeeper had hung in the hall at Weymouth Street. He had kissed her lightly on the corner of the mouth—that wide, sweet, serious young mouth which she rouged to a pale rose, matching the almond-shaped nails. Glynis had charming, well-kept hands. He saw her face grow scarlet, and her eyes widen as though with fear. She broke away and he laughed it off by saying, 'Silly, nice little thing.' But he wanted, all the rest of that day, to snatch her back, to make her give him kiss for kiss. Not mistletoe kisses. Deep, passionate, significant ones as between a man and woman who are in love.

And suddenly Grant-Tally knew that he had fallen irrationally in love with his secretary-receptionist.

A young medical student threaded his way through the dancing couples and waylaid the famous Mr. Grant-Tally.

'This is for you, sir, urgent, and I believe there's a car waiting for the answer.'

Steven drew Glynis to one side. He was a little glad this interruption had come. He had been experiencing an unusual insanity and was half afraid he might lose his head and kiss Glyn's incredibly lovely little face right there in front of all St. Martha's Hospital.

When he had read the note his expression changed. Glyn watching knew what it meant.

The swift reversal from 'playboy' to surgeon. Frowning, he said:

'I must go at once.'

'Emergency op, sir?' asked the student sympathetically.

'Not exactly,' said Steven, and turned to Glynis.

Her heart was beating somewhat quickly. She, too, had been enjoying that dance with every fibre of her being. And if he left the dance—well, there was no denying that for her the dance would be over. That was the maddening part of it.

He said:

'I'd rather like you to come with me, Glyn. I'll explain as we go.'

'Work?' she said.

'Work,' he said grimly.

Without hesitation she followed him, found the camel-hair coat and scarf to put over the demure black evening dress which her mother had given her for Christmas—the only gay note was struck by the wide rose-pink sash swathed around the hips trailing at one side. Then she followed her employer out of the hospital and into the frosty starlit night where a big black and silver Rolls-Royce waited for them!

CHAPTER TWO

A chauffeur drove them swiftly away from the hospital down the Whitechapel Road towards the West End. Glynis, glancing at her wristwatch, saw that it was nearly midnight. She glanced at Steven. He wore a thick light-grey coat, collar turned up, and a soft hat on the side of his head. He was reading the letter again, and she did not speak for he was obviously immersed and very serious. She wondered what it was all about. Waiting with her usual discretion for him to make the first move, she thought of the sequence of events which had led up to her becoming this man's personal secretary.

Glynis' father was a dentist. He had been operated on in St. Martha's twice and his life saved. That was how Glynis had first come to know the place and love it. She had always wanted to be a nurse. It used to be a joke in the family even when Glynis was small, because she went around with tiny bits of sticking plaster and bandage in her pockets and in her small grave way attended to the hurts (either real or imaginary) of animals, grown-ups, and other children.

Her father used to ruffle the thick shining hair and laugh. 'Little Nurse Glyn,' he would call her.

He had quite liked the idea of seeing his only daughter join the famous teaching hospital. But her mother, more ambitious, had hoped that her beautiful Glyn would marry a rich man and lead an exciting life. That is the ambition of most mothers. And Mrs. Thorne had lived and worked through two world wars and always had to struggle, as the wife of a dentist in Barnet. She had wanted something more for her child who had been born with such superlative good looks. Glynis, herself, knew that Mummy had been bitterly disappointed because there was no ambition of that kind within her to lift that dazzling loveliness of hers to the high peaks of social success.

Mrs. Thorne complained:

'I can't understand it—Glyn's so painfully shy and retiring. She seems to prefer a domestic life. It just isn't *natural.*'

But to Mr. Thorne it was perfectly natural. Glyn had inherited those qualities from him. He had always been a shy, retiring man, devoted to his home.

Glynis' first year as a probationer at St. Martha's had been a mixture of great happiness and bitter disappointment. All her innate love of nursing and medicine was there to form a buffer between her and the grim spectres of pain and death which must necessarily haunt a hospital and make life difficult to bear at times. But she did not even mind the most painful and detestable forms of nursing. She was immensely popular in the wards, and with her fellow nurses. Nobody was jealous of Glyn because she looked so angelic in her little white Dora cap, and with the pale blue cotton frock rolled up above her elbows and her flushed serious face.

Then the blow had fallen. A slight weakness of back which Glyn had always had as a child began to show itself more seriously. She struggled on for a few months until pain and discomfort conquered even her passionate longing to qualify as a nurse. The Matron had had finally to tell her that she must give up nursing as a career. The heavy lifting and carrying were just things that Glyn couldn't take on.

'A little rest and care and you'll soon be normal again, but much as I want to keep you on my staff, my dear, there isn't one single doctor that you've seen who does not tell you that you are *not* physically cut out to *be* a nurse.'

So, in tears, Glynis had left St. Martha's and gone home and thought her life was finished. Such devilish irony—all the will in the world, and that stupid weak flesh of hers! But of course it was as Matron had prophesied—she soon recovered health and strength. She could not risk hurting her back again. So she took a course in shorthand and typewriting, and looked for the next best thing to nursing—a

13

job in a doctor's house.

Robin Gellow, who had continued to see her and take her out and never stopped asking her to marry him, was actually the means of her becoming Steven Grant-Tally's receptionist. He had heard Steve saying that his own 'treasure' was leaving and Robin had thought it the job for Glyn.

She hadn't been so sure. She knew Steven, of course. Almost her first evening in the nurses' Common Room she had heard him being discussed. He was the big E.N.T. surgeon consultant here and quite an amazing person, because he was barely thirty-one. Brilliant Steven who had raced away with the honours when he qualified at St. Martha's at the age of twenty-one.

Glyn had listened to her colleagues 'raving' about Steve and as a result was immediately biased against him. But when she had seen him for the first time coming down the ward in his white gown, examining patients with a little crowd of students reverently following, and listening, she had to admit that most of the nice things she had heard about him were justified. But when he glanced at her, smiled and said, *'You're new here, aren't you, Nurse?'* her face had gone crimson. She had remained tongue-tied. But at a hospital dinner later on he had managed to draw her into a discussion, and he had told her that he had found her shyness most intriguing. It was so rare, he said.

14

After that—well, she continued to admire him from afar and to blush when she met or talked to him.

Eighteen months later she took Robin's advice and applied for that job.

Now a whole year had passed since she had been accepted by Steve as his secretary-receptionist in the big beautiful house in Weymouth Street where he had his consulting rooms.

Suddenly she was jolted out of these reminiscences.

Steve said:

'I feel rather a cad taking you away from the party. I had better explain. It is rather a difficult case.'

'I don't mind leaving the party if I can help,' she said.

He told her that the car belonged to Lord Marradine.

Her eyes widened.

'Not the peer who married a film star?'

'That's it.'

Glynis puckered her brows. She seemed to remember that she had read something in the paper lately about the wealthy young peer who had married a beautiful Swedish film actress. They had been living in Washington, where Marradine held a diplomatic job. Both had returned with severe sinus trouble and both became Grant-Tally's patients.

More of Steve's rich paying propositions,

Glynis thought to herself.

Why, she asked herself, had she such a queer aversion to money and titles? Certainly it was not jealousy. But she was *afraid* of riches.

Steve was telling her about tonight. Anna—Lady Marradine—had enchanted the family by producing a fine son and heir. Young Aubrey, Steve said, must be about twelve months old now. It appeared he had been ailing for a week or two, and only tonight developed a serious ear condition.

This note was from Lord Marradine imploring Steve to go to them at once. A sudden rise in the baby's temperature had startled them and was made all the more catastrophic by the fact that the Nannie was away for a day or two, and the doctor in charge of the case was also out of town.

Glynis nodded her head. So that was it! A child's life was at stake. Well, obviously Steve would answer that call for rich or poor.

He went on to tell her that he had asked *her* to accompany him because Marradine's note said that his wife was in a 'state' and unable to cope with the situation.

'I'll see to the little boy—and you can look after Mamma,' Steve said with a dry laugh.

'I'll do what I can.'

'You generally do, but I find the way you belittle yourself very aggravating at times,' he said suddenly. His gaze was on her. He saw her

16

cheeks colour.

'Well, that's better than thinking that I am the world's wonder,' she muttered.

He put his tongue in his cheek.

'Is that a dig at me? Do you know at times I think you've got something up against me. What is it?'

'Nothing.' (She seemed to be saying that nebulous word all evening.)

'Come clean,' he said grimly.

She took a breath and suddenly grew bold— braver than usual, by virtue of the fact that she felt so strongly about Steve.

'I wish you didn't waste so much time on rich patients,' she broke out. 'You're so brilliant at your work—I'm sure you could do tremendous things, in research—or—or . . . Oh, I don't know, I suppose I just *hate* specialists as a whole. I'm silly and bigoted and *awful*, daring to criticize *you*,' she added with a thumping heart.

Then Steven said: '

Not at all. What you have just said interests me enormously. I don't think it's quite true that I waste all my talents on the idle rich. There aren't so many rich people, you know. The Chancellor of the Exchequer sees to that. And I do, you know, give quite a lot of time to unpaid jobs. However, we won't discuss my work. How I choose to behave as a surgeon is my own business. But how I appear to you *as a man* is another. I don't want to be quite as

17

lousy a fellow as you infer.'

The green, silky-lashed eyes she turned to him now were soft and full of unusual emotion.

'Oh, Steve, you're *not* lousy—I didn't mean . . . Oh, I'm just funny—I don't really understand myself,' she trailed off lamely.

'No, and I don't understand you either,' he said, 'except that you seem to be eaten up by a lot of hopeless ideals and illusions about life.'

'They're not hopeless. And if I have illusions, I want to keep them,' she began to protest.

'You're a perfectionist,' he broke in. 'So am I as far as my job is concerned. And perhaps I don't give enough thought to ideals. You're an amazing little creature, Glyn. Beautiful as an angel—and . . .'

'And dumb,' she finished for him drily, 'that's Glynis Thorne.'

'Don't be absurd. You're shy. But I may say you've broken through it tonight, and almost for the first time I feel I really know you.'

'Don't let's go on talking about me.'

But now a stubborn desire to probe further into her mind and to be reinstated in her good graces seized Steven Grant-Tally. He rapped out a question:

'What do you ask of life? What do you really *want*? What sort of man *would* you marry?'

'Oh, please, Steve . . .'

'No, answer me, Glynis, I want to know.'

She bit her lip. She was trembling violently. His deep interest in her was so totally unexpected. It seemed neither the time nor the place for the discussion. But bit by bit he dragged the answers from her. And finally he knew. Glynis wanted a quiet life in a backwater with a man she could love with all her heart and who would give his whole life and love to her. English home life, in fact, with a family, he reflected.

'Dear me,' at length he said, 'how divinely simple it sounds, and coming from the lips of one whose face might cause a riot on the screen and who might be the world's pin-up girl—how ironic!'

'But that's just it, I don't want to be a pin-up girl'; she was almost on the verge of tears. 'I don't want fame or fortune or success like you do.'

Suddenly he seized her fingers. He pressed them together between his. She thought: *'How hard and warm and strong his hands are . . .* the hands of one of the cleverest surgeons of the day.'

'Glynis,' said Steven, 'you've worked with me long enough to know that even if I don't share your simple beliefs and ideals, I'm not a bad fellow.'

Such humility coming from Steven Grant-Tally completely shattered her.

'Oh, Steve!' she whispered.

19

There was no thought in his mind then except to get near her and yet nearer—or to endear himself to her—to make her will subservient to his. *To love her.*

The Rolls was purring smoothly through the frosty night. In another moment they would be turning into Park Lane. Suddenly she found herself in his arms. He was kissing her—not lightly as he had done under the mistletoe—but with deep insistent passion. A passion that roused a throbbing response in her. All her defences were down. She was in that split second utterly and completely his—her arms around his neck and her rose-red mouth giving him all the warmth and sweetness that he wanted. Then he lifted his head and said in a hushed voice:

'Dear life, I knew it. I've been in love with you for the last month or two. I've tried not to give myself time to think so. But I can't help myself. I want to marry you. Any objections?'

That was altogether too sudden and alarming for Glynis. She gasped:

'Steve, you must be out of your mind!'

'True enough,' he said and laughed, but it was a laugh that had a happy sound. To her immense astonishment and delight she realized that she had the power to make this great man happy. The idea had a simplicity that appealed to all that was in her. Now he began to say a lot of other things. She was beautiful and good and sweet. Every darned thing any man needed. She was going to make the perfect doctor's wife and he wasn't going to wait long for her, either.

Real 'Grant-Tally' stuff, she told herself, unable to forget his background. The autocrat. The spoiled successful hero of the medical world. Her senses were whirling. That long kiss that they had exchanged had left her weak and shaken. But she could still keep her head. Thank goodness she had her early hospital training to help her, she thought. It had taught her control—and caution. She began to argue with him.

How could she *ever* make a fitting wife for such a man? Oh, what did her lovely face and figure *matter*? She wasn't the right *person* for him. He needed a sparkling companion—a social light—a perfect hostess to help entertain for him. Above all a woman who would enjoy the success that she would share with such a man as Steven.

'You know I couldn't cope,' she wailed. 'I've just been telling you, Steve. I couldn't stand the *pace*. It would frighten me. Every time I speak to Lady Barley—your sister, I mean— I'm terrified of doing or saying the wrong thing. All these women in your and her set are so poised, so clever; they talk about the South of France, and these dress shows and first nights, and things I've never been able to afford to do. I don't speak their *language*. I should never, never marry *you*.'

But he pulled her back into his arms and looked down into the wonderful green eyes that were no longer the colour of ice-water, but dark with passionate feeling.

He was very much in love with her in a way that he had not loved a woman since he was a boy.

He said:

'What you've got to tell me is whether you love *me* or not? Or do you despise me because I'm successful and rich and my private patients have titles?' he asked humorously.

'Oh, how can you even *suggest* that I *despise* you?' she cried. 'It's just that your sort of background is so different from the one I'm used to.'

'Well, my dear angel, you must forgive me if I'm not a poor struggling G.P. in the East End, and accept me for what I am,' he said on the same note of good humour. 'I love you. *Do you love me?* Please answer that.'

The answer was torn from her very heart.

'*Yes.* But—'

'Darling,' he broke in triumphantly, 'then there are not to be any "buts". Marry me you must.'

'No—' she began again.

'The debate will continue, my sweet,' he interrupted her. 'We've reached our destination.'

Like one in a dream, she stepped out of the Rolls and followed him into the handsome block of flats where two very unhappy patients waited for Mr. Grant-Tally.

CHAPTER THREE

And that was how it all started—Steven's seemingly ridiculous desire to marry his demure little secretary. But her apprehension concerning the matter persisted.

Glyn said to her mother that next day:

'You see, Mummy, I'm terribly in love with him, which makes matters much harder for me.'

Mrs. Thorne, who had never been as beautiful as her daughter but was still a good-looking woman in her late forties, regarded the girl as she would an extraordinary phenomenon.

'You really are incomprehensible, Glyn. That wonderful man and all that he can offer you, yet you shrink from even getting engaged. Do you understand her, Bertie?' She turned to Glynis' father, who had been listening to the two women talking during the family breakfast this Sunday morning.

'Yes, I think I do, my dear,' he said, 'Glyn doesn't move in Mr. Grant-Tally's world and she doesn't altogether approve of the social life he leads. She doesn't think their marriage would work.'

'Well, she'd *make* it work if she had any sense,' declared Mrs. Thorne, 'and anyway it's not natural for a girl in love to try and get out of marrying a man.'

Glynis looked out of the window at the frost-whitened garden of the little house in Barnet where she had spent most of her life.

'I'm worried, Mummy, not only because I'm afraid Steve might get bored with me as a wife, but because I couldn't stand what I know would be in store for me.'

'And what is that, pray?' asked Sylvia Thorne—coldly, her patience sorely tried by this daughter so different from her pleasure-loving self.

Glynis tried to explain. She *did* love Steve. Despite all the differences of their background and ideal—she loved him. But if she became his wife she would never get that little home she had always wanted and all those children. If she *had* children, Steve was the sort of man who would want her to have a nurse; she would have to leave them and go out to the social functions with him, and give all the parties the wife of a leading specialist would have to give. She wouldn't be able to take her children to some little seaside place for holidays alone with Steve. She knew his tastes. He'd want her to send them to Frinton with Nurse while they flew to the Bermudas, or lay on the beach in Italy or France covered in sun-tan oil and spent the nights at the Casino—as

24

he liked to do. She had set her heart on having a husband who would come home to her every night, and even if they could afford domestic help, they would fix things so that she could do all sorts of little things for him and feel that it was a real *home*; not an elegant hotel. Of course she didn't expect Mummy to sympathize because she adored meeting new people and going places and didn't know what it was to be shy. Besides, Steve would always get called out for some rush job or have to go to some special dinner—or medical conference. He'd never be at home, and she, his wife, would be forced to share him with his friends. They'd lead a whirl of a social life, like Lady Barley. Glynis would *hate* it.

Mr. Thorne listened to this in sympathetic silence. Mrs. Thorne shrugged her shoulders, nonplussed. Then she said:

'So you are throwing up this wonderful chance?'

For a moment Glynis did not answer. She was really very tired. She had slept badly last night—her mind seething with the memory of all the things that had happened. She had remained in a daze while she and Steve were in the Marradines' flat. There they had spent a somewhat chaotic hour. Steve, professional and cool, had introduced her to the Marradines as his nurse assistant, whom he had brought in case she was needed.

Little Aubrey Marradine was in fact

25

seriously ill. His beautiful Swedish mother had broken down completely, partly through sheer terror of losing her son, and partly because she knew nothing about children at all. Lord Marradine was a nice boy but dithering with nerves, and the baby had been crying—a high-pitched wail of pain and fatigue—for practically the whole day. Glynis was detailed to sit beside the bedside of the weeping Anna. Of course the girl's mind immediately leapt to the thousands of small homes where competent, hard-working mothers looked after their own children so well. But Steve showed up in his best light tonight. Glyn was quite edified by the sight of him dealing with the child, by the tenderness with which he handled the poor screaming little patient. It all ended as Glynis expected. The Marradine Rolls took them speeding to the clinic in Harley Street where Steve sent most of his patients. An immediate operation was necessary. But Steve would not let Glynis go.

'Wait for me. I won't be long and I'll drive you back to the hospital. You're staying there tonight, aren't you?' he said.

Later, the grateful Marradines (informed that their son would live and there was no further need to worry) detailed their chauffeur to drive the pair back to St. Martha's. Steve was in a jubilant mood but looked very tired, Glynis thought, and was remorseful because she had said so many hard things to him earlier this evening. Then he tried again to argue her into marrying him.

'You say you love me—give me a chance,' he begged her.

She would not have been human if she had not in the long run given way. And in his arms once more, with all the intoxication of his lips against her mouth, and on her throat, and hearing his husky voice tell her that there would never be anyone else—she told him she would think it over.

She was thrilled and troubled in turn. Could it be true, she wondered, that she was no longer only Mr. Grant-Tally's receptionist, *but the girl he loved and wanted to marry*?

Suddenly she drew in her breath as though she had reached a vital decision.

'I promised I'd ring Steve after lunch,' she said to her parents. 'He had to dash down to his sister's country cottage for a lunch party. They have a lovely place in Bray. He wanted me to go with him but I told him I'd rather stay in my own home today and think things over quietly.'

Mrs. Thorne looked pained. Mr. Thorne nodded.

'Quite right. Don't let 'em rush you into it. I dare say it is all very tempting but much better not to get married unless you're a hundred per cent sure it will be a success.'

Which were precisely the words that Glynis repeated to Steve, himself, on the 'phone an hour later. He agreed; but he was still determined to make her give in.

'I swear you shall have your real home and your domestic life, and anything else you want,' he said with the recklessness of a man who was now head over heels in love, and ready to promise anything.

Glynis, thrilled by the sound of his eager voice and her own longing to see him again, took the plunge.

'All right, Steve, I will marry you.'

'Glyn *darling!*'

'I will, but let's be engaged for a bit and don't ask me to marry you too soon,' she qualified the acceptance. 'Let me see first if I fit in with your family and friends and your whole life—will you?'

'You'll be a huge success and never regret it,' he said with a boyish excitement which made her feel quite unworthy.

She could not begin to adjust herself to this new state of affairs. But her heart beat to the tune of his name. 'Steve! *Steve, my Steve!*' she kept thinking.

When she broke the news of her engagement to her parents her father kissed her and said:

'All happiness, my pet. Mr. Grant-Tally is a fine man and I'm sure things will work out.'

Sylvia Thorne embraced her daughter rapturously.

'It's the most sensible thing you've *ever*

done, you funny girl!' she exclaimed.

Glyn's shining eyes held a look of slight bewilderment.

'Is it?' she said slowly under her breath.

But she stopped wondering when she next saw Steve. Much to her surprise and delight he swept down to the little house in Barnet, driving his own long sleek black Jaguar. The car which so frequently stood outside the house in Weymouth Street, and which all his colleagues recognized as his.

He was as excited as Glynis had ever seen him and she had to believe that he was really in love with her even though she genuinely failed to understand why she had been singled out for such an honour. Now she hushed the voice of doubt and gave herself wholly up to the joys of being Steve's girl. He endeared himself to both her parents by throwing off the cloak of the successful surgeon.

He was delightfully simple; just like an ordinary young man meeting the parents of his girl-friend for the first time. Mrs. Thorne, quite bowled over by his charm, to say nothing of his position, insisted on him remaining to supper.

'Mummy's a superb cook so you won't miss anything if you do,' Glynis encouraged him.

'A boiled egg is good enough for me,' he said.

They all laughed. Mr. Thorne watched the great surgeon with one arm around Glynis, and one possessive hand holding hers. He thought to himself that Steven Grant-Tally was really a very nice fellow. But this being in love was a dangerous thing. Under its influence men and women didn't always show up in their real colours. He could rely on Glynis being true to herself. But how far would the great Steven be prepared to meet her on her level and give her that moderate domestic life she craved, or be tolerant of that incurable love she had of retirement, despite all the lure of her beauty? *How would those two really mix?*

There was no answer to the question now. Time alone would tell, and Mr. Thorne had to confess that Steve certainly drew Glynis out and she was quite radiant before he drove away later that evening.

It was agreed that she should keep on her job until he could find a substitute for her. But after they acknowledged their engagement (which he planned to do next week) it would be too awkward for her to go on being his secretary. That was the first rub for Glyn. She adored her work. Steve had laughed at her when she said so.

'I've never met such a girl; I think it's high time you took a rest and spent a bit more of your time enjoying yourself.'

Somehow that remark frightened her.

Steven couldn't understand that she regarded her work as enjoyment, even though he admitted that he was absorbed by his own.

Which, of course, he was, or he would not be so good at it. But he was a man, and a beautiful young girl, in his opinion, should be allowed more pleasure—and more leisure. Glynis did not have to be as extravagant and as crazy as Anna Marradine, but surely she would like to spend a few weeks looking at clothes, getting together a marvellous trousseau, preparing for a wonderful wedding, he said.

Glyn had not wanted to spoil his obvious delight in her or his prospects for this 'wonderful wedding'. She supposed she really was quite unlike the average girl who would be crazy about the whole idea. But there were other shy retiring girls in the world, she tried to reassure herself, and fled for conference with one of them. Alma Jackson, who was a probationer at St. Martha's, and was Glyn's best friend. She had none of Glyn's beauty, but a similar temperament. Alma was the first person at St. Martha's to learn of Glyn's engagement to Steven.

'I'm absolutely thunderstruck,' the young nurse confessed. 'I didn't think our big surgeon was a marrying man. But of course I quite understand him falling for you.'

'But do you think it *suitable*?' asked Glynis. 'I refuse to be dazzled, Alma. I want to go carefully for his sake more than mine. *I love him*, you see. Mummy doesn't understand it when I say so. She thinks if I was really in love I'd dash into marriage like a mad thing. But it's *because* I love him so much that I'm afraid. I couldn't bear *him* to be disappointed. Do you understand?' And Alma, like Glynis' father, said that she did. But she was less apprehensive about it than her friend.

'Love does marvellous things to you, my dear,' she laughed. 'You know how I've changed since I became engaged to Dickie.' (Dickie was a young regular officer, at present serving in Singapore.)

'Well, I'm certainly going to give it a chance because I adore the ground he walks on,' said Glynis in a low voice. 'Don't tell anybody, Alma, until our engagement's actually announced.'

Alma laughed again.

'Dear old panic-stricken Glynis! I may be a frightened mouse, but you're worse.'

'The frightened mouse' went to her work on Monday morning feeling, indeed, quite panic-stricken. She put on her white overall, buttoning it with trembling fingers. First she sorted the papers on the Big Man's desk, answered one or two telephone calls, made one or two appointments, cancelled another, and all the time kept glancing out of the window watching for the Jaguar.

Down the street at length it rolled, and into the room, in his usual rush, came Steven himself—carrying a case of instruments. To Glyn's immense relief he started off by being entirely professional.

'Has that chloromycetin come in? Good. Is my consultation with Dr. Pinking at eleven o'clock or twelve?—I can't remember. Clean out this case, please, Glynis—it's getting a bit mucky. Dear life! What a day! Muggy and foul. I loathe after Christmas.'

He chattered on, picked up a letter which Glynis had opened and laid before him and muttered:

'So my prognosis was correct about that Scott child. I've never seen such tonsils—and her Mum would keep putting it off.'

Glyn stood mute, watching, wondering if things were any different and if there had ever been a passage of love between her and this man. Then suddenly Steve looked up. His whole face changed. He had very light clear grey eyes, and they changed to a deeper colour. Standing up he swept her into his arms and buried his face against her hair.

'My sweet! My *sweet* little love! I wish the whole world could see Grant-Tally with his secretary now. Such goings-on in the consulting room! You know I'm crazy about you, don't you? I wish I hadn't got to do any work but could just put you in the Jag. and drive you out of town to some lovely, lonely spot.'

She surrendered to his kiss. She was wildly, ecstatically happy and proud. But in another moment the telephone rang again and Steven was back in his chair. There was no more time for personal affairs until just before he had to keep his first appointment. Then he said:

'We're celebrating our engagement tonight, darling, and I want your Mamma—who by the way is a gorgeous cook—to put the announcement in all the papers. Will she?'

'I'll tell her,' said Glynis.

'Kitty suggests throwing an engagement party for us at the Caprice tonight. Would you like that?'

Glynis had never been to the Caprice but she knew about it. One of the chic restaurants where Society and the Stage gathered. She pictured that dinner-party, with Lady Barley as hostess. Everybody so frightfully smart and amusing. Oh, that wasn't what she wanted at all. She wanted a quiet little dinner alone with *him.*

Flushed and doubtful, she told him so. Whereupon Steve laughed, kissed the top of her nose and said she could have whatever she liked.

'If you wish we'll have just a quiet meal at Thurloe Square with Kitty and Paul. I'd like you to get to know them, and I want to show *you* off!'

That seemed to her rather sweet of him. And after all she *must* get to know her future sister-in-law. Sir Paul Barley was rather nice and friendly. He was in the Foreign Office.

Just before Steven rushed away, Glynis touched his arm and asked:

'What did Lady B—I mean Kitty—say when you told her about us?'

'What could she say—or think—except that I'm going to have the most beautiful wife in the world?' said Steven extravagantly, and, seizing his case, hurried out to his waiting car.

In actual fact Lady Barley had expressed quite a lot of other opinions which Steven would not have liked to repeat to Glyn. They had almost fought last night. Kitty had a special girl-friend lined up for her handsome brother. She had told Steve outright that he was a fool to be marrying his secretary.

'You've fallen for that lovely little face and she won't make you a suitable wife at all, and I think you're *mad*! What you need is a wife who will help you in your career.'

To which Steven replied:

'You leave the choice of a wife to *me*, Kits. And when you get to know Glyn you'll see that she's just the one who can help me. But she's painfully shy, and you must be nice and tactful, and not queer my pitch.'

Now Kitty Barley was, herself, quite a clever woman; a year younger than Steven, thin and handsome like him, with his black springing hair and deep-set grey eyes. Her main hobbies were racing and sailing and she had a passion for poker parties. She was a noted leader of fashion. She asked only one thing of the world—that she should be amused. She could be a good friend and an unscrupulous enemy.

Success was the breath of life to her and she wanted to further her brother's career by marrying him to her rich attractive friend, Rhona Chayney. Kitty had often met Glynis Thorne in his consulting rooms, in the capacity of receptionist. She had always thought Glyn's pretty face a danger, but hoped that Steven would be too sensible to fall for it. Of course, in Kitty's opinion, he was quite crazy to want to marry Glyn, and if she could queer *that* particular pitch—she was going to do so!

So Glynis was shy and needed diplomacy, did she? Kitty asked herself grimly. This morning, when Glyn telephoned to suggest the quiet meal *en famille* instead of the party at the Caprice which Lady Barley had planned, her ladyship was furious. If Steven was going to marry the girl—then why not do it with a splash and exploit the wretched girl's good looks? Kitty wasn't going to have this nonsense. She was perfectly charming to Glynis over the telephone. She offered hearty congratulations and said how much they looked forward to seeing her this evening.

'Don't bother to change, wear any little thing. I shall only put on an old rag myself.'

But the moment Glynis had said thank you and good-bye, Kitty Barley marched into her writing room where a visiting secretary was sending out two or three hundred invitations to a cocktail party the Barleys were giving early on in February.

'Ring up every newspaper—morning and evening—and tell them to get busy with reporters and cameras. Say that the great Mr. Grant-Tally, M.D., F.R.C.S., is celebrating his engagement here tonight to a Miss Glynis Thorne, and they might like to take some photographs of them,' she said.

The girl gave a little gasp.

'My word, Lady Barley, won't there be a rush? There's been such a *lot* about Mr. Grant-Tally in the papers since he was flown out to India to operate on the Maharajah of Jed-Pura.'

'Quite so,' said Kitty drily, and thought, 'I reckon when shy little Miss Thorne arrives here, she'll have to face a *battery*.'

CHAPTER FOUR

Lady Barley's secretary carried out her ladyship's orders and found an interested Press. Features Editors were only too willing to send representatives to Lady Barley's beautiful house in Thurloe Street tonight. Her distinguished brother was 'news' at the moment, and, as the secretary had remarked, he had been news since his spectacular flight to Bombay to save the life of a Maharajah.

Having achieved this somewhat malicious object, Kitty Barley salved her conscience by telling herself that whatever she did was for 'poor Steve's sake'. He had become 'poor Steve' in her scheming brain since he had told her he meant to marry Glynis.

Kitty then turned her thoughts to Rhona Chayney . . . Rhona who was so passionately in love with Steve and whom Kitty had set her heart on her brother marrying.

She had a very difficult and unattractive job ahead of her, but she did it, anything rather than that Rhona should hear the news elsewhere or see it in tomorrow's papers, which would be such a shock for her.

She dialled the number of Rhona's fabulous penthouse which overlooked Hyde Park.

Rhona had a low rather husky voice. She was in bed and answered Kitty languidly.

'Aren't I lazy—only just woken up. Good morning, Kitty, my angel.'

'You won't "angel" me when I tell you the horrible news,' said Lady Barley gloomily.

And, indeed, a moment later Rhona's voice came over the wires no longer languid and good-tempered, but feverish and horror-stricken.

'Oh, it can't be true! He *can't* be going to marry somebody else.'

'Yes, and that little secretary of his, too!'

A pause. Then came Rhona's anguished voice with an underlying note of rage.

'You mean his receptionist? Yes—I know. I saw her the other day. She's pretty, but . . . Oh,

Kitty, *Kitty*, I can't *believe* it!'

Lady Barley was not a sentimental woman. She was a matter-of-fact worldly person and in her heart of hearts she always thought Rhona inclined to exaggerate, to dramatize herself. On the other hand this must be a ghastly blow for her. Now Rhona was sobbing. A broken voice said:

'This will *kill* me. You must do something about it. Come and see me—now at once, Kitty!'

It was most inconvenient for Kitty to go round to Rhona's flat at the beginning of a busy morning, but she rang through to her garage and told them to get out her car at once. Under no circumstances was she going to risk losing Rhona as a friend. She was far too valuable. Besides, all was not yet lost just because Steven was about to announce his engagement. Engagements were made to be broken, Kitty told herself grimly.

Rhona Chayney had been Kitty's bridesmaid. Within a month of Kitty's wedding she had married Paul's best man, Noel. He had been a young barrister of singular charm but with no private means. Rhona, however, had just inherited a considerable fortune from her grandfather and was one of England's richest débutantes. She had more than enough.

She had been brought up by doting grandparents and spoiled from birth. She had been known to brag that she had never had to do a day's work in her life. She had even escaped being hauled into any of the Women's Services during the War because of her youth and the fact that her grandparents had shipped her out to Canada at the beginning of 1940. She was a dark-haired, dark-browed girl with a pale skin that rarely flushed, a sulky mouth and a quick passionate temper. Rhona, like her friend Kitty, could be a good friend but a bitter enemy. She was vain and self-opinionated but had one trait that endeared her to her friends. She was exceedingly generous. The trouble with Rhona was that she indulged this money-spending to a point of mad extravagance and at times her generosity became embarrassing. It was always Rhona who paid. It suited Kitty who was also extravagant and had not nearly so much to waste on her parties and clothes. Rhona adored her and lavished presents on her.

It was rumoured in their circle that her marriage had failed because Noel had always been forced into the background by his wife, and been made to feel that everything—their house, their parties, their holidays—were financed by her. He had grown to resent it. Fortunately perhaps for both of them he died suddenly of unsuspected cardiac trouble before their disagreements could develop into more serious rupture. Rhona, having led him a dance for years, now mourned him in her passionate way—went round her circle garbed in black and wearing Noel's miniature on a locket. Then, as suddenly and passionately as she had wanted Noel in the first place, she ceased to mourn and fell in love with Steven Grant-Tally. Having decided that he must be her second husband—she went 'all out' to get him.

Kitty had done her best to help. She thought it an excellent match for her brother. A successful surgeon and a wealthy widow of his own age, only one year younger in fact. But she knew there were certain prejudices first to be conquered in Steve. He had, of course, known Rhona for years. He admired her good looks, that rather voluptuous curving mouth, the long raven hair swept up at the back with combs, in Spanish fashion; and she generally wore long dangling ear-rings; she had small white ears. She was thin—too thin—but beautiful in an exotic feverish fashion. And he liked her for her extreme generosity. But he had always told Kitty he was 'scared of Rhona'. She was what he called a 'predatory type of female', and he suspected that she had made poor Noel Chayney's life a burden to him, with her excessive wealth. But Kitty, ever hopeful, continued to throw them together.

Last Easter they had all of them spent a week at Le Touquet. Rhona had been at her best; soft, a little *triste*—and very effective that *triste* air could be with her large dark eyes and hollowed cheeks and the 'sad lonely young

41

widow' touch. Kitty had watched her brother and her friend and fancied she saw Steve weakening. He had spent an entire evening dancing with Rhona and the next morning an excited Rhona announced that he had been far more friendly towards her than usual—and had made a little love to her as they walked together in the moonlight on the way back to the hotel from the Casino.

He had kissed her good night and told her she had a disturbing effect on him. That was enough to send Rhona's hopes soaring up to ecstatic peaks. Kitty then saw to it that the two met on every occasion; at theatres; at her home or in Rhona's magnificent penthouse overlooking Hyde Park. She gave chic little dinners there for which she was famous.

Only the other day Kitty had urged Steve to propose to Rhona.

'My dear Kits,' he had laughed, and protested: 'Rhona has a vast fortune. She can marry any one of our impoverished dukes or earls—why me?'

'You know perfectly well she adores you and that she is interested in your career and that she'll further it for you.'

Steve had shrugged his shoulders. Then when Kitty reproached him and intimated that 'poor Rhona was very unhappy' he said he was still a little 'scared of Rhona', although there had been moments, he admitted, when he had found her company stimulating.

'And her Rolls-Bentley is terrific,' he had added with a grin. 'If I ever marry Rhona it'll be to get that Rolls. But joking apart, Kits, I don't want to marry the fantastic Rhona or anybody else.'

That was what he had said. And look what he had done about his own secretary, Kitty thought angrily, and could have wept both for Rhona and her ambitious self.

She found Rhona in her sumptuous bed, no longer weeping, but looking deathly, her large dark eyes tragic and full of bitter resentment. Kitty, who liked fresh air, was a little overpowered by the stifling heat and perfume, and Rhona's theatrical grief. There were moments when she sympathized with Rhona's dead husband. But Kitty—ever the opportunist—looked with respect at the magnificent trappings of this room—the rich white satin, the gilt, the painted Italian ceiling and rare furniture. There were flowers everywhere. Rhona was so very *rich*. Steve was quite right when he said she could have made a brilliant marriage. Why bother about *him*? Even a distinguished surgeon like himself would be 'small fry' for her. But Rhona always seemed to fall in love with men who had nothing to offer her. That was pathetic and quite charming in its way. But there was a bit of the spider touch about her, Kitty reflected; once in the golden web Rhona's victims were apt to be devoured.

Could she, Kitty asked herself, as she sat and watched her friend smoking and sipping champagne (it was only eleven o'clock) really believe that Steve would be happy with this fantastic young woman? The answer always was that Rhona was a prize—a financial asset of such magnitude that it outweighed all on the deficit side. She also had her beauty, and she knew how to exploit it. Kitty wished that Steve could see her now, with her long black hair flowing over exquisite marble shoulders, and those great sorrowful doe eyes. Niobe drowning in her own tears! What a lovely, mad, hypocritical but fascinating personality she was!

Rhona began to moan that she couldn't *bear* it. She couldn't *live* if Steve married that little ex-nurse. She would die of a broken heart.

'Nonsense, darling,' said Lady Barley, unable to endure this exaggeration. 'People don't die of broken hearts.'

Rhona eyed her friend sullenly through her sweeping black lashes.

'I found the most wonderful Brazilian diamond yesterday at Boucheron's. I was so excited about it. Now I don't care. *You* can have it.'

'Nonsense,' repeated Kitty, but felt hopeful that Rhona might stick to that promise. Thousands of pounds meant nothing to her. She was so *lucky*. Most of her American grandfather's fortune was tied up in the States.

Rhona's income might be curtailed over here but she could go to New York (which she did) whenever she wished and purchase just what she wanted.

'Steve's a fool!' Kitty muttered.

'What are we going to *do* about it? I thought he was getting fonder of me—he showed every sign of it. What has that girl got that I haven't?'

'Nothing, darling. But I tell you Steve will soon find it out, and when the reaction comes—*that* will be your big moment.'

'Meanwhile have I got to watch him with that awful girl—what's her name—Glynis?'

'Leave it to me,' said Kitty firmly. 'She has certain drawbacks which will soon begin to annoy Steven. I'm going to see that this crazy affair doesn't last long. But we must be subtle and not put Steve's back up. You as well as I. I know it's hard for you to practise self-control; you're so impulsive, darling—but will you *please* behave as I suggest? If you make any sign that Steve has upset you and embarrass him, you'll scare him right off for good. I have all sorts of ideas. Leave it to me. Now listen . . .'

And Rhona pulled herself out of her 'Greek tragedy act' and listened while Kitty told her about this evening.

'You're a very old friend and you often pop in to see us—no reason why you shouldn't pop in tonight. You're not supposed to know

45

anything about the engagement. Just put on your most heavenly dress and your sable jacket and come in about half past nine or quarter to ten—say to tell me some special news. Yes . . . to show me the Brazilian diamond. Be your scintillating self—express surprise about Glynis, of course, but be particularly nice to her and convey only by the merest flicker of an eyelash to Steve that you still love him. Do you think you can do this? Have you the strength?'

'Oh, I don't know!' groaned Rhona. 'It will drive me crazy to watch them together.'

But before Kitty Barley had left the exotic penthouse she felt that she had got Rhona in control again. Everything was now arranged. And Kitty, having kissed and comforted the distracted Rhona, went off to order the dinner and buy special flowers for tonight.

CHAPTER FIVE

Glynis only saw her newly-acquired fiancé alone once more that day at the end of his afternoon's appointments. When she had shown the last patient out—a famous singer whom Steven was treating for laryngitis—he 'buzzed' on the intercom for her. She walked from her office into his room. She wrinkled her nose as she gave him a shy smile.

'M'm, your soprano uses rather nice

perfume and plenty of it.'

'I'll send you a bottle—remind me, Miss Thorne,' he said and grinned back at her. He was taking some instruments out of a cabinet and glanced at her over his shoulder as he did so. 'It's been a hell of a day, my sweet,' he added. 'I haven't had time to tell you how much I love you. But I do. You'd better run home now. I'm going off to that consultation at Hendon.'

'I'll see you tonight,' she said, 'but you know I'm absolutely petrified.'

'Please don't be, my darling,' he said, came up to her, took her in his arms for a moment, and put his cheek against hers. 'Everybody who meets you is bound to love you. And I've promised you that our dinner is to be an exceedingly quiet family affair. It couldn't scare even my little mouse.'

'You're the second person who's called me a mouse today,' said Glyn with a laugh. 'It sounds awful.'

The telephone rang. Glynis, true to her training, immediately answered the call, then passed the instrument over to Steven.

'St. Martha's—Sister Bates.'

She waited, and heard Steven's authoritative but ever charming voice.

'Oh, yes, Sister . . . M'm, what a nuisance. Well, we said at the time there was a danger of it. Is she in pain? Yes, she could have another shot right away. A sixth ought to do the trick.

47

I'll be in to see her tomorrow.'

That was that. Steve hung up and cocked an eyebrow at Glynis.

'That was the old girl I operated on yesterday—from the Elizabeth II Ward. That growth in the throat was malignant, you know.'

'Poor old thing,' said Glynis.

'I'm off,' said Steven, reaching for his coat. 'I'll fetch you about half past seven. Kitty never dines until eight-thirty.'

After he had gone Glynis tried—as she had been trying all day—to orientate herself. She was still so incredulous of being the chosen future wife of Steven Grant-Tally. She felt hopelessly at sea. And even that little time of dining seemed to put a gulf between Steven and herself. Dinner at eight-thirty! At home it was high tea at six-thirty, only occasionally Mummy entertained and people came in for a meal at seven.

She caught the usual Green Line bus to Barnet. Steven had said this afternoon that he would try and get an hour off tomorrow so that they could buy the engagement ring. It might always be like this—the fantastically busy Steven could only snatch the odd hour to give to her.

'I love him so much,' she thought, as she journeyed through the cold blue twilight towards Golders Green, and en route for home. 'I love to remember the strength of his arms, his kisses, the slight aroma of cigar smoke that clings to his coat (Steven is so fond of cigars), and occasionally that familiar smell of anaesthetic when he comes in from the operating theatre. The half-amused, tender look in those marvellous grey eyes when I say something he thinks funny. The desire in them when he kisses me. That electric shock of passionate love and longing that springs to life when we touch hands. The switch-over from successful surgeon to man-in-love. All those things are fast becoming my life . . .'

The breath of life to her, in fact. Her sun, her moon and her stars. And yet through the rosy cloud of romance in which she was now floating helplessly and hopelessly . . . there broke the light of a terrifying knowledge that it *just wouldn't work.*

On this night when she was to meet his sister for the first time as his promised wife, everything that was deep down in Glynis rebelled against her own apprehensions.

'*It must work,*' she told herself. 'I worship the ground he walks on. There could never be any other man for me.'

Once home she swept away fears and was gayer than her mother had ever seen her while she bathed and dressed. There was terrific excitement in the air. A long discussion as to what she was to wear. Dear life! There were only two dresses to choose from. She knew that when Lady Barley spoke about 'an old rag', it would probably be a Dior model that she had worn twice. She couldn't compete, so why try?

Mrs. Thorne moaned:

'If only we'd known this was going to happen, I'd have asked Dad to buy you something special.'

That fired Glynis' pride. She retorted:

'I won't pander to it. If Steve loves me, he and his people must take me as they find me.'

'Quite right, too!' said Mr. Thorne, who always backed his daughter up.

'Well, you're both very stupid,' declared Mrs. Thorne. 'If Glyn's circumstances are going to alter so must she—and her appearance—and lots of things. She owes it to Steven.'

Glynis was too happy tonight to continue the debate. It was treading on dangerous ground. Finally she decided to wear not the flowered silk Mummy suggested, for it was too summery for a January night, but her full black quilted skirt (which was two years old) and a black pullover, the monotony relieved by a triangular-shaped green stole with bobbles. She put on a wide green belt. It showed off the extreme slenderness of her waist. She really looked charming after she had fixed on her gold ear-rings and necklace. And not too unfashionable, even though nothing she had could be called expensive. And she deplored the fact that her black satin evening shoes were so worn. However, she had those new nylons that Aunt Pat had given her for Christmas. A dab of scent from Mummy's bottle and then (oh, horrors!) the old camel-hair coat. No rich furs for little Glynis. However, her hair held the gold lustre of youth and health and the radiance of her delicately powdered face with its flush of excitement made even her father whistle at her when she was ready.

'No need for *you* to fear rivals, Glyn.'

Mrs. Thorne hung around grumbling and muttering. Glynis gave her a wicked grin.

'She was only a dentist's daughter . . .' she began.

'*Only*!' repeated Mr. Thorne, and gave her a dark scowl. 'You may be going to marry a famous specialist, but I bet he can't extract a tooth like your old dad.'

'Silly! And you can't take out *tonsils*,' giggled Glynis.

Then came the time when Steven arrived. He was half an hour late to begin with. He barely had time to apologize to his future in-laws, or to notice what Glynis was wearing under that coat. He hustled her into the car and off they sped through the night that had become unseasonably warm and muggy. There was a slight drizzle.

Steve was doing some grumbling now. He had far too much to do. He wanted more time for *her.*

Glynis bit her lip and sighed.

'I don't believe you'll have time even for a honeymoon *if and when* we do get married.'

At once he pulled up the car—dead.

'What do you mean by "if"?'

'Oh, Steve, do drive on—we're late—your sister will be furious,' she laughed nervously.

'Not a step further until you tell me what you meant by that "*if*".'

Her green limpid eyes glowed at him through the dusk. He was so possessive, he so obviously cared deeply for her, yet he was so far out of her reach, she thought.

'I didn't mean "*if*",' at length she gave in— 'that is, not if you go on wanting me, darling.'

'Well, I do, and I always shall. Tell me you love me—at once. I've had a hard day and I need some gentle treatment.'

'I love you,' Glynis whispered. 'You don't know how much.'

'I daren't kiss you because of your lipstick, but later on, oh, my adorable little Glyn! I really did not know I had it in me to be so fond of anybody.'

'Don't tell me you've never had a love affair before me, because I shan't believe you, darling.'

'I won't say anything of the sort. It wouldn't be true.'

'Have you kissed heaps and heaps of girls?'

'Thousands,' he laughed and started the car up again.

Strangely enough, in that moment he had an

uncomfortable remembrance of a night in Le Touquet, walking through a palm-filled flower garden outside the Casino when for a moment he had committed the folly of kissing Rhona Chayney. The flame of ardour that he had woken on her lips had filled him with disquiet. His senses had been stirred, he admitted. How magnificent she had looked that night, her wonderful black hair piled on her small head and wearing a white velvet suit that spelt Paris, and her white Arctic furs and famous sapphires. A man could be excused for losing his head over Rhona. She had 'bags of glamour'. Yet he could not begin to love her, nor want her for a wife. It was this quiet, lovely, idealistic young girl beside him here this evening who appealed to the finest and best in Steven.

As he turned the Jaguar into Thurloe Square and neared his sister's house he received a shock There were several cars already outside, and on the doorstep a small crowd of men with cameras and flashlights gathered—unmistakably reporters.

'Good heavens!' exclaimed Steven.

Glynis stared at the little crowd. She felt as though a cold hand touched her.

'Oh, Steve—what does it mean?'

'It looks as though someone has given us away. If it's Kitty I'll wring her neck. The gentlemen of the Press await us, my sweet.'

'Oh, no!' she breathed and hung back.

53

'Come on, poppet, you've got to get used to it,' he said.

He, himself, was quite used to being photographed and fêted. There had been movie cameras and a good deal more besides when he had taken that trip to India. He felt Glynis' cold hand trembling in his as he helped her out of the car.

'You promised this was going to be a quiet family affair,' she whispered resentfully.

'I meant it to be,' he whispered back.

'I don't believe it. I think you arranged this. I'm livid with you,' she said under her breath, her cheeks scarlet.

'Chin up, darling'—he squeezed her fingers—'let's put on a good show.'

Glynis choked. She was now very conscious of her shabby coat and shoes. Everything had been such a chaotic rush—she had had no time to buy anything new. It was her birthday on February 2nd, and Daddy had been going to give her a nylon fur coat, but that was too late for *tonight*. Was it *true* that Steve had not arranged this public reception? Oh, how she loathed the idea of cameras, of all these men peering at her, and of seeing her own photograph in the papers tomorrow.

But the victim was thrown to the wolves. On the doorstep with Steven beside her, Glynis went through what was to her such agony, although Steven with his easy charm answered all the questions 'the boys' put to him.

'Yes, Miss Thorne has been my receptionist for about a year. Yes, I hope for a wedding in the early spring . . .' Then flashes of light, Glyn shaking, blinking, trying to smile, to appear dignified. Glyn, answering questions, too:

'Yes, I'm the daughter of Mr. Albert Thorne of Rudge Crest, Barnet. No, I'm not a fully trained nurse, but I've had some training . . .'

Then it was over. The reporters thanked Mr. Grant-Tally for the interview and rushed off to their various offices.

In the wide hall of the handsome Georgian house Lady Barley greeted her brother, innocent-eyed.

'Oh, you poor darlings—did you get caught? I can't think who tipped them the wink. Don't be so cross, Steve.'

'Well, I promised Glyn this was to be a quiet affair.'

'So it is,' she said sweetly. 'Only dinner with Paul and myself. How late you two are! Come upstairs and have a drink. Miss Thorne, you must be frozen. Maria, take the Signorina's coat.'

Still shaking, Glynis slipped out of the coat and the Italian maid took it from her as though surprised to receive anything that wasn't mink or sable, Glynis reflected. She felt her pulses fluttering with nerves. It had been a bad beginning—all that publicity. Kitty tucked an arm through hers as they walked up the wide handsome staircase and was being friendly and effusive.

'Such a delightful surprise, Glynis. I do congratulate you. We always thought that Steve—or, well—' She broke off as though she had decided not to tell Glynis *what* she had thought.

Glynis cast a glance at her. It was the first time she had seen Steve's sister without a hat. She bore a slight resemblance to him, but there was something about her manner that made Glynis suspicious of her sincerity. She had always thought Lady Barley affected. Too many 'darlings'. And was that wonderfully cut black dress 'the old rag' she had promised to wear? She looked terribly smart, Glynis thought. She was so poised—so much mistress of herself. Glynis tried to smooth out a creased skirt and pat a wave of hair into place. Lady Barley said:

'You look *charming*. What a *marvellous* colour your hair is, no wonder Steve fell in love with you. We're all so thrilled he means to get married at last.'

Steven, with a man's complete lack of intuition, thought:

'Good old Kitty—she's going to do her stuff. I don't think she knew about those reporters.'

But Glynis—hypersensitive as usual—thought:

'I believe Lady Barley arranged it!'

Now she was in the drawing-room, where a huge fire burned in the Adam fireplace, over which hung a portrait of Kitty by a famous contemporary painter. Glynis took a swift look round. Certainly everything was in perfect taste: glorious expensive flowers, bookcases full of leather-bound books, drinks on the table. Paul Barley—a tall, thin man with prematurely grey hair and a tired face—was mixing cocktails, stirring ice in a glass beaker. But he gave Glynis what she felt to be a really warm welcome.

'Steve's a lucky chap,' he said. 'I was told you were a beautiful girl, but that's putting it mildly. Steve'—he turned to his brother-in-law—'she looks like one of those Leonardo angels.'

'She *is* a Leonardo angel,' smiled Steven.

'Oh, don't, please,' said Glyn, and was all confusion and flaming colour. She was given a seat by the fire. She sat there trying to tuck the offending shoes well out of sight. She hoped no one would take any more notice of her. She refused the dry Martini her host handed to her.

'N-no, thank you, Sir Paul!'

'Oh, look here—we're going to be sort of related—do drop the title, please,' he murmured.

That further embarrassed Glynis. Then Kitty said sweetly:

'Don't you drink, Glynis? I *am* disappointed. Paul suggested we had the *Château Lafite* tonight—it's Steve's favourite wine. He's a connoisseur, you know, and he'll be sad if you don't drink a little, tonight of all nights. Or would you prefer champagne? It's the thing for festive occasions, I know, but Steve hates it. He much prefers good wines, don't you?'

She chatted on. Most of what she said about red and white wines, vintages and what you chose for certain food passed completely over Glynis' head. Mummy and Daddy had the odd glass of sherry and very occasionally a cheap South African wine for a celebration, but in these hard times, as Daddy said, a wine cellar was impossible. (Except for people like Sir Paul and Lady Barley, thought Glynis.) Well— she would have to learn to know Steve's tastes, and to her horror now, his sister was calling him an 'old gourmet, too. Mad about French cooking. Did she ever watch Philip Harben on the television?' asked Kitty. *They* did on occasions. That was one thing Glynis *could* discuss. The family *did* have a TV set. Daddy had bought it for Mummy's birthday last year. But the Thornes were not particularly fond of food or interested in Continental dishes.

'I shall have to go to cookery classes now and become a *cordon bleu* so that I shall know how to feed my important husband,' she thought.

Kitty was delighted when Steven expressed disappointment, not because Glynis rejected the Martini, but because she wouldn't appreciate the vintage red wine which was served with the pheasant. Nor the Napoleon brandy afterwards. And another moment of malicious pleasure was in store for Kitty when the young, unsophisticated girl asked for milk with her coffee. She saw Steve ruffle the shining hair. He said:

'Try it black first, duckie—it's so good in this house. Milk spoils it.'

Scarlet, Glynis sipped the black French coffee which was far too bitter and strong for her liking. But Steven had two cups and relished it. They were all little things—but they assumed a colossal importance for Glynis as she was just beginning to know him. Steven was totally unaware of her attitude of mind. He, himself, was thoroughly happy, because he was in love with the exquisite young girl whom his brother-in-law called a 'Leonardo angel'. Paul painted as a hobby. He expressed a burning wish to paint Glynis as soon as she would sit for him. Steve kept looking fondly at her, too, and thinking how beautiful and gentle and how altogether adorable she was. He had no idea what her clothes had cost but liked the quaint green shawl that made her eyes take on a dark emerald hue.

He was enjoying this evening. Toasts to the engaged pair had been drunk, and Glynis at dinner, to please everybody, had sipped a little wine. Her heart had beaten with tremendous pride as she clinked her goblet against Steve's and his lips formed the word:

'*Darling!*'

But Kitty Barley's mind seethed with resentment at what she felt to be an intrusion by this inexperienced little 'nurse-typist' for whom Steve had fallen. She had some education; her beauty was undeniable, a sweet manner except for that dreary shyness, but oh, those shoes . . . that cheap skirt and scarf . . . not taste. Pure Suburbia and she could *never* take her proper place as the future Lady Grant-Tally (which she would eventually become).

Kitty felt that she was being a hypocrite every time she smiled or enthused over Glynis; she felt disloyal to Steve, too; but she was delighted that she had asked Rhona here. Rhona would put Glyn right in the back of the picture. Surely Steve, even if temporarily infatuated, must see that for himself.

Glynis looked longingly at the Sèvres clock on the mantel-piece. She felt heavy-eyed and flushed from the unaccustomed wine and rich food. She longed to get away—to be alone and quiet somewhere with Steve. But he seemed happy—enjoying himself hugely. With cigar, brandy, and she, herself, beside him on the chesterfield, he obviously had no desire to leave his sister's drawing-room.

Once he leaned down and whispered:

'It isn't nearly as bad as you thought it would be, eh? They're not eating you up, are they, sweet?'

'N-no, they're charming,' she stammered, 'but I—'

'I know,' he interrupted and put a hand over hers and his fine grey eyes looked down at her caressingly. 'We'll go in a second. I want to be alone with you, too.'

Her heart jumped. At such moments she felt wildly happy. He was all hers. But his sister frankly terrified her. The long-drawn-out dinner had been a torture, in case she did or said the wrong thing. She kept feeling that Lady Barley was criticizing her inwardly, no matter how sweetly she smiled, and that there was a hidden barb in all her personal remarks.

At half past ten Kitty was beginning to grow restless and to think Rhona did not intend to come, which would have added to Glynis' discomfiture. Steve, too, rose to his feet and pulled Glynis on to hers and said he must 'drive her home'.

Before Kitty could reply, one of the Italian maids knocked on the door and came in.

'The Signora Chayney,' she said.

Paul Barley looked at his wife, surprised.

'Rhona—at this hour?'

'Oh, you know she comes in at all hours to see us. She knows nothing about Steve and our party tonight. But now she's here, she *must* meet Glynis,' said Lady Barley smoothly.

Steven bent down to Glynis.

'Sorry, sweet—we'll have to stay awhile. We

61

must present you to the great Rhona. Mrs. Chayney—Kitty's bridesmaid who is now widowed.'

Glynis nodded. He moved forward to greet the visitor, cigar in hand. Kitty managed to say a word in Glynis' ear.

'Be nice to my poor Rhona, she was terribly fond of brother Steve,' she murmured. 'This will upset her a bit, I fear.'

Glynis, bitterly disappointed that her departure with Steve had been postponed, froze a little as she took in the poignant meaning of the whispered remark (said half in earnest, half in jest, she supposed).

Then a woman came into the drawing-room. Glided in, Glynis thought, like a mannequin, on high narrow heels. An amazing-looking woman of thirty, with a thin graceful body; wearing a narrow sheath of a short black skirt that showed perfect legs; a small head emerging from the collar of a rich sable jacket like a *Vogue* cover, Glynis told herself, and one of those tiny Paris hats on dark swept-up hair; diamond drop ear-rings and one huge diamond ring; perfect gloves and expensive bag. The *dernier cri* . . . she was the very essence of sophisticated womanhood.

'May I introduce my friend Mrs. Chayney,' said Kitty gaily. 'Rhona—this is Glynis Thorne; we are celebrating Steve's and her engagement this very evening. You are the first to know, darling.'

62

CHAPTER SIX

Steven Grant-Tally, like a great many very clever men, had a slightly vague attitude of mind towards things outside the circle of his particular genius. He could, at times, be annoyingly preoccupied.

He was, in fact, too busy and successful—often too rushed to brood over what was past. The unfortunate evening was over. He was alone with his little Love. His lovely Glynis had her foibles and complexities—well, who hadn't? he asked himself. He wanted to carry out her wishes as far as possible. But he was positively amazed by her attitude. He began to wonder if it was possible that jealousy caused it; faint jealousy of Rhona, perhaps.

They had reached a bridge spanning the Serpentine. He pulled up the Jaguar to one side, switched off and took both Glynis' hands in his. He pulled off the little green gloves, then drawing each hand in turn up to his lips, kissed the palms.

'Darling,' he said in a low tone. 'Darling, anybody would think you've gone dead cold on me. Glyn, my *sweetest* love, what on earth is wrong?'

She was moved by his appeal and his lingering kisses on her hands. But not yet could she find it in her to forgive completely the failure of what should have been a glorious celebration. And when she said so, Steven began to protest indignantly.

'I didn't know those boys were coming—I swear it. I hadn't the slightest idea.'

'You must have done—'

He interrupted, a little crossly:

'Darling, I *didn't*—you must accept my word.'

She looked up at him, then down.

'Very well,' she whispered.

But her eyes filled with tears again and she turned to the rather dreary vista of water and bare trees on this bleak January night. The drizzle had given place to a steady rain through which the lamp-lights danced in an iridescent haze.

The whole situation depressed her. Now Steven, too, caught and felt in full the tang of her depression. He made an earnest bid to understand what was really worrying her. His questions met with confused results. It had meant a great deal to Glynis to have a month of privacy, and now she had been robbed of it, she said, though it became very obvious to Steven that she was really worried about that neurotic young fool Robin Gellow, and she did *not* like Rhona Chayney. Nothing, either, would convince her that she had a friend in his sister, although, she said, she liked Paul very much—*he* had been sweet and kind.

'Look, darling,' said Steven. 'You are being

a little unduly sensitive. I'm sure Kitty adored you. She said so.'

'Did she?' said Glynis, almost inaudibly, and bit her quivering underlip.

'Though I'm afraid it *must* have been Kit who gave us away. But she meant well—she thought a splash would be good for me, and you must remember, darling, most girls would have thoroughly enjoyed it.'

Those words held a reproach which roused Glynis to protest once more.

'But I'm not *like* other girls—you know I'm terribly anti-publicity. I warned you, Steven, when you asked me to marry you.'

'Are you trying to break with me?' he asked suddenly.

But the very thought of saying farewell to him tore through all the defences Glynis had tried to put up. She burst into tears and flung herself into his arms.

'No, no, Steve, I love you—darling, I adore you—you know I do. It isn't that,' she sobbed. 'But everything went so wrong, and when I met Mrs. Chayney—she's terribly in love with you—I felt you ought to be marrying *her*, not me.'

Steven strained the trembling young figure close to him and covered her hair with kisses. That beautiful burnt-gold hair that never failed to excite his admiration, his desire. Now he felt in his own element again. The dominant male—better able to understand

and comfort. So long as she loved him, nothing else mattered—no obstacles were too great. Admitted, with her funny little nervous temperament and dislike of notabilities, he said, there *were* obstacles to be got over. But she could do it—and he would help her—and he on his side would try to see things from *her* point of view. But they must go on loving each other. It would be a betrayal of a very real love that had sprung to life between them if they let it slip at the first fence. He'd talk to Kitty tomorrow and make quite sure *she* understood things, too; as for Rhona—Steven admitted that Rhona was attached to him but he had never dreamt of marrying her. It had never even entered his mind. Her wealth and her chic, her wit, and that generosity for which she was famed, were all obvious assets to a man who was in the running for her. But he, Steven, was not. He did not want a rich amusing wife. He wanted his adorable, practical little Glynis.

Glynis would have been inhuman had she not responded with all her fervent young heart. So they kissed and clung blindly. Taxis and private cars passed them. The rain spattered against the windscreen. Glynis and Steven did not care. It was one of those enchanted moments that transport those who love into realms which shut out the fear of future misunderstandings.

They did not hear—nor would they have cared much had they heard—the conversation that was taking place at this same hour between Kitty and her husband.

Paul Barley sat in his dressing-gown on his wife's bed, finishing a last cigarette. Kitty was creaming her face. Her brown waving hair was confined under a blue silk net. She looked older and even haggard seen thus, but she did not mind if Paul thought so. His feelings, however, were rarely revealed to her these days. He had been madly in love with her when they married. She had so much charm. That Grant-Tally charm which Steven had in such quantity.

Kitty had been a beautiful, merry and apparently good-natured girl when Paul (then struggling to make his way in the Foreign Office) first met her ten years ago. They had spent much of the time abroad moving from one Legation to another. Kitty, always well dressed and the perfect hostess, had been spoiled, and her mad extravagance had, of course, nearly ruined their personal happiness as well as Paul's financial status. Now that he had curbed her expenditure and begun to criticize her mode of life, she had fallen out of love with him. She resented what she called his 'meanness' and shut her eyes to his worth, his intrinsic goodness. So there was little left between them of the old warmth and only a 'keeping up of appearances' in public. The fact that there had been no children had made matters worse. Even Steven did not know quite how badly this marriage was going. But Paul believed in the sanctity of the marriage tie and he believed, somewhat hopelessly, that one day Kitty would come to her senses and they must find happiness together again.

He liked others to be happy, too. He said, quietly:

'You ought to leave those two alone, Kit. Glynis is charming.'

Kitty stopped patting skin-food into her long throat and her fine eyes flashed. How she hated Paul when he dared air his opinions, and especially if he admired other women.

'Oh!' she snapped. 'So you found Glynis charming, did you? Well, I found her a bore, and she is *not* in our circle and—'

'She may be all the better for that,' broke in Paul drily.

She was furious with him. What did he know about Glynis Thorne, anyhow? she cried. Like all men, he was taken in by a pretty face. Oh, she granted that Glynis had intelligence, too. But she was penniless.

Steven didn't need money? Of course he did! His expenses were enormous. A lot of his work was hospital stuff, unpaid. Nobody could make enough money now, and so on and so on. Until Paul, looking tired to death, drew a long deep sigh and got up.

'So,' he nodded, 'you want to break them up—make life unbearable for that poor child as only you can, in your clever way, then try and push Rhona into Steven's lap again.'

'Well,' Kitty glared, 'what of it? Rhona was absolutely broken tonight by the shock of finding out about Steven.'

'She'll have to turn her attentions elsewhere, my dear.'

'Oh, you don't understand—so don't interfere,' Kitty exclaimed.

Her glittering eyes turned to her small bureau and seemed to see all too plainly that pile of unpaid bills which she dared not bring to Paul's notice. She had sent Rhona home promising faithfully to do her utmost to break things up between Glynis and Steve if she could.

She meant to keep that promise. Rhona was more in love with Steve than ever; perhaps because a woman of her type wants so badly what she cannot get. But Paul was warning his wife:

'Don't *you* interfere, my dear, with those two. Glynis is the nicest girl Steve has ever produced, and if he marries her I reckon it will be the making of him. He doesn't want your fabulous widow. He wants sweetness and kindness in his home. Most men do,' he added bitterly, and got up and walked out of the room, painfully aware of his own ruined happiness.

But Kitty, once in bed, immediately telephoned the penthouse in Grosvenor Square and spoke to the cherished friend who was of such vast importance in her life. Rhona's rich voice sounded husky, as though she had been crying. She answered sullenly:

'Steve hardly noticed me. Oh, Kit, if he *marries* that girl—'

'He won't, darling,' broke in Lady Barley. 'Don't upset yourself. I have a strong hunch that he *won't*.'

CHAPTER SEVEN

That day in which the newspapers chronicled Steven's engagement to Glynis was by no means one of unsullied delight for her. Steven went out of town early; perhaps fortunately for him he was called away in consultation for a serious case in Bournemouth and left London by an early train. He had 'phoned her to apologize because the purchase of the ring must now wait. She had said she quite understood. She was on her way in a Green Line bus from Barnet to town when she saw her own face in her morning paper (a close-up) in one of the leading dailies, side by side with one of Steven. Then the two of them standing on the doorstep of the Barleys' house. Steve, handsome, confident, smiling; Glynis, a half-smile on her lips, shyly clinging to his arm.

Famous specialist announces engagement to

his secretary-receptionist. Mr. Steven Grant-Tally outside the home of his sister, Lady Barley, with his fiancée, Miss Glynis Thorne.

There followed a brief résumé of Steven's latest triumphs of surgical skill in his own field, then details about Glynis.

Miss Thorne is the daughter of a well-known Barnet dental surgeon. A year ago she began training as a nurse at St. Martha's Hospital, but had to resign owing to ill-health.

Glynis' cheeks went scarlet. Hastily she folded up the paper, and glanced sideways at her travelling companions, most of whom were reading their own dailies. She was terrified one of them might recognize her. She thought: *'Isn't it awful how this limelight scares me?* For Steve's sake I *must* try to get used to it.'

Her first telephone call after she reached Steven's consulting room and began to sort out correspondence was from Alma.

'I thought you told me to keep the news a deadly secret, my dear? Why, the whole hospital is *buzzing!*'

'Oh, lord!' groaned Glynis. 'I *did* mean it to be a secret but someone gave us away.'

Said Alma: 'When I met Sister Bates this morning she was clutching the *Daily Express.* She held it up so I could see your and Steve's photos.'

Glynis swallowed. Sister Bates had been in charge of the Elizabeth II Ward which Her Majesty had opened during Coronation Year and where Glynis had been working just before her breakdown. A most capable woman, Miss Bates, but scarcely the romantic type. All men were wolves in her opinion and all young nurses in her charge lambs who not only went to the slaughter but dashed to it in wanton haste. Somewhere at the back of her throat Glynis repressed the desire to giggle at the memory.

'Oh, what *did* old Bates say?'

Alma was giggling too.

'Nothing—she just *looked.*'

But a lot of others in the hospital were thrilled, Alma added. Matron, herself, had told somebody who told somebody else who told Alma that she thought Glynis would make a good wife for a famous man. And the probationers were all tickled to death. But Robin Gellow . . .

Then, at the mention of that name, Glynis stopped laughing. Her charming flushed face with its crown of deep gold hair, and the delightful tip-tilted nose, took on a grave look.

'Oh, Alma, have you seen him?'

Alma had, and admitted he looked like death. He had walked past her in the corridor after breakfast and she had gone up to him and asked him if he knew, and he had given her a grim look and said: *'Oh yes. A nice surprise for us all, isn't it?*' Alma had wanted to break it to him gently, but he had read it first.

'But, of course, that little cat, Moira Thomas, thrust the paper in front of his nose at breakfast,' ended Alma.

Glynis was not surprised. She and the young red-haired probationer, Moira Thomas, had been rather antipathetic and Moira had tried in vain to catch Robin's eye. Hence her antagonism to Glynis. Oh dear, how complicated life was, Glynis reflected, and felt somewhat subdued as Alma volunteered the further information that Robin had apparently 'come over queer' during 'Out-Patients' and Dr. Snook, the Senior Physician, had sent him off duty. He called it 'a touch of malaria'. Robin had contracted malaria in the Far East doing his National Service. But Alma knew that it was because he was so upset about Glynis and Steve.

'You're coming round to supper, aren't you? Everyone is expecting you and you'll get a grand reception—they're all dying to congratulate you,' Alma ended. 'Don't be scared off—I'll hold your hand.'

They ended on a light note. But as Glynis returned to her desk to sort letters and deal with Steve's correspondence she felt heavy-hearted about Robin. He had received the shock in just the sudden way she had least desired. She had tried to telephone him last night, late though it was when she got home,

73

but unfortunately he had been off-duty and one of his friends told her Robin had gone down to Brighton on his motor-bike to see his widowed mother. He had said he might stay the night in Brighton, so Glynis had not been able to contact him.

The memory of the highly-strung young man who was so desperately in love with her never failed to worry Glynis. He was so nice in so many ways and so devoted to his mother, who, in turn, worshipped him. It seemed tragic that he should possess that other neurotic side. No sense of humour; none of Steven's buoyancy or zest for life. Robin took everything far too seriously, including himself, Glynis thought. Now the fat was in the fire and she was sure she would be hearing in person from Robin all too soon. He had sworn never to give up the attempt to make her change her mind.

She was, however, surprised and disturbed when, later that afternoon, she answered the bell and found him on the doorstep—hatless, fair hair tossed by the wind and damp with rain; an old mackintosh over one arm. He looked, as Alma had described, 'like death', and a little wild-eyed.

'What do you want, Robin?' she asked by way of greeting. She was nervous. There were two other doctors who shared this house with Steve and whose consulting rooms were in use. Patients were coming in and out all the time. The telephone-bell rang constantly. Afternoons were always busy. It was no time or place for her to try to soothe a disappointed suitor.

But Robin Gellow pushed past her.

'I want a word with the great Grant-Tally,' he said.

Glynis closed the heavy front door which had a wrought-iron grille across plate glass. She felt her pulses jerking a trifle nervously, but she spoke in her quiet way:

'He is not in. Come and talk to me for a moment—but not for long, Robin. I still have an arrears of letters and a report to copy out for the Chief before he gets back.'

Robin walked into the consulting room. For a moment he looked bitterly around him at the handsome rosewood desk and the carved chair usually occupied by Steven; at the book-lined walls, the modern cabinets full of gleaming instruments. And at an oil-painting of the late Sir Campion—one-time Senior Surgeon Consultant of St. Martha's—hanging over the marble, fluted fireplace. Robin said:

'The Chief's room, eh?—where he interviews his wealthy patients and rakes in the shekels. Humph!'

Glynis bit her lip. She let the bitter remark pass. She knew this mood of Robin's. He disappointed her—as he always had done. Once she had liked his outlook—his absorption in humanity and his total disregard for fame. She had thought his aims high, and so like her own that they might have made a go of it. Only when their friendship developed had she discovered that he was a crank without tolerance. Also that he suffered from an inferiority complex because his father had died an undischarged bankrupt and his mother had only just managed to allow him enough out of the wreckage to finish his medical training. A more courageous and normal type of young man might have got through these troubles and remained calm and cheerful. But Robin had grown introspective. When he first met Glynis, her fresh shy charm and radiant beauty coupled with her own ideology had thrilled him and done him a power of good. But unfortunately her inability to return his passion had recently had a bad effect.

She tried now, however, to be patient and tactful.

'You need not like Steve if you don't want to, nor need you wish me good luck, but do be honest and admit that Steve does plenty of work among the poor as well as the rich,' she said.

'So now you defend him? Once you had no use for the great Grant-Tally.'

'Never quite that,' she said, flushing. 'I always admired him. I knew he had a wonderfully kind and generous side. What I said was that I wished he had not become a successful *specialist.* I thought that might spoil him.'

'So you eventually decided to love him as you've never loved before,' sneered Robin.

She gave a quick worried look at the boy's miserable face. He looked badly in need of sleep. She said in a low voice:

'Robin, don't let this upset you so much. If I've fallen in love with Steve and he with me, it just can't be helped. It's one of those things.'

'And I aided and abetted it—I suggested that you might make a good receptionist for him and got you the post. I must have been crackers.'

She thought:

'My poor Robin, you *will* be crackers if you don't get a grip on yourself.'

'Oh, why the hell should this have happened?' he broke out. 'You, the one person in the world I cared for and needed. Much more than *he* needs you.'

'That may not be true, Robin, for all you know. Why not accept the fact, anyhow, and be generous and wish me happiness with Steve?'

'You've changed your mind about him, haven't you, and about entering the high Society which you used to say you hated?'

'I still don't care for it—but I love *him*.'

The words seemed to madden Robin. He flung his mackintosh on a chair and, suddenly striding to her side, seized the slim young figure in the white overall and kissed her on the lips. It was the first kiss she had ever received from Robin. It was brutal and offended her bitterly. She tore herself away and drew the back of her hand across her hurt lips.

'That was *beastly* of you—unforgivable. Please go, Robin—at once—and don't come near me again.'

He stood shaking, his eyes bloodshot.

'You've wrecked everything for me—you and your wonderful Chief. I won't be able to do another stroke of work. I'll resign from St. Martha's and from the profession. Between you you've ruined my life.'

'I think I'd like an explanation of those words,' cut in a cool deep voice from the doorway.

Glynis swung round. She was shaking—nerves all on edge. She was perturbed to see Steven himself walk into the room. He shut the door behind him. He put down the case he carried and flung hat and gloves on to the desk. Then with his overcoat still on, he walked up to Robin, who glared defiantly at him.

'What are you doing here, Gellow?' Steven asked quietly. 'Having a day off from hospital or something? And why this attitude towards Glynis?'

The younger man stood motionless a moment. He was pale and breathed unevenly. Somehow the sight of Steven—he had slipped an arm around Glynis; he was so handsome, so self-confident, and now so intimately associated with the girl—tantalized Robin beyond bearing.

'Oh, *God!*' he said in a choked voice, turned, and leaving his mackintosh on the chair, rushed out of the room. They heard the front door slam.

Steven frowned and, moving to a window, opened it as though to let in some fresh air.

'Phew!' he said. 'May I ask what that was about?'

Glynis was upset but quite in control of herself. She said:

'I'm sorry you heard it all.'

'Only the tail-end, obviously. He seems to have a burning grievance against us, and me in particular. Why?'

Glynis looked unhappy.

'You must excuse him—he's a bit unbalanced, I think.'

'You said last night that he might take our engagement badly.'

'So he *has.*'

Steven flung off his coat, rummaged among some papers on his desk, glanced at his telephone pad, then gave Glynis a quick, wry smile.

'I suppose I must forgive the fellow if he's very much in love with you and feel sorry for him. But he ought to know how to take a licking.'

'He'll soon get over it, I hope,' said Glynis.

'You shouldn't, of course, be so very attractive, my darling,' said Steven, and walked up and caught and held her close for a moment. He breathed in the fragrance of her hair. 'I've been thinking of you all the way back—and reaching a definite conclusion,' he added.

She relaxed in his embrace, feeling secure again. The unpleasant scene with Robin had affected her more than she had thought. It was good to feel Steve's arms around her again.

But when she heard what conclusions he had come to, her heart sank. She was besieged with doubts and fears again. He wanted her to marry him at once.

'Why wait? The cat's out of the bag so far as publicity is concerned. Let's just creep quietly away and get married, darling,' he said.

She could so easily have said 'yes'. The impulsive, passionate side of her wanted him now. But the retiring, sensible Glynis clung firmly to her old ideas. It was all too sudden, she said—they *must* stay engaged for a time. They shouldn't rush things; it might prove fatal . . . it was for their future happiness if they waited . . .

Steven listened, marvelling at the wisdom in this girl's small pretty head, and knowing deep in his heart that she was right. Yet this afternoon, following that scene with young Gellow, she seemed more than ever desirable to him and in need of his love and protection.

But in the long run, he agreed. Sighing, he kissed the warm rose-lips and let her go.

'Right as usual, my love. But I wish sometimes you were not such a practical little thing.'

'You'll never know how madly my heart's beating,' she laughed wryly.

An hour later she was at St. Martha's. It had been agreed that Steve should meet her there for a small party. Matron and some of the sisters had invited them to dinner and supper in celebration of the engagement. After all, Mr. Grant-Tally was a St. Martha's man and Glynis an ex-probationer. Matron had a romantic streak under the hard crust of professional etiquette and discipline.

The moment Glynis appeared in the nurses' comfortable, warm Common Room, which had recently been modernized, she was surrounded by the section of white-capped, cheerful members of the staff who knew her best. Kisses and handshakes were exchanged. Matron finally appeared herself and touched Glynis' velvet, rosy cheek with her lips.

'Congratulations, my dear. You're a lucky girl. And you've got a *wonderful* man.'

'And what a surgeon!' put in one of the theatre sisters with an envious sigh.

'He's so jolly good-*looking*,' came from a young probationer to whom Steven had long been a heart-throb.

Glynis felt warm, happy and infinitely

fortunate. She sat there smoking a cigarette and sipping the sherry that had been produced for the occasion. They were all waiting for the Big Man. Steven had had to see a patient upon whom he had operated yesterday and then go home to change. No striped trousers and black tonight—just a lounge suit he had told Glynis. It was going to be an informal evening.

Glynis found herself the very centre of attention, and as most of it coming from the nursing staff was genuinely friendly and Alma was there beside her, she did not feel quite so shy as usual. But she could not stop remembering Robin Gellow. Nobody seemed to have seen him. It was generally believed that he had retired with one of his worst attacks of malaria.

Glynis confided in Alma.

'I must say I'm a bit worried—he looked *awful* when he rushed out of Steve's consulting room this afternoon.'

'Oh, forget him—and enjoy yourself. This is *your* night, duckie,' counselled little Alma.

Two of the fourth-year medical students dropped in for a sherry. One, Harold Brennan, was a particular friend of Robin's. As he entered the Common Room he saw Glynis sitting there, the light from a standard lamp behind her turning her crisp short hair to living gold, slim legs crossed, long green eyes crinkled with laughter. Brennan's face was unsmiling as he watched her.

'Say, it's the first time I've seen young Glynis looking quite so glamorous. I don't think the great Tally is doing too badly.'

'No, but I know someone who is,' said Harold Brennan, and walking up to Glynis, handed her a letter in an open envelope.

'Good evening, Glynis. You might like to read this,' he said drily.

Surprised, and with her smile fading, Glynis returned young Brennan's greeting and took the letter. It was addressed to Harold.

'I found it in his room when I went to see if he was coming along to your party,' added Brennan.

Now the 'party spirit' vanished for the girl. Her face grew pale, then crimson, as she glanced through the hysterical scrawl Robin had left for his friend. It was a diatribe against women in general, and the evil effect they have on men; and against Glynis in particular. One long paragraph stood out, smashing all Glynis' newly acquired self-confidence; the happiness that was bubbling up in her heart tonight among her St. Martha's hospital friends.

It said:

Tell Glynis she has done something to me by this sudden decision of hers to marry G.-T. I know she owes me nothing—except I always hoped she'd change her mind and marry me. But what hits me is the way she's blinding herself to facts, and they're facts she believed in before she

let G.-T. talk her out of them. He and his big success and rich friends are not her cup of tea. And she's never going to be his, either. If she marries him it'll fail as sure as I write this. Anyhow, it's a bitter blow to me and I can't take it. I can't stay in the hospital and watch him take Glynis out of my reach. Even if it means ruining my career—I'm quitting. I'm going down to my mother. I shan't come back to St. Martha's. I know you'll say I'm out of my mind. Perhaps I am. Say good-bye to her for me. Tell her if it's the last thing I ask—I beg her not to marry Grant-Tally. It won't work. Forgive me if you think I'm too cowardly to face up to disappointment. Maybe I am.
Robin.

Glynis finished the letter. She knew that Harold was looking at her with reproach, as though his friend's shameful cowardice was, indeed, her fault. She knew, too, that many inquisitive pairs of eyes were being focused on her. Her heart grew heavy as lead. Her eyes stung with tears.

'Oh!' she said under her breath. 'It wasn't fair of him to write like that.'

'What is it, duckie?' put in Alma anxiously.

Glynis did not reply. One or two of the things Robin had written were stinging her.

'Blinding herself to facts . . . facts she believed in before she let G.-T. talk her out of them.'

Was that not true? Hadn't she felt, all the

84

way along, that she and Steve were ill-assorted? Yet she loved him and he loved her. Could anything be more difficult?

But '*it won't work . . .*' Robin had written. The same fatal words she had repeated so often to herself, yet been trying so hard to forget.

She could no longer stay in the room full of the chattering, laughing medical staff, all wanting to talk to her about Steven. She thrust the offending letter written by Robin back into Harold's hands, and made her way blindly into the white corridor. It smelt of rubber flooring, disinfectants and anaesthetics.

She stood still a moment, fighting with her tears.

She heard Brennan's voice behind her.

'I say, I'm sorry if I've upset you, but I thought you ought to see what the poor devil wrote.'

Glynis swung round.

'Yes, you did as he asked and let me know what he said. If I'd at any time encouraged Robin to think I was fond of him, I'd blame myself. But I can't. I never, never gave Robin any hope.'

'All the same,' said Brennan, who was a hard-headed and loyal young man, 'I think you ought to try and get him to come back. He's a neurotic chap, but this walking-out is madness. He *can't* be allowed to ruin his career.'

'You know I'd do anything to help,' said

Glynis, her lower lip quivering. 'But what can I do?'

'Well, personally, I think you and I together might see him and persuade him to come back.'

'But I can't go all the way down to Brighton—' began Glynis.

'Not even if you think Robin's career is at stake?' broke in young Brennan. 'After all, you are *indirectly* concerned.'

'But—but Steven wouldn't allow it,' Glynis began to stammer.

Again Brennan interrupted.

'Mr. Grant-Tally has everything in the world—his success, money, the *lot*. Is he such an egotist that he won't understand how essential it is you should use all your influence to get Robin back to his job?'

Now it was Glynis' turn to defend Steve.

'I'm sure if Steven thought it the right thing, he'd be the first to suggest I went.'

'Then do it, Glynis. Let's get the first train to Brighton—there are masses of them—let's go down and bring that poor misguided idiot back to St. Martha's.'

'But Steven—' began Glynis, and stopped. A night sister was approaching, waving a piece of paper at her.

'Glynis Thorne, a message has just come through to you over the phone from Mr. Grant-Tally.'

Glynis, her heart beating miserably fast,

took the slip of paper. As she read it, she felt even more wretched. Fate seemed to be conspiring against her—to wreck the impromptu hospital party that was being thrown for Steve and herself tonight.

This message was to tell her that Steve could not come. (A forerunner of other nights ahead of broken appointments; those sudden crises and dramas and disappointments that beset the wife of a famous doctor, she told herself.)

Unavoidably detained; got to see patient dangerously ill. Forgive me, will be too late to make it, see you tomorrow.

So Steve wasn't coming at all. If she *wanted* to accompany Harold Brennan on his mission of mercy to Brighton—if she felt at *all* responsible for Robin—well, there was no reason why she shouldn't go with him now.

CHAPTER EIGHT

Glynis had to do quite a bit of quick thinking. It was no light matter—careering down to Brighton with Harold Brennan to try and talk poor Robin back into a reasonable state of mind. It was half past six. Harold, glancing at his watch, said that if they made a dash for it they could get the seven o'clock from Victoria.

Glynis gasped.

'But what will . . . will *they* say?' She nodded towards the door of the Common Room.

Brennan's rather stubborn long-chinned face grew more stubborn. He was nothing if not a devoted friend and he had always liked Robin. He thought the fellow was making a darned idiot of himself over this girl—lovely and desirable though she might be—and no woman in young Brennan's unromantic estimation was worth chucking away your career for. He said:

'What the blazes do *they* matter? It's Robin who counts. If we can bring him back tonight all will be well. But if Snooker' (*this was Mr. Snook, Senior House Physician*) 'pops in to Robin's room tomorrow morning to see how the malaria is and finds him missing, there'll be a bust-up. Robin will have *had* it. You know it, Glynis. Your precious G.-T. would be the first to condemn him.'

'Why do you speak of Steven in that sneering way?' she demanded hotly, indignantly. 'Is he to blame as well as me for all this? I can't help it if—if a man f-falls in love with me in such a c-crazy way,' she added, stammering. 'And neither is it Steven's fault.'

'Oh, Tally's all right—he's a fine chap and all that—I didn't mean to be disparaging,' muttered Brennan. 'I'm just worried nuts about old Robin. Do be a sport and come with

88

me, Glynis. Between us I'm positive we can influence him into coming back with us.'

At this psychological moment the door opened and Moira Thomas came into the corridor. She was a thin, small girl with beautiful red hair and a white skin, but her looks were spoiled by a snub nose and small prim mouth. But she had character, and she had always had a passion for Robin Gellow— the curious kind of love that so often the weak inspire in the strong. She marched straight up to Glynis.

'I've just heard about Robin,' she said.

'Who told you . . .' began Brennan.

Moira mentioned the Canadian student's name and added:

'Robin hasn't got malaria. He's done a bunk because of her,' she ended on a bitter note— nodding her head at Glynis.

Now it was Glynis' turn to show spirit. Pale but composed she said:

'Look, Moira—I know you're very fond of Robin and it's only natural you're upset, but I'm *not* taking the blame. Why should I? We never had an understanding—whatever you may think—and I had every right to become engaged to someone else.'

The little red-headed nurse, bitterly jealous and envious of Glynis' breath-taking beauty— as she had been in the days when they were nurses together—sneered at her.

'Yes—and what a chance for you. Who

blames you for accepting? You'll soon be coming to patronize us girls, all wrapped in rich furs—the beautiful Mrs. Grant-Tally.'

The malice in this hurt Glynis deeply. She had on the whole received friendly, sincere good wishes from the staff at St. Martha's—but even one or two poisoned darts found a mark in Glynis' ultra-sensitive heart. She went scarlet.

'I'm not going to demean myself by making any comment, Moira,' she said in a low voice.

'Oh, listen, you two!' interrupted Harold. 'This is no time for petty wrangling. Robin's whole career is at stake.'

'Where is he?' Moira swung round to Harold. He told her, and taking her further into his confidence, explained what he was trying to make Glynis do. Then it was Moira's turn to cool down and show the human and genuine side of her nature. She caught Glynis by the arm. Her eyes filled with tears.

'Oh, Glynis—forget the stupid things I said—I didn't mean them. It's only that I've always hated it because Robin was in love with you, and he means so much to me . . .' She gulped. *Please*, Glynis, if you have any influence, use it tonight. Make him come back. Please, *please* make him come.'

Glynis softened but still hesitated. Moira added:

'Think if it was *your* boyfriend. If your Steven went and had a nervous breakdown like

Robin and was temporarily all to pieces, and I was the only one who could influence him—wouldn't you beg *me* to go?'

Glynis had to agree that she would. And she could see now that the little nurse who disliked and envied her was the victim of her own thwarted unreciprocated love. It was enough to decide Glynis. That and the thought of what it would mean to *her* if Steven was on the verge of ruining his life. She surrendered.

'All right—I'll go with Harold,' she said.

'Oh, thank you, thank you!' Moira was in tears now. 'Bring Robin back—don't let him wreck his career. He's weak but he's so good at his job and so lovable—honestly he is. You're happy with Steven Grant-Tally. You can afford to be generous, Glynis.'

Glynis' eyes brimmed suddenly. She seized one of Moira's hands and said:

'Don't worry—I'll do all I can. I will—honestly.'

The next half an hour was chaotic. To Matron and the nursing staff Glynis made the excuse that she had received 'bad news' which necessitated her going off at once—she begged to be forgiven and hoped she and Steve would be given another chance to celebrate at the hospital. She then rushed off with Harold. They caught the seven o'clock train from Victoria.

All the way to Brighton Brennan talked of Robin; his neurosis; future possible treatment

91

for him at St. Martha's in the psychiatry ward. Glynis did most of the listening. But she was haunted by the pathetic remembrance of Moira's usually hard blue eyes full of tears and that appeal from the heart: *'Bring him back!'*

It couldn't be much fun being in Moira's shoes, Glynis thought—loving without return—wanting only the reward of knowing all was well with the beloved being. That was *true* love. That, Glynis thought, was how she would want to love Steve. Selflessly. Prepared to give him up even though he appeared to love her in return—unless she could be quite certain that marriage to her was the best thing for *him*.

They reached Brighton in an hour. It was cold, windy and unpleasant as they left the station. Harold was like most students—not well off—but Glynis insisted that they took a taxi and that she paid for it. The Gellows lived in a flat in Clifton Road, which was only a few minutes' drive in a streamlined taxi up the hill from the station. They were both thankful to see a light shining through the frosted glass of the Gellows' front door when they reached it. A slightly built woman opened this door to them. She had ash-grey hair and blue eyes and they could see at once that she was Robin's mother. She had the same delicate bone-structure and over-sensitive lips, and nervous manner. But Mrs. Gellow was good-looking and in her early fifties.

She looked enquiringly from the tall boy in tweeds and mackintosh to the very beautiful girl with the gold-bright hair in the camel-hair coat. Harold introduced himself.

'My name's Brennan. This is Miss Glynis Thorne. You may have heard of us from Robin. We're friends of his from St. Martha's. At least *I* am.'

The last slightly sinister remark was resented by Glynis.

'We're both his friends,' she added.

Mrs. Gellow's face flushed. Her lips trembled and she looked as though she was about to cry. Her fingers plucked at the cameo brooch which she wore pinned to a blue woolly cardigan she was wearing.

'Oh, yes—do come in!' she said. 'Please . . . I—I don't think Robin expected you, did he? No! And I don't know whether he'll even see you. Ever since he arrived home an hour or so ago he's been locked in his bedroom. He's shut even me out. I can't get a word out of him except that he's left St. Martha's for good and won't go back. Oh, dear, he's been in a most *dreadful* state ever since he saw about that girl's engagement—'

She broke off. She had ushered Harold and Glynis into a small lounge which was quite attractively furnished in modern style with unvarnished oak, with green linen curtains and covers and a green flowered carpet. An electric fire burned in the grate. Over the

93

mantelpiece hung a painting of a baby boy with a mass of fair curls. A plump smiling child. Somehow the sight of that portrait—so obviously the young Robin—touched Glynis to the quick.

'Oh, Mrs. Gellow!' she exclaimed, unwrapping her headscarf. 'I'm so very sorry about all this. It's simply awful—for you particularly. But it isn't my fault—really it isn't. It—it just *happened.*'

Then Robin's mother, staring, flushed a deep pink, as her gaze travelled over the girl.

'Why, *of course. You* are the Glynis he talks of all the time. It's your photo that was in the papers this morning—with a St. Martha's surgeon. So it's all *your* fault my boy is in such a terrible state of mind!'

And with those words she sat down in a chair and put a hand to her eyes and fumbled in her pocket for a handkerchief which she found, then blew her nose noisily.

Harold glanced at Glynis. He saw her flush and turn away. He was beginning to feel sorry for her. It was he now who started to speak in her defence. It was not her fault, he told Mrs. Gellow. A girl couldn't be blamed if a chap fell for her and she couldn't return it. Robin, himself, had always told him, Harold, that Glynis had not encouraged him. It was just that he had this blind passion for her and he had refused to lose hope until he actually knew that she was going to marry someone else. But

94

Glynis was in her rights to become engaged to any man she liked. She had come down here tonight to try, like himself, Brennan added, to persuade Robin to look at things sensibly.

'Everyone at St. Martha's thinks he's laid up with malaria. But he can go back with us on the next train and no one will know a thing about it. We'll smuggle him through the back way—Out-Patients' entrance or something.'

Mrs. Gellow was weeping. She looked frantic with worry. Dabbing at her eyes, blinking at poor Glynis over the handkerchief, she said:

'Oh, well, I can't blame you if you *didn't* lead him on, Miss Thorne.'

'She didn't, Mum—I've told you that dozens of times. You can take my word for it.'

They all turned round. Robin stood in the doorway. He wore old flannels and a polo-necked pullover. His hair was rough—his eyes red-rimmed with lack of sleep. He was colourless. Glynis looked at him, silently shocked and distressed. He used to be a boy who could laugh and be cheerful at times. It seemed to her so tragic that his love for her should have turned him into this. *'It only shows,'* she thought *'how carefully I* personally *have got to be about Steve—what a power for good or evil love can be in this life . . .'*

Then Harold moved towards his friend. Robin backed away.

'Why are you here, Hal? And with Glyn?'

Harold said:

'I'd like to chat with you, Robbie. So would Glynis.'

Robin eyed Glynis sullenly.

'You're wasting your time—' he began.

Mrs. Gellow interrupted. Rising, with handkerchief to her lips, she hurried past him, saying:

'You'd better listen to your friends—they know what is good for you. You're behaving very badly, Rob, and you're *killing* me.'

'Oh God, I'm sorry!' he muttered, and sinking into a chair, hid his face in his hands.

Glynis' heart beat quickly. Suddenly all her courage, her innate sympathy for suffering human beings, came to the fore and conquered her nervousness. She made a sign to Harold to follow Mrs. Gellow, intimating that she would like to talk to Robin alone. He nodded and walked out of the room.

'That's the girl,' his eyes said, encouraging her.

Left alone, Glynis took off her coat, seated herself on the arm of the chair, and put an arm lightly round the young doctor's shoulders.

'Now, Robin,' she said in a firm voice, 'let's talk this thing out. You can't refuse to go back to St. Martha's. You just can't—not only for your own and your nice mother's sakes, but for mine. If you go under now I'll never forgive myself, and nobody at St. Martha's will ever forgive me, either—even though I'm not really to blame. Do you want to do that to someone you say you love very much? *Do* you, Robin?'

At this same moment, Steven Grant-Tally emerged from the Matron's sitting-room and made his way towards the front hall to a telephone box. He was a surprised and somewhat harassed man. He had not been as long with his patient as anticipated and had thought he might still find Glynis 'celebrating', so he had come on to St. Martha's. Not only did he find no party in progress but was told that some mysterious bad news had reached his fiancee and that she had excused herself from the cocktail party and vanished.

Steven's first inclination was to telephone Glynis' family in Barnet. But as he was about to enter the telephone booth, one of the probationers whom he did not even know by name—a red-haired, plain little thing, he thought—waylaid him. Hot-cheeked and obviously nervous, she apologized for daring to interfere but thought he might like to know what had happened to Miss Thorne.

'I—I'm about the only one who kn-knows about Nurse Thorne—I mean M-Miss Thorne,' she stammered.

Steven smiled in his kindliest fashion. Nobody could be more charming than he when he wanted to put one of the nursing junior staff at ease. The warmth in those handsome eyes made Moira Thomas begin to feel she understood why Glynis had 'fallen' for the famous E.N.T. man. As briefly as possible she told him the story of Robin Gellow. Steven listened, frowning. That infernal fellow Gellow again—he really was 'a pain in the neck', Steven told himself, but questioning Moira further he was positively amazed to hear that Glynis had rushed down to Brighton by train to Gellow's home.

'I think this is rather a poor show, Nurse,' began Steven, a trifle pompously. 'I don't see why Miss Thorne should have been dragged into the affair. After all, she is going to marry me, you know, and if every disappointed boyfriend behaved like this, the world would be a sorry place.'

Moira trembled. But she had enough character to stick to her guns. She said:

'Oh, honestly, sir—she *had* to go. As Mr. Brennan said as well as me, she is the only one who has any influence over Robin, and he is at the beginning of his career—he must be brought to his senses.'

Steven hummed and hawed, but gradually melted. He began to feel sorry for all these inhibited young people with their personal griefs and disasters and to remember what such disasters can mean to emotional youth. He also mentally took off his hat to Glynis for going down to Brighton with Harold Brennan. It must have been a tricky decision for her to make. Suddenly he said:

'Look here, Nurse Thomas, I can see you're

all for saving friend Robin from catastrophe. I presume he means a lot to you—eh?'

Moira swallowed and nodded.

'Yes, sir.'

'Right—then we must and will bring him to his senses—in fact I also must join in and do a bit of interfering!' said Steven with his kindly smile again. 'Does Gellow happen to be on the 'phone?'

Moira said that he was and that she knew his mother's number.

'Good,' said Steven. 'Then 'phone through and speak to Glynis and tell her to stay there till I come. Say that I'm driving down to Brighton right away to see Gellow, then bringing her and young Brennan back by car. We may all have a bite down there. It's past eight now, you know.'

Moira gasped.

'Oh, how marvellous of you! And you will bring Robin, too?'

'Even if I have to sock him one and lay him out and bring back his unconscious form,' said Steven cheerfully.

Moira, almost speechless with excitement, darted into the telephone box to put through that toll-call to Brighton.

CHAPTER NINE

Much later that night, driving in the beautiful powerful Jaguar down the Brighton Road, headlamps projecting a broad white path on the wet road, Glynis thought this must be one of the happiest moments of her life—*so* far.

She sat snuggled very comfortably under a rug close to Steven; his left hand over hers; his right—in leather gauntlet—on the wheel, a cigarette between his lips. On the small back seat, not so comfortable but quite content, two young men sat bolt upright, also smoking, and carrying on a conversation which had nothing to do with personal triumphs or disasters but (so Glynis and Steven gathered when they heard snatches of it) dealt with the prevailing tendency on the part of the medical profession, as a whole, to make too free a use of penicillin.

Now and then Glynis giggled and whispered to Steve:

'Did you hear that, Steve? Aren't you going to argue?'

And Steve whispered back:

'Not on your life, darling. No sensible medicine man of experience ever dares to suggest that a fourth-year student or his newly qualified friend might conceivably be wrong.'

They giggled together now.

Oh, it was a wonderful evening! Glynis thought ecstatically. The rain had cleared up. The sky, full of ragged clouds, was bright with moonlight now. They had left the glittering lights on Brighton sea-front far behind them. They had come over the Dyke and were now well on their route, passing over Bolney cross-roads.

It was past midnight. Terribly late, Glynis reflected. She was terribly tired, too, but too content to be troubled by mere fatigue. It was delicious to sit so close to Steve and feel his fingers closing over hers—breathe in the odour of the Turkish cigarette he was smoking—to rub her cheek now and then against his shoulder. She loved him more than ever tonight. He had been absolutely marvellous about Robin. Everyone said so. Robin's mother in particular. Mrs. Gellow's last words to Glynis had been:

'If Mr. Grant-Tally is a good example of a St. Martha's man, I'm proud to feel my son is also one.'

And she had been proud too when Robin fought down those demons of despair in his mind and conquered. She had thanked Glynis with all her heart for the part she had played. But she knew—and so did they all—it had really been Steve's doing that won Robin over in the end.

Never would Glynis forget her astonishment when she had taken that 'phone call from

Nurse Thomas and heard that Steven was on his way down to Brighton. She had been so afraid he might be angry and resent her coming here. Yet Moira assured her he was not and that he had expressed a wish to join in the concerted effort to get Rob back to St. Martha's.

Glynis had been thankful when Steven walked into the flat. She had had a difficult hour or so with Robin, who had broken down and wept in his weak fashion, bathing her hands in his tears. She had pleaded with him—appealed to his common sense—tried every argument—without definite results. First he would go back—then he wouldn't. First his life was wrecked—no use without her—then he admitted he had his mother to think of. Then he broke down again.

When Steven arrived Glynis was looking exhausted and almost at the end of her resources. Steve, too, was tired. He had had a long, trying day. But he was cheerful and full of common sense and from the start he treated Robin as he would have done a cherished friend. That the boy's mind was sick and that he was in need of a psychoanalyst might be true—but tonight Steven tried his own methods of dealing with Robin. And it was a simple and homely one—so simple that it amazed even the girl who thought she knew him. She had not credited even Steven with quite so much 'horse sense'. Nor for a moment

102

did he exhibit any wish to be treated by Robin with the respect or fear in which a newly qualified man might accord a famous surgeon. He assured him from the start that his visit was 'off the record'.

When Robin had first seen him he was furious and all out to sneer and defy. But within a few moments Steven had him under control. He sent Harold Brennan for beer and two glasses.

'I'm thirsty and what Robin and I both need is a couple of pints and some quiet conversation,' he said.

Glynis left the room, struggling with her tears. She joined Robin's mother and Harold in the next room. They were equally depressed. They none of them knew what Steven said to Robin: except once, when the voices were raised and penetrated through the walls. Then Robin was heard to say:

'Why should you care a damn? Let me go—'

And from Steven:

'Sit down, you young fool, and don't make such an ass of yourself. Why *shouldn't* I care? I'm a St. Martha's man too, aren't I? And we both love Glynis. When you love somebody you don't try to wreck them. She didn't want to wreck you—why do you want to hurt her now—and me too! *I've* never done you any harm. If you persist in this damn-fool attitude you'll have the whole world getting wind of it and the papers suggesting you walked out on your hospital job because Glynis and I double-crossed you.'

From Robin hoarsely:

'I've never blamed either you or Glynis.'

Steven:

'Then pull yourself together, man, for lord's sake. Oh, to the devil with these histrionics. Have some more beer. Come on—pour it out and give me some and stop grousing. It isn't you, you know, or I, who count—or even Glynis, really. It's that mother of yours. Tell me about her and your father. She looks a sweetie. How long have you two been alone down here in this nice flat?'

Later Mrs. Gellow said to Glynis:

'Mr. Grant-Tally isn't a bit what one might imagine. He was so human with Robin. Robin says he talked so much of his father and me, and in the end he made Robin feel ashamed he'd ever *dreamed* of hurting me by quitting his work. Mr. Grant-Tally brought things right back into perspective for Robin. The boy was quite like his old self after he finished that talk.'

So it had seemed to Glynis. Poor Robin was a bit shaken and subdued—but a man whose brain-storm had passed. He was ready for action again. Like some of the poor chaps Steven had seen on active service, he told Glynis later on. They'd go to pieces and crawl on the ground and swear they'd never be forced into action again. But the fears would pass. The 'coward' would suddenly brace himself and in the end be just the chap to win a V.C.

Robin had won his battle. He was going back to St. Martha's. He had given his mother his solemn promise; and given it to Glynis and Harold, too. Ashamed of himself, but a man again, and thought Steven Grant-Tally one of the finest men he had ever met.

'No wonder you clinched matters with *him*,' he said to Glynis. 'I didn't know he was such a hell of a nice chap. I am sorry I caused you all such a lot of trouble. But there's no need to worry about me any more.'

No need to worry about him—perhaps not, Glynis had thought at the time. But there was still need to worry about *herself* . . . and Steve.

The rest of the evening, however, had been sheer delight. Steven, in crashing form, had taken them all—including Mrs. Gellow—to a late meal at a big hotel in Hove. Full of food, wine, and with a gay spirit prevailing, they took Mrs. Gellow home again and were now making their return journey.

They dropped the two young men at St. Martha's; then on Steven drove to Barnet. Once alone with him Glynis said:

'Darling, your vitality shakes me—you're older than I am yet you seem twice as full of energy. How many miles have you driven today? Over a hundred—and after all that operating. I really *am* full of admiration.'

'Quite right, too. I like being admired,' he laughed, and stopped the car and kissed her warmly and lingeringly. 'I think you're a darling. I'm not surprised Gellow had a brain-storm,' he whispered against her lips. 'Don't ever run out on *me*, my love.'

'I couldn't!' she whispered. 'Unless . . .'

'Unless—what?'

She gulped.

'Unless—it was best for you . . .' she began.

'Subject forbidden. Good night, Precious Heart. Tomorrow we buy that engagement ring, and the shorter our engagement is, the better I shall be pleased. It *has* been a day, I grant you, and I am exhausted. Home to bed. Good night, my adorable one . . .'

How could any girl be anything but madly happy when a man like Steven Grant-Tally said things like that—and seemed to mean them? Glynis could quite well see that if she was going to stick to her belief that a period of waiting was essential between two such different people, she would have to exert all her strength of mind. For that fervent young heart of hers clamoured for him. Every time he held and kissed her, she was wholly, madly in love.

Steven let nothing stand in the way of the purchase of that important ring the next morning. It was altogether an exciting day, beginning with a note from Robin brought round from St. Martha's (no doubt by himself before he started work), saying:

Thanks a million. I can never be grateful enough to you, G.-T., and Hal. Good luck and bless you.

And a letter from Brighton the following day from Mrs. Gellow, too, which Glynis thought especially nice.

I thank you and your wonderful surgeon from the bottom of my heart. I know now why Robin loved you so much.

Flattery of this kind did not go to Glynis' head. On the contrary it made her feel extraordinarily humble, and the impact of too much admiration or *largesse* spent on her always scared her a little.

As she said to her mother when that busy day ended and she was home again:

'It's funny, Mum, the right things always seem to happen to the wrong people, or *vice versa*. I mean *I* was really born to get quietly engaged to some nice young man who'd never been heard of, and look at *this*!'

'*This*' was a huge post—most unusual for the Thorne family. Photographers begging to be allowed to photograph Miss Glynis Thorne. Printed cards for Mrs. Thorne touting for wedding receptions. Fashion houses, shoemakers, modistes and private dressmakers all 'wondering if Miss Thorne would like suggestions about her trousseau'.

Sylvia Thorne was, of course, in her element.

'It really *is* going to be exciting, Glyn, although I don't know how or where we can give the wedding reception. There'll be such *hundreds* of guests on the Grant-Tally side. Our lounge is big, but not big enough.'

'We don't need to discuss it yet,' said Glynis hurriedly and picked up Sinbad, her mother's Persian cat, who had long been a member of the family. She buried her face against the silky grey-blue fur. Sinbad, in a bad humour, mewed and ran his claws over the back of her hand. She let him go, sighing:

'You wouldn't think anybody as beautiful to look at as Sinbad could be so cruel and treacherous at times. But the world's full of cruel treacherous people who look wonderful.'

'My *dearest* Glyn, you do say the most extraordinary things!' exclaimed her mother, opening another advertisement which had just come through the letter-box. 'What people do you know who are beautiful and have claws like Sinbad's?'

Glynis did not answer, but in that moment the memory of Mrs. Chayney leapt to her mind. Rhona Chayney's thin hands and long pointed nails. *She* might very well answer to that description.

After the long tiring day she wanted nothing

more than to have a hot bath and go to bed. She had just slipped between the sheets and switched off her lamp when her mother rushed into her bedroom.

'I hate to disturb you, darling, but it's Lady Barley on the 'phone. What a charming woman she is! She sounds *so friendly*. She's asked Dad and I—I mean Dad and *me*—I'm always so silly about that—to dinner next week. Won't it be a thrill? She wants to speak to you.'

Rather crossly, Glynis muttered: 'Didn't you tell her that I've gone to bed?'

But Mrs. Thorne had switched on the light and brooked no nonsense.

'Don't be silly, darling. I expect the Barleys are only just finishing dinner. You said how late they dined the other night.'

Glynis, who remained in awe of Steven's sophisticated sister, went grumbling to the telephone, which was in her father's study.

She answered and then heard Kitty's voice with all that charm that could so easily 'bamboozle Mummy', as Glyn put it.

'You weren't in bed, my poor sweet, were you?'

'Yes,' said Glynis, who was determined not to 'pretend'. A little laugh from Kitty.

'How naughty of me to wake you. I never dreamt—'

'That's quite all right, Lady B—I mean, Kitty,' said Glynis, 'but I was very late last

109

night, and had rather a lot to do today. I'm a person who needs a lot of sleep.'

'Very sensible of you, darling. I wish I could make Steve go to bed. He never does. He's one of the sitters-up-all-night type.'

'That's one in the eye for *you*, Glynis, my girl,' thought Glynis. 'Oil trying to mix with water again, and her ladyship knows it.'

Kitty babbled on. How she had heard when Steve got home this evening that they had chosen a perfectly *wonderful* ring but that it had to be made smaller for Glyn's slender finger, so she hadn't got it yet. A fine emerald, he had told her, set in platinum with baguette diamonds on either side. Steve was being quite poetic, Kitty said, and had announced during dinner that the ring was the same colour as Glynis' eyes.

'*Madly* extravagant, I hear,' she finished with the laugh that Glynis found so affected.

'I'm afraid it was,' said Glynis. 'I didn't want him to spend so much. I'd have been quite happy with something less.'

'Oh, you mustn't be so modest, dear. It will never suit Steve. I'm afraid, as a family, we have a passion for the most lovely things.'

Glynis found this difficult to reply to.

Kitty went on:

'Look here, darling, we all want some really good photographs of you. I wonder if you would let me take you along to my favourite man—he's the most *wonderful* photographer in

London—just off Park Lane.'

Glynis spoke up bravely now.

'I don't think Mummy can afford the West End prices, Kitty, but I'll get some done down here. We've got one or two quite good men.'

'*Not* in the suburbs, darling, please. Let it be a West End portrait for Steve.'

Whether Kitty knew it or not, that was the worst sort of remark she could have made. Glynis had been very happy this last day or two, but it would take more than forty-eight hours to wipe out the ideals and principles of her lifetime. At once she was up in arms.

'I'm afraid I'm going to disappoint you, but I *am* suburban, you know, Kitty—if you like to call it that—and I don't want to be turned into a Society "deb", and I don't think it would be fair to my parents to launch out into all kinds of unnecessary expense. Besides—'

'Darling Glynis, you needn't be quite so sensitive. I didn't mean to offend you, nor ask you to become a débutante but—Oh, very well, Steve shall speak to you.'

Glynis, who was sleepy and cross and desperately anxious not to start an argument on these lines with him, began to protest. But Kitty had handed over to her brother. She heard Steven's delightful voice:

'Hullo, my angel. I hear you've been dragged out of your little bed. What a shame! What's all this about your not wanting to come up and be photographed?'

CHAPTER TEN

When Glynis started to explain that she would far rather have her photograph taken in Barnet, Steven, like his sister, would not hear of it. He shared Kitty's views about the photograph—that it was essential that his Glynis should be photographed by one of the famous London men.

It was useless for Glynis to go on protesting, but she was determined to pay the account herself, however much it was. Steven took the wind out of her sails by saying the most romantic and tender things to her and then:

'Good night, my sweet love. Sleep well! . . .'

The confused Glynis was then handed over to Kitty again, who, victorious, and more than ever effusive and charming, invited her to lunch and said, 'Good night, darling.'

'*Darling* . . .' Glynis muttered the word darkly to herself and returned to bed. It was all so trying, because Kitty was going to be her sister-in-law—a close relationship. She would have to *learn* to like her, Glynis reflected. She knew that she was probably 'too touchy' and stubborn. But the thought of that lunch and being dragged around town by Kitty held nothing for Glynis but gloom.

Her mother, hearing what Glynis had to say, was, of course, ecstatic. 'I think you're so

112

lucky. Lady Barley might have had other plans for her brother, but she is being *sweet* to you.'

'Saccharin,' growled Glynis.

'I just don't understand you,' said Mrs. Thorne.

Sometimes Glynis felt that she did not understand herself. But through all the setbacks, her admiration and love for Steve took precedence.

*   *   *

She saw him for only a few moments that following morning. It was his day at St. Martha's. He would be operating all morning. He rushed with his customary haste into his consulting room at ten o'clock, kissed her hand, and immediately started to dictate an urgent letter to a professor of pathology.

Glynis wanted to throw herself into his arms and say: *'Can't I get out of lunching with Kitty and go with you to some quiet place where we can talk?'* She wanted to say: *I absolutely adore you . . .'* She wanted to step into his car and drive with him into the country. But she said nothing and went on with the second letter.

He even forgot to say good-bye, because an important call came through for him from a big West End clinic just as he was leaving. She heard him say:

'I don't agree with Simpson. I think the child's on the young side. I much prefer to wait

113

till he's four. Oh well, Simpson and I will argue that out later . . . Tell him I'll be there at five o'clock.'

Then, looking very preoccupied (the conversation had obviously irritated him), Steven picked up case, gloves and coat and rushed out.

Glynis stood at the window and watched him drive away. At no time did she care for this Harley Street, Wimpole Street, Weymouth Street district, with their long rows of tall houses, all marked by doctor's plates. Much as she loved working for Steve, she had never quite accustomed herself to this consulting ground, as she termed it, for people who had money to spend—or even if they hadn't— preferred to spend it on specialists rather than go to the hospitals. She supposed she was 'hospital minded' because of her passionate love of nursing. But already Steven had made it clear to her that once they were married he would probably buy a house in this part of London. Here she would live—Mrs. Grant-Tally of the future. (That sent shudders down her spine!) She, who had so much wanted to be just—Nurse Thorne.

Just before one o'clock Lady Barley swept in, *soignée* and handsome, in Persian lamb coat and tiny pancake hat. She was niceness itself to Glyn.

'Come along, darling—we're going to have a cosy lunch together and a long chat.'

Glynis found herself at the Ritz.

It was the first time she had ever lunched there. It was quite a thrill to see the big beautiful room with its many windows facing the Park. Lady Barley appeared to be well known. The *maître d'hôtel* led her at once to a window table, and said that he had her favourite dish for lunch.

Fascinated, Glynis listened and watched, while Lady Barley ordered the menu, and envied the ease, the poise that Steven's sister possessed, and which she felt that she, Glynis, should try to acquire if she was to make the right sort of wife for him. She accepted the sherry and settled down to enjoy her lunch.

'I really must get to know and understand Kitty better, then perhaps I'll like her,' she decided. 'We *should* have something in common, as we both love Steve.'

Unfortunately Glynis' good intentions received a setback, for they had scarcely finished their *Sole Bonne-femme* before Rhona Chayney walked into the restaurant. She was alone, but spotted Kitty and made for her table. Whether it was manoeuvred or not, Glynis had no idea, but Kitty at once invited Rhona to join them. The lunch became a trio, and Glynis sat quietly eating, listening to a lot of frothy social chatter between the two women. Kitty was going to Sandown Races tomorrow, Rhona was taking her in the Rolls-Bentley.

'You ought to come with us, darling,' said Kitty gaily, turning her attention to the young girl.

Glynis reminded her that she had a job. Kitty sighed that it was a pity because racing was such fun. Glynis said that she didn't think she'd care much for it, whereupon Kitty gave a theatrical laugh, and said:

'Darling, I can see you'll have to be terribly self-sacrificing over a lot of things when you're married to Steven—racing is one of his pet hobbies.'

'I shouldn't have thought he had much time for it,' said Glynis drily.

'Oh, he gets off from his work now and again, you know—we had some wonderful days at Ascot last summer, didn't we, Rhona?' put in Kitty, glancing at Rhona.

Glynis felt as she had done on the first night she met Mrs. Chayney, that here was a woman who might be a definite menace in her life. Rhona looked wonderful—superb mink coat—tiny coq-feather hat—exquisite gloves and bag. But Rhona looked at Steven's choice and hated her for her fresh youthful beauty which marked her out from a great many other women in this room who were twice as well dressed, and twice as heavily made up. She hated, too, that slight touch of dignity about Glynis. 'The little suburban girl' could hold her own, shy though she was. Her strangely beautiful green eyes looked very penetratingly into Rhona's discontented ones and Rhona thought: *'What an uncomfortable way the girl has of staring!'*

It was Rhona, rather than Glynis, who felt uneasy during the rest of that meal. Without knowing why, Glynis felt that the two women, no matter how gaily they smiled or included her in their gossip, were 'getting at her' in some sort of way.

'They neither of them like me,' Glynis reflected. But she felt that she would die rather than let them see that she knew it. Delicately she discussed Steven.

'He's very anxious for us to be married soon, you know,' she announced during the coffee.

Rhona whitened under her rouge but continued to throw Glynis dazzling smiles.

'How thrilling, my dear. Have you fixed the date?'

Glynis, twining hot slim hands in her lap, grinned back.

'I should think some time next month.'

'What about your trousseau?' asked Kitty, with a horrible mental picture of her bills and of the way that Rhona might react to this announcement. She had hoped for a long engagement which would give Steven plenty of time in which to change his mind, even if Glynis didn't change hers.

'Oh, Mummy will see to my clothes,' announced Glynis coolly.

A moment's silence. Then from Rhona:

'You must let me introduce you to someone I know who can get the Dior and Balmain models over from Paris for you.'

This was where Glynis held her own—loyal to her upbringing and her convictions.

'Mummy will have her own ideas, thanks awfully, Mrs. Chayney. I'm quite sure we shall be able to manage without the terribly expensive model-houses. Anyhow, one can get their patterns, you know, and have the dresses made at home.'

'Yes, of course,' said Rhona with a sickly smile.

But when Glynis left Rhona and Kitty alone for a moment in the vestibule, Rhona Chayney no longer pretended. She gripped Kitty's arm in a vice and spoke to her in a strangled voice.

'It's absolutely *intolerable*—that little nobody! . . . I don't care how beautiful she is. Steve must be raving. Are you going to stand for it, Kitty?'

'Darling, I can't break Steven's engagement for him,' said Kitty with a brief unhappy laugh.

'Kitty,' interrupted Rhona, 'whose side are you on? Oh, *heavens*!' She broke off, and pulling a gold, diamond-crested case from her bag with trembling fingers, opened it and found a cigarette. Kitty applied her lighter to it and said, nervously:

'Don't upset yourself, Rhona, please. You know perfectly well I'm on your side. I'm going to do everything I possibly can. You know I'd be the happiest woman in London if it were only *you.*'

'Well, it has got to be me in the end,' said Rhona, and jerked on a suede glove so roughly that it slit across the thumb.

She did not go with the other two to the photographer's. That next hour was by no means Glynis' idea of fun. Kitty seemed to have swung from a gay mood to a difficult one and snapped at Glynis whenever she tried to suggest how she personally wanted to be photographed.

The famous photographer raved about her beauty, her profile and her figure until Glynis was covered with embarrassment. She wondered when the ordeal was over if the results would be at all what Steven wanted. She feared that she had either looked scared to death or simply artificial with what she called a 'toothy smile'. Afterwards Kitty wanted to take her along to Bond Street.

'I do so want to introduce you to my favourite lingerie shop. You must give them an order for your trousseau, darling. They'll do you heavenly nightgowns.'

'What sort of price?' asked Glynis doubtfully.

'Well, the hand-made, real satin or chiffon are from twenty to thirty guineas.'

Then Glynis laughed.

'Kitty dear, I can't *begin* to afford a

trousseau like that, honestly I can't. But please don't worry about it, let me cope with my clothes by myself.'

'Steve will be disappointed—he asked me to take you around—'

'I'll explain to Steve,' broke in Glynis.

And that was as far as Kitty could get with her interference today. She was a little surprised and put out to find that Glynis was not to be as easily managed as one might think from that quiet, shy façade of hers.

Just before they parted, Kitty said:

'I'll be seeing you when your parents dine with us at Thurloe Square next week, but I don't know whether Steven told you—Rhona's giving one of her supper parties in the penthouse the day after tomorrow and we're all invited. She gives the most *exciting* parties in London—divine food and drink and there's generally dancing and roulette afterwards.'

It scarcely sounded the sort of evening that Glynis would enjoy, but Kitty made haste to tell her how much Steven wanted to go. Then suddenly Glynis looked Kitty straight in the eyes with that frankness that Rhona had found so 'awkward' and said:

'Does Steven like Mrs. Chayney very much?'

Kitty's lashes fluttered. She gave her most insincere laugh.

'Darling, what a question!'

'Well, *does* he? I'd like to know.'

They were driving back to Weymouth

Street. It was nearly four o'clock. Steven had insisted on Glynis taking the afternoon off but she wanted to slip into the consulting room to see if he wanted anything.

Kitty answered:

'My *dear*—it doesn't do to delve too deeply into the past. But I think I told you on the night you dined with us that Steve's engagement has been a great blow to poor Rhona.'

A little devil of stubbornness made Glynis persist with her questioning.

'I agree, and the past doesn't concern me, but I just want to know. I hate undercurrents. Is it supposed to be common knowledge that Mrs. Chayney was in love with Steve? I mean, did *Steve* know it too and were they—were they . . .' Now words failed her. She sat silent, flushed, unhappy.

But Kitty Barley felt that this was the moment to be subtle and, having inferred so much, to say no more.

'If I were you I'd just not worry about it at all, darling,' she said in a hard bright voice. 'And if you want my advice don't bring the subject up with Steven. Just be *tactful*.'

What all that meant, Glynis had not the slightest idea. It might have meant everything—or nothing.

As she walked into the consulting room she felt disgruntled, and she had no wish whatsoever to go to Rhona's 'exciting party'. She wished that Rhona Chayney had never had anything to do with Steven in the past. Why *should* she be so upset about the engagement? After all, Steven had told her, Glynis, the other night that he had never even dreamt of asking Rhona to marry him. Yet . . .

Glynis realized suddenly that she was jealous. A fine thing, she told herself grimly. Not much use being jealous if she meant to marry an attractive, popular man like Steven. She had a sudden enormous desire to fly into the comfort of his arms and be reassured. But he had not come back. A telephone call from the clinic informed her that Mr. Grant-Tally was doing an emergency operation and would be very late, so Miss Thorne was not to wait.

Glynis went home feeling curiously flat. It was as though she was being constantly alienated from the man whom she loved so much and with whom she wanted to be so close. It should be possible for two people in love to be very close, she reflected. Yet there seemed a thousand outside circumstances, invisible yet factual, always drawing a blind down between Steven and herself.

She had never felt more deeply and humanly in love or more in need of him than tonight. She was filled with a frantic longing to bind him to her irrevocably—not to risk losing him for any reason at all.

Later that night when Steven 'phoned her she answered the call in an unusual mood of softness and subjugation.

She answered his questions about the photograph and the lunch with Kitty, then with cheeks hot and heart fluttering, blurted out:

'You know the other day you said that you wanted us to get married quickly. That is, you said you saw no reason why we should wait too long?'

'Yes, darling. I remember very well. You were very sensible, my angel, and said you thought it would be a good thing for us to have a long engagement.'

Now the rapidity of her own breathing almost choked Glynis. She said:

'How far did you really agree with me?'

'Darling, I told you at the time, if it's your wish to wait, it's mine.'

'Do you still think it—sensible?'

'Possibly. But one spends one's life having to be sensible and suddenly life slips away. I used to regard myself as a cautious man. Perhaps falling in love with you has somewhat altered my viewpoint. I don't know that I *want* to be sensible about you.'

'You mean . . . you'd like us to get married at once, but you agree it might be silly?' she said huskily.

Steven appeared to hesitate. His voice sounded surprised now.

'This is all very unlike you, my sweet. What's the matter? Have you suddenly decided that it might be a good plan for us to go mad and rush into the nearest register-office?'

She hesitated and was lost.

'No, of course not,' she said in a suffocated voice.

He laughed. She could see that he thought she had been joking. Yet she had been on the verge of saying: *'Yes, let's get married tomorrow or the day after. I love you so—I'm terrified of losing you. I don't care how different we are—let me come to you now—at once.'*

But the moment passed. Steven, manlike, swung from romance to business. He told her about a special appointment he wanted her to make with a firm of surgical instrument makers as soon as she got up to town tomorrow.

'When can I see you—outside work?' she finally asked, swallowing hard.

'Let's see—aren't we invited *to* a party Rhona Chayney's giving? Kitty said something about it.'

'Yes, but not till next week,' said Glynis bleakly. 'She said you wanted to go.'

'Well, whatever her failings are, Rhona is a genius at giving parties—I think you ought to sample one,' said Steven.

'Yes, of course,' Glynis forced herself to say, 'but . . . when can I see you *alone*?'

'Shall I come down right now and see you—' he began.

'Of course not,' she broke in. 'You must be terribly tired. Tomorrow night, perhaps.'

'Of course. We'll go out together tomorrow and have a quiet evening, angel.' Then: 'Oh, *dear life*! I can't!' he suddenly groaned.

'Why?' Glynis, bitterly disappointed, bit an underlip that was inclined to tremble.

'Does my estimable secretary not remember that the poor perishing surgeon has to go up to Manchester for that conference at the Royal Free? I shan't be back in time. I shall probably have to stay on to dinner with the boys.'

A moment's silence, then Glynis said:

'Oh yes, I remember now.'

He bade her good night tenderly, and told her that he loved her to distraction. Then he put down the receiver.

He was lost to her again, she thought dully. Now he would have after-dinner drinks with his sister and brother-in-law. He would be absorbed into their *milieu*—which was of course, *his own*. And for Glynis tomorrow would be like any other day. She would just see him for a second, snatch a word and a kiss.

Oh why, *why*, hadn't she had the courage to say 'yes' just now when he had asked her if she would like to reverse all her opinions and get married at once? He would have agreed. Of that she was sure.

She had meant to spend the evening discussing her trousseau with her mother, but instead she pleaded a headache and went to her room to fight all the old secret demons of doubt and apprehension.

CHAPTER ELEVEN

That next morning Mrs. Thorne heard about the party that was to be held by the famous Mrs. Chayney. Her photographs were regularly to be seen in Society journals and she had even been introduced as a reigning beauty one night on the TV, so Mrs. Thorne was delighted that her daughter was to be the guest of so notable a London hostess. She then started what Glynis called one of her 'nagging sessions' about what dress Glyn was to wear. It *could not* be the one she had worn at the hospital ball. It just wasn't one hundred per cent. Glynis was *sure* to be noticed and photographed, and so on, until Glynis suddenly gave in, but with a rather dogged determination to show everybody—including her mother—that she could hold her own in spite of all the Society hostesses in town.

'But you'll have to do some jolly hard work, Mum. The party is on Monday, isn't it? Four days' time. I know little Miss Potts will do all the machining and Alma's a marvellous needlewoman—she's coming tomorrow for supper—she'll help. You work terribly fast and I can sew all Saturday and Sunday. Okay, we'll show them. And it'll only cost the price of the material.'

Carried away on the tide of enthusiasm,

Sylvia Thorne cordially agreed. There wouldn't be time to 'finish off' properly, but they could and would 'run up a little frock' such as the retiring Glynis had never before dreamed of wearing.

First, out to buy a woman's magazine that had a Dior pattern for a strapless ballet-length evening dress. Then the material which Mrs. Thorne, rushing up to town, found in Oxford Street—creamy satin with a pattern of gold thread, and the price made mother and daughter gasp. But they laughed over it. The whole dress wasn't going to cost even a quarter of what the original Paris model would do.

Finally it was achieved after an exciting, breathless four days of loving labour, with assistance from the local dressmaker, Miss Potts, who had adored Glynis since she was born, and from the faithful Alma. When they first saw Glynis in the lovely dress they all broke into 'Oohs' and 'Aahs'. Glynis stared at herself in a long mirror and suddenly felt, as she described it, 'a million dollars'. Then Mrs. Thorne rushed upstairs to find the *pièce de résistance*—her grandmother's white lace mantilla, bought on a honeymoon in Seville in 1890. That, over Glynis' bright gold head (or pretty shoulders), and the picture of elegance was complete. Glynis then walked with exaggerated dramatic grace up and down the room, and Alma made everybody laugh by exclaiming:

'Oh, *Glyn*, if only Christian Dior himself could see you, he'd want you for one of his models.'

'No thank you!' Glynis laughed back. 'Nothing like that for me.'

But she was glad she had decided to make this dress. The gamble had 'come off'. It was going to startle not only Steven, but all those well-dressed women friends of his.

It certainly did startle Lady Barley on the night, and still more so the hostess.

Steven, manlike, had little idea what he was looking at when he first saw Glynis without her coat and walked with her into Rhona's drawing-room. He only knew that she looked a dream of beauty and chic in that cream-satin dress. When she lifted it a little it showed a frill of foamy lace, and a glimpse of slim leg and small feet in gold sandals.

'Darling, what a *dress!* I can't tell you how marvellous you look tonight—I'm quite stunned!'

He held her hand tightly in his. It was the hand that now bore his engagement ring. The exquisite emerald glittered, and Glynis, who had only received it that morning from the jewellers, could not stop looking at it. She had never before worn anything of such value. She was terrified in case she might lose it. She thrilled to the admiration in Steven's eyes, but she was feminine enough to feel that her big moment was when Kitty saw her, and for a second the mask fell away and her face broke into lines of sheer astonishment.

Kitty exclaimed:

'My *dear,* you *are* an extravagant little monkey—and you never told me that you were going to get yourself such a lovely model. It's a Dior—I recognize it from the collection.'

'It's *divine!*' put in the astonished and angry Rhona. Her smile cracked a little. She and Kitty had meant to patronize Steven's fiancée tonight. They had imagined she would appear in one of her 'off the peg' English evening dresses which Rhona despised, whilst *she* would ravish Steven's eye (and everybody else's) with her own amazing gown which had been the highlight of the collection in a leading Paris house.

Certainly Rhona looked her most attractive. Silver-grey satin, her corsage trimmed with narrow bands of mink, and a hem of the same rich dark fur on the wide flowing skirt. Wonderful sapphires and diamonds around the lovely throat . . . sapphire bracelet and ear-rings . . . her dark smooth hair in loose fashionable waves. She was the picture of sophistication.

Kitty wore black Chantilly lace and was equally chic. The room was, in fact, full of glamorous women but this was the proud moment of Glynis' life. For she knew that even if there were dresses here that must have cost over a hundred pounds, there was none more beautiful than her home-made 'Dior'. But it was a sad moment for Rhona. One by one her guests murmured to her:

'My *dear*, what a beautiful girl Steven Grant-Tally is marrying.'

At one juncture of the party Rhona whispered fiercely in Kitty's ear:

'If anybody else tells me how beautiful Glynis Thorne is I shall have one of my black-outs and put an end to this party. I wish I had never *held* it. How did she *get* that dress? I suppose Steven paid for it!'

Kitty had no answer to this spiteful remark. She wavered between being annoyed over Glynis' triumph and secretly a little pleased. It was beginning to irk her that she was so heavily in debt to her dearest Rhona. She could see that all this was finally going to come between her and the brother to whom she was really attached. The party was spoiled for Kitty, and Paul Barley made things worse by murmuring to her:

'Your little nobody from Barnet seems to be a great success.'

Glynis' triumph was only temporary, however. Rhona worked hard to make that certain. She immediately tore Glynis from Steven's protective side and handed her over to a certain South American who was a close friend of Rhona's, and who had strict orders to monopolize as much of Miss Thorne's attention as he could. Señor Rodrigo Canillo was only too delighted. He performed his task with avidity. But Glynis did her best to get away from him. He was far too sleek; held her far too tightly while they danced and paid her far too many fulsome compliments.

'Ah, Señorita, you are the true emblem of the English rose, with your pink and white beauty!' he sighed, and brought his head so close down to hers that she could smell the powerful odour of the brilliantine that plastered his hair.

Frantically she searched the room for Steven. But when she saw him he was dancing with Rhona. Glynis sucked her lower lip as she saw how closely Mrs. Chayney clung to him. Her huge dark eyes looked with melting softness up into his. Somehow the sight made Glynis uneasy, try as she would to conquer the sensation. It was so obvious to her that this night's silent duel between Rhona Chayney and herself must be the forerunner of many others. It was an atmosphere abhorrent to Glynis. She was fundamentally too simple and sincere to breathe easily in it. The party was marvellous—that she admitted. She ought to be enjoying it. It was on a lavish scale.

The two huge sitting-rooms of the flat had been thrown into one, transformed into an exotic garden fringed with palm trees in little tubs. An awning of striped red and white silk was looped across the ceiling. A hired South American band, behind a bank of magnificent flowers, played intimate lilting dance music. The sweeping gold satin curtains framing the six windows had been drawn back, so that one could look down over the Park and across to the glittering lights of London for miles. There was endless champagne; the supper was a work of art; every woman who sat down at the table found a present on her plate—some expensive trifle from Paris. Glynis had been given a tiny Russian leather booklet with gilt clasp and marked with her initials—a novelty powder-compact. And in an adjoining room, for those who did not like dancing, roulette was being played. Glynis adored dancing; she had no desire to gamble, but Rhona, with a well-simulated air of friendliness, sent her off with Canillo and insisted on her taking her seat at the tables with him. She sat there bored to death but trying to be polite while Rodrigo showed her how to stake her chips.

Glynis, by midnight, realized that she had only been allowed one dance with Steven and she had hardly seen him. Rhona had commandeered him for supper. He seemed happy enough when Glynis did see him— dancing or chatting, smoking a cigar with one or two men here whom he seemed to know well.

Glynis began to feel tired. She drank so little—her vitality flagged quickly. She kept on refusing the champagne Rodrigo tried to force on her. Then suddenly, while Glynis was gloomily watching Rodrigo stake a lot of money on a number, and she was wishing passionately that she could find Steven and be taken home, the dance music abruptly stopped. Then somebody rushed into the roulette room and announced that the hostess had fainted. She had dropped down suddenly while dancing with Steven Grant-Tally . . .

Glynis stood up. She felt suddenly cold and apprehensive. Ignoring the Señor, who had begun to speak to her, she made her way through the crowded smoky room, out into the wide passage of Rhona's elegant penthouse. She was just in time to see Steven carrying the slender figure in grey into a bedroom, the door of which was held open by a scared-looking Italian maid.

Instinctively Glynis thought:

'I don't believe she really fainted. I don't believe it . . .'

Now she saw Kitty running into Rhona's bedroom. Glynis waited outside with that heavy, suspicious, horrid feeling that Mrs. Chayney had staged the faint because she was not getting enough attention and she, Glynis, was getting too much.

After what seemed a long time Steven emerged from the room. He was wiping a perspiring, frowning face. As he saw Glynis' radiant young figure, however, his brow cleared. He came up to her.

'Oh, hello, darling. This *is* a pity. I'm afraid

133

the party's over.'

'I couldn't care less, but is Mrs. Chayney really ill?' asked Glynis.

'I'm not sure yet what's wrong. She appears to be in great pain.'

'Well, you're a doctor—don't you *know*?' asked Glynis.

The hard tone of voice was so unlike Glynis' usual one that it surprised Steven. He hesitated a moment before answering. The candid truth was (though he would not admit it) that he did *not* know what was wrong with Rhona. She had fainted very suddenly. When he had laid her on her sumptuous bed she had seemed to recover consciousness—lifted her lashes and whispered:

'Oh, my *head*! . . . don't leave me . . . I'm frightened . . . *Steve* . . . stay with me . . . the pain is awful.'

He had tried to reassure her in his most professional manner. He had to decide that as there was no other doctor present he must attend to her and do what he could until her own doctor, to whom they had telephoned, arrived.

Her fingers clutched at his so feverishly and she had so piteously begged him not to leave her, he had to say that he wouldn't. He had just come out and was explaining to Glynis to give the key of his car to one of the manservants. He wanted his case up here. He needed a stethoscope.

'What's wrong with Mrs. Chayney?' Glynis asked again in a low voice.

'I tell you I don't know, darling. But it's pretty late anyhow—everyone is going home.'

'Then I'd better go too,' she said.

'No, of course not—wait for me,' he said. 'I'm driving you home.'

Then he was gone. Glynis, still *quite* unable to feel any sympathy for Rhona, drew near to the bedroom door. She saw Kitty Barley sitting on the edge of her friend's bed. What they were saying to each other Glynis could not hear, but she suddenly caught sight of Rhona Chayney's face. *And she was smiling.* She did not look in the least ill or as though she was in pain—only as though she was sharing some private joke with Kitty.

Glynis turned and walked away. Her cheeks were flaming. She thought:

'So I was right. It *was* a put-up job. And Steven's own sister is on it. How *horrible* of them! And how could Steven be so blind?'

She knew that as a doctor he was bound to give Rhona the benefit of the doubt if she told him that she was 'in agony', but somehow it nauseated Glynis to think that he could be drawn into such an absurd affair, that a designing woman could so easily 'pull the wool' over his eyes. She had the sudden feeling that nothing could ever be right in the future between her and Steven so long as those two women dominated his—and her—life—the life

135

she was to share with Steven.

She knew Rhona's practitioner by name. He was what she always termed 'the rich man's pet'—the sort of doctor who did not take his job too seriously and was only too pleased to have a wealthy patient like Rhona Chayney and pander to her neurosis. But Glynis still had a mental picture of that beautifully made-up face creased with laughter, when Rhona had thought she was alone with Kitty Barley.

Glynis also had another unpleasant memory—of Señor Canillo's parting words to her. They had not made things any better for Glynis.

'Lucky the *muy bonnita* Señora Chayney had your *medico* right here to minister to her. And you—wonderful, beautiful English rose— you are not at all jealous, eh?'

'Why, should I be?' Glynis had flung at him, furiously.

The Señor had bowed and shrugged.

'Ah—it is well known . . . the Señora Chayney is one of your fiancé's *devotees.*'

'One of Steven's devotees!'

Glynis had repeated the words to herself indignantly and left the Senor in a hurry. She felt unable to restrain herself any longer. She broke out to Steven:

'I don't think Mrs. Chayney was ill at all.'

Later, Mrs. Chayney's own doctor arrived and took over from the eminent throat consultant. By now all the guests, including the

Barleys, had left the penthouse. There was an air of melancholy about the empty reception rooms full of wilting flowers—despite the magnificence. The atmosphere was still thick with smoke and reeking of perfume. Glynis, who had been staring over the rooftops up at a sickle moon, suddenly threw open one of the windows. An ice-cold draught blew in upon her flushed face. Steven came up behind her and quickly shut the window.

'You'll catch a chill, my darling. Come along—I'll take you home now.'

She turned and faced him, a resentment which she despised yet could not cure robbing her of the childish happiness and victory experienced earlier this evening. Steven, oblivious of her mood, began to talk about 'poor Rhona'; her terrible attacks of headache and how troubled her own physician was about them. Glynis twisted her lips.

Steven gave a laugh full of genuine humour and affection and tried to pull her towards him.

'Oh, how adorably feminine you are! Am I right in thinking even *loosely*, as they say in *What's My Line*, that my darling Glynis is jealous?'

'Perhaps I am—and with cause!' exclaimed Glynis, choking.

He pulled her towards him and tried to kiss her.

'Nonsense, angel. Whatever you do, you

must never be jealous of your husband's patients.'

'She isn't your patient.'

'No, darling, but what's all this about? You were a huge success tonight and I was immensely proud of you, and Rhona couldn't have been nicer about you. She—'

'Oh, be quiet!' Glynis said between clenched teeth. 'I . . . I *hate* that woman.'

'But that's absurd—she's quite a wonderful person in her way and—'

But again Glynis interrupted. She was in the grip of a strong emotion that she was unable to control.

'I tell you I don't like her and I don't trust her. And if we're ever going to get married I refuse to see any more of her—ever!'

Now Steven was thoroughly startled and not a little perturbed. He let go of her hands.

'Glynis, my darling, you're just being very silly about Rhona Chayney, aren't you? Surely you're not going to shelve a very old friend— my own sister's closest friend in fact—just because you have some ridiculous idea that you don't like her?'

CHAPTER TWELVE

Glynis had never heard quite such a tone from Steven before. She walked towards the row of blue and pink hydrangeas behind which the dance band had been grouped. Irrelevantly her mind turned to the beauty and sadness of the flowers that seemed to her to be hanging their great heads for lack of air and water. She wanted to rush out of this overheated magnificence and take the flowers with her. She did not know what to answer Steven. She had a thousand things to say, but no words came. His coldness had stricken her. Yet deep within her she was afraid that she had been unreasonable. No matter what she thought about Rhona Cheyney, the woman *was* an old family friend.

Steven, frowning, tugged at his stiff white collar. He was not in the best of humours. He was tired. The hour was late. He had no wish to quarrel with Glynis. Either he must be very stupid or it was that vague trait in his character that had made him oblivious that Glynis had been feeling like this all evening, he thought gloomily. As he had just told her, he did not know what actually was wrong with Rhona, he might even have had a suspicion that her dramatic swoon and all those tears and groans afterwards were not altogether genuine. Rhona loved to dramatize herself. He could remember her having scenes with her husband while he was alive, embarrassing them all. At the same time he had felt sorry for her since her widowhood, and she had always been kindness itself to Kitty and himself. And he would not have been human if the man in him had not responded a little to her obvious devotion. But at the same time Steven was not inexperienced. It was queer—Rhona seemed to have all the dazzling qualities a successful man could want in the woman he married, yet he knew that Rhona had never had for him that particular alchemy that holds a man bewitched for the rest of his life. It was that magic which he had found with Glynis. He did not doubt that she loved him too. He could and must be tolerant, he told himself, of the difficulty with which Glynis was adjusting herself to the new environment in which he wanted to place her. But he was not prepared to be dictated to about his friendships.

He broke out:

'Glynis, you have no cause for being jealous—I've told you so before. What's getting you down so particularly tonight? Why, for instance, should you jump to the conclusion that Rhona was not ill?'

Glynis hunched a shoulder.

'Oh well, if you think she was—you're a doctor—I have no right to question it. I apologize.'

He looked at her doubtfully as he pulled a cigarette from his case and lit it. Glynis stood with her back to him. It was a very straight, defiant young back and gave him no encouragement. He could not help but admire the way this young and immature girl stood up to life and adhered to her principles. But jealousy of Rhona was—if flattering—a nuisance, he reflected.

Glynis was thinking: *'I'm not going to tell him that I saw Rhona and Kitty laughing and I know that the whole thing was a put-up job. If he wants Mrs. Chayney's friendship so much, let him have it.'*

And suddenly she swung round. He thought that she looked exceedingly beautiful in that strapless satin dress. Her throat and shoulders were a flawless white. But the young face was white, too, without any of the usual bright colour. The sight sent all *his* anger flying to the winds.

'Glynis—darling—' he began.

'I'd like to go home, Steven,' she broke in.

'Well, certainly we can't stay here all night. Come along then,' he said with a short laugh.

'Glynis,' he added in a low, changed voice, 'you look so lovely, my dear. Much too lovely to wear that cold expression. Darling, we mustn't quarrel—it's too absurd. We can't allow anybody, including poor Rhona, to come between us.'

'Poor Rhona.' The words irked her. Yet she was so much in love with Steven that her efforts to remain impervious to his charm weakened. So also did her resolve to issue further ultimatums to him. With a catch in her throat she said:

'Oh, Steven—I don't want to quarrel,

either—but I do wish Rhona Chayney didn't matter to you *at all.*'

Now, manlike, he was appeased and happy because she had capitulated. He had no desire to probe deeper. All his life Steven had got what he wanted—both success and triumphs—easily. He wanted his love life—his marriage—to be just as simple and rewarding. He was prepared to battle to exhaustion pitch in order to defeat pain—and stave off death—and mend the broken bodies of the sick. But everything else in his life must be gloriously easy. He swept Glynis into his arms, and covered her face and throat with passionate kisses.

'Do get Rhona off your mind, angel—just regard her as an old friend. And remember that you are my heart's delight'—he gave a little laugh and now set a swift warm kiss on the cream of one rounded, girlish shoulder.

Then Glynis was lost. She shivered under the passion of his lips. However much she disagreed with Steven over the small things, in this way she was his, wholly and entirely. He was irresistible to her. What he was saying now was true—where there was real love there must also be trust.

'When you're my wife, you'll probably see a lot of glamorous women coming into my consulting room to consult me about their throats or noses or ears, but they are not glamour girls to *me*—they are just my patients, and, as such, I am interested. But for no other reason. You understand?'

She clung to him, her face hidden against his chest.

'Oh yes, darling, you make me feel an awful idiot. I am not really jealous of your patients at all—nor ever will be. There's just something particular about Rhona Chayney that I can't stand.'

'Poor Rhona,' said Steven lightly.

This time she tried not to let what he said annoy her. Full of generous impulse, she added: 'And *of course*, I don't insist on your breaking your friendship with her. Forget that I ever said that.'

'I knew you did not mean it,' he said, relieved and delighted.

His pleasure was her reward. She squeezed his hand. 'Let's go,' she whispered.

In the car, driving back to Barnet, Steven was the one to issue an ultimatum.

'Glynis, I think the trouble is that both of us are a bit on edge. I never see enough of you and you ought not really to be working for me any more. It's all unnatural. Let's get married at once. Then you'll see how much better everything will be.'

Leaning near him, she felt utterly dependent on him for her happiness. It was just what she had felt the other night—this desire to be with him altogether. It *would* be better then. It must . . . or she might as well say good-bye to him for ever.

The time had come for her to turn a deaf ear to any of the warning voices in her innermost being. The sort of voices that said:

'You will be happy in a wonderful crazy sort of way with this wonderful man—but it won't be your way and he won't belong only to you but to his career and to all his patients. To his family and friends. You'll hardly ever see him. He'll find it difficult to get time off—to take you anywhere—even at weekends. You'll have to share him with the whole world. How will you like that, Glynis Thorne? You, who wanted the simple life!'

She wouldn't like it, of course. But she would accept it as the penalty of loving such a man.

Before they had reached Rudge Crest—the quiet home which had been hers for so many years—the die was cast. Glynis had silenced the voices and doubts and fears—for better or for worse, she told herself wryly. For she had agreed with Steven that the best thing they could do was to get married at once. And *'at once'* meant in four or five weeks' time. Glynis must have at least a small trousseau, she said, and Steven in fact needed a few weeks in which to make his own preparations. He was due for a holiday shortly. He would take it in February, so that they could have their honeymoon. They might fly to Majorca. He had a wealthy patient with a house out there,

144

who might offer to lend it to them. How about a couple of weeks in the sunshine?

Glynis was swept right off her feet as she listened to Steven making his plans. It was all so wildly exciting. She sat speechless while he talked in airy casual fashion about booking their flight to Majorca, then getting a furnished flat somewhere until they had time to settle on a house of their own.

'I suppose we ought to have our own home ready before we marry, but it will give you something to do, choosing it, won't it, darling?'

When she found her voice, it was only to say:

'Steven, *darling*, it sounds too marvellous!'

'Then it's settled,' he said, relieved. 'And we're never going to say a harsh word to each other again, and everything is going to be quite splendid.'

He had stopped the car outside her home. For a moment they clung and kissed. Tenderly he smoothed the rich hair back from her forehead. His pulses stirred at the warmth and surrender of her in his arms.

He whispered: 'I don't want to have to say "good-night" to you much longer. I want you with me always, my darling little love.'

It was only later that she recalled that little word '*always*'—knowing that he had meant it, that it was as he wished it to be—but knowing too that with Steven Grant-Tally it could never be '*always*' except in his mind and his heart.

145

That was the lesson which she had yet to learn. All that mattered now was that they wanted to be together and she promised to discuss the whole thing with her parents, and fix the date for the wedding in the middle of February.

When Kitty Barley rang her friend Rhona that next morning to tell her that the date of Steven's marriage to Glynis was fixed and that there seemed little hope now that they would change their minds, Rhona's disappointment and bitterness knew no bounds. She went to her bed with an illness that was not merely staged; it was a sickness of the mind. She worked herself up into a state bordering on a nervous breakdown. She said that she never wanted to see Steven again and that she was finished with Kitty too. She retired forthwith into an expensive nursing home and everybody in their immediate circle was informed that Mrs. Chayney had had a complete nervous collapse.

Kitty was herself reduced by this to a state of nerves. *She could not afford to fall out with Rhona.* Nor could she endure the thought that Glynis had won the day. Matters were made worse for her by virtue of the fact that Paul was worse off at this moment than at any other time of his life. His private investments were on the downgrade, and he talked of cutting expenses rather than increasing Kitty's allowance. She knew that if in an ordinary way she asked Steve for a personal loan, she would get it. Steven was an affectionate brother and not ungenerous. Although he made a lot of money, he, too, was finding taxation a drain. His expenses were huge. And the magnitude of the debt she owed to Rhona would have appalled him—she dared not let either husband or brother know about it. She could only hope and pray that Rhona would emerge from this temporary seclusion and restore her to favour again. These hopes at least were fulfilled.

Suddenly Rhona sent for her banished friend. Rhona had apparently decided that she was 'cured' and returned to her flat, which was, as usual, full of magnificent flowers from her admirers and hangers-on. She kissed and welcomed Kitty as though there had never been a break between them. It left Lady Barley wondering what mischief Rhona was up to now.

'I've been terribly upset because you would not see me in the home, Rhona darling,' Kitty began. 'I really don't see why you should have blamed *me* because—'

But Rhona silenced her. Feeling better for her 'rest' and using a pale make-up which made her look rather fragile, she said:

'We won't refer to the past, dear. Naturally Steven's marriage will *kill* me, but I am going to try to put a good face on it. I have made up my mind to do all I can to help that poor little thing he is marrying. She needs my help.'

Lady Barley, used though she was to her friend's acting capabilities and various affectations, bit her lip. She felt distinctly apprehensive. When she knew, she felt more than a little conscience-stricken. She had seen a lot of her future sister-in-law these last two weeks. True, she and that child had nothing much in common, but Kitty could not deny the fact that Glynis was very sweet and had a lot of character, and that given a chance she might make a charming wife for Steven. But after an hour with Rhona, Kitty knew that what Rhona called her decision to be 'nice to the poor little thing' might cause a serious rift between those two even after they were married. They were now so much in love—it worried Lady Barley. But she could not afford to murmur a single protest.

CHAPTER THIRTEEN

'Come and have a last look at the presents before you go to bed, darling,' said Sylvia Thorne.

She was immensely excited and thrilled. She laughingly told Glynis that she believed she was more thrilled than the prospective bride herself. Glynis seemed so very calm. Perhaps, the mother thought, it was because—like most girls in her place—she was very tired after all the endless preparations for the wedding.

At last, thought Glynis, as arm in arm with her mother she walked into the dining-room to look at the loaded table (sideboard too). *At last* it was about to dawn—this Great Day of her life. Her calmness was not superficial. She did not feel the usual apprehension this evening. She thought of the new life facing her with deep inner satisfaction. She only prayed that she wouldn't develop 'nerves' when the big moment came.

Mrs. Thorne pointed to a magnificent canteen of silver from 'Sir Paul and Lady Barley', inscribed *'All our love and good wishes to you both. Kitty and Paul.'* To a hand-painted French dessert service from 'Aunt Marjorie'— Mrs. Thorne's sister, who was the old maid of the family, and much the best off.

'Thank goodness you can produce that for Lady Barley from our side—it's antique,' Sylvia Thorne said proudly.

That immediately induced Glynis to pick up one of the smaller, more homely, gifts, and say:

'And your *dear* Lady Barley can see *this* one and like it, too. It only cost a pound or less, but at least it was sent by somebody who really knows and loves me.'

Mrs. Thorne ignored the remark. She knew that she need never expect sympathy from Glynis when she chose to be a snob.

She kept pointing, however, to more

valuable objects in that glittering display.

'What wonderful things—how *terribly* well off all Steven's relatives and friends must be. Aren't *you* a *lucky* girl?'

Glynis' charming face only creased into a small secretive smile. She had, if anything, been overwhelmed by the hundreds of wedding presents that had poured in. Now she said:

'I'm worried about this wedding being held at St. Paul's. I always meant it to take place here in Barnet in the church where we are known and I was christened. Why did I ever give in about it?'

'Darling, it would have been nice from the sentimental point of view,' said Mrs. Thorne, 'but you *must* think of Steven. We just couldn't expect to hold a suitable reception here. And Daddy agreed. Don't start regretting any of the arrangements, *please.*'

'He's been marvellous,' murmured Glynis.

'Darling, a pin has just dropped out of your hair,' said Mrs. Thorne, anxious that the crisp shining hair should look its best tomorrow. Glynis had had a 'set' late this afternoon. Fondly the mother regarded her. It suited the child to be a little pale and ethereal, she decided—with those strange limpid green eyes of hers. Where *did* she get them from? Mrs. Thorne often wondered, and wondered, too, how she and Bertie had ever managed to produce between them a daughter of such

150

dazzling good looks.

'Well, I'm off, Mum,' said Glynis. 'Come and tuck me up.'

In the hall she met her father. He smiled at her over his glasses.

'*"Here comes the bride!"* . . .' he hummed.

She hugged him, her eyes suddenly wet.

'Not yet—but I shall be awfully proud to go up the aisle on your arm, darling Daddy. You've been more than generous. I am worried about it. Two hundred and fifty guests—and a reception in Knightsbridge—oh, dear!'

'Don't you worry your pretty head about that. We've only one child and we're going to do her well,' broke in Mr. Thorne, but he added: 'I'm going to miss you, my darling.'

'Oh, Daddy,' said Glynis tremulously, 'shall I ever be able to live up to my new environment?'

'Of course. Take it in your stride. Only one thing really matters—that you two love each other—and stay in love.'

Glynis agreed with this and repeated it to herself that night when she lay in bed with her lamp still switched on, thinking. She and Steven loved each other terribly. They must never let that love grow less. Never change.

He had telephoned her this evening, earlier than usual. The telephone was about the only contact she had with him regularly during these hectic weeks of shopping and fittings. As

151

ill-luck would have it, he seemed to have been busier than usual, too. But he had come down at week-ends to Barnet and she had dined several times at Thurloe Square. She had even gone shopping with Kitty and found her future sister-in-law trying to be genuinely helpful. As for Rhona Chayney—Glynis had heard that Rhona had been in a nursing home for some time. Then had come her acceptance of the wedding invitation and a present which Glynis had been forced to admire whether she wanted to or not—a set of exquisite Georgian glasses for the dinner-table. A set for every kind of wine. They were goblets of such beauty and value that Glynis gasped as she unwrapped them. She tapped her thumbnail against the glass and listened to the ringing note. With it came a formal card and a little note written in the friendliest terms. *'I do hope these will be useful for the many lovely parties which I know you will give for Steven.'*

Mrs. Thorne was ecstatic. Glynis remained a trifle quiet, wondering about those parties. It would be difficult for her to try and entertain for Steven in the grand manner. But Glynis determined, for Steven's sake, to fight down her prejudices and wrote Rhona a warm note of thanks.

This was followed by further friendly advances from Rhona which culminated in an unexpected way.

About a week ago Kitty had lunched with

Glynis and with a well-assumed gaiety, said:

'Darling, the luckiest thing has happened. Rhona Chayney is going to America after the wedding and has offered Steve her perfectly wonderful penthouse (as you know, it's a fairy-tale flat) rent free to you two for as long as you want it—anyhow, till your house is ready.'

At once, instinctively, Glynis revolted from this idea. The mere thought of living there, breathing in Rhona's atmosphere, among her things, was abhorrent to her. But she was given small chance to refuse.

'I've just 'phoned Steve,' Kitty went on. 'He asked me to ask you if you'd like it to accept—he seemed to think you mightn't like it. But *why not*, darling?'

Glynis was scarlet. Her heart beat fast. She did not meet Kitty's inquisitive gaze. She did not want Kitty or anyone else to think for one moment that she so greatly disliked and resented Rhona Chayney. She could see that Steve had been worried about the offer, too. Quietly she asked:

'Did Steve want to accept?'

'Naturally—who wouldn't, my pet? Such a glorious flat and Rhona's own chef and maids flung in. You know how fabulously rich she is—one need never mind accepting favours from her.'

'I mind,' said Glynis bluntly.

At once Kitty gave her metallic laugh and said, pretending to joke:

153

'Dear Glynis, surely you are not jealous of a girl-friend Steve is shelving for *you*?'

That made Glynis angry and at once determined to show that she was too confident of Steven's love to be jealous.

'If Steve wants us to take the penthouse while Rhona is in America—that's okey by me,' she said.

'Then it's all settled,' said Kitty happily.

But she knew perfectly well that Glynis was far from happy about it. The last place in which the young girl would want to start her married life was that particular flat—even if its owner would be at the other side of the Atlantic.

But Glynis had her reward when Steven next saw her.

'I was so afraid you might wish to turn down Rhona's offer—but it really will be a lovely place to come home to, darling, and I've no scruples about going there if you like the idea. She usually keeps the place shut up when she's abroad. Such a waste. I'm delighted you are so sensible about it. Do write and thank her, darling.'

So Glynis wrote the letter.

Tonight Steven had told her that all was now arranged for their honeymoon.

They were staying tomorrow night in town and flying, the next morning, to Majorca. There would be one change at Barcelona. They should reach Palma by the afternoon.

'My holiday's safe—two whole weeks, thank heaven,' he had ended with that warm note in his voice which always made her feel breathless. 'Fennymore is going to look after my patients for me.'

Richard Fennymore, another ear, nose and throat specialist, who had been at Cambridge and St. Martha's with Steve, was to be best man tomorrow.

Steven had ended:

'For the last time, good night, Miss Thorne. Tomorrow I shall *not* be 'phoning you.'

That had brought the stars into her eyes and the hot happy colour to her face. She had answered:

'Good night, *darlingest* Steve. I'm so happy.'

'Not worried about the Press boys who'll fight at the church door to get a good picture of my lovely bride?' he had asked a bit anxiously.

And she replied:

'No, I'll be all right. I may get cold feet tomorrow, but tonight I'm feeling terrifically brave.'

So she was, she thought—brave and gay, without one tremor of anxiety. There was so much to be thrilled about. In two days' time she and Steve would probably be dancing in their luxurious hotel in Majorca. They were going on to Paris before coming home—Paris as Steve's wife. What a prospect! she thought, and her brain reeled a trifle dizzily. She wondered if all brides felt as dizzy—as unbelieving of their luck.

One of the nicest things that had happened lately was the party that they gave at St. Martha's for Steven and herself a week ago. She had got through it all without feeling at all embarrassed by her exalted position at, the side of 'the great man'. And it had been such a joy to see how well Robin Gellow looked. He seemed to have settled down to his job and was quite a changed being. There was also a strong rumour among the nurses that he had been taking the red-haired Moira out quite a bit. That pleased Glynis.

She looked around her room and sighed. She could hardly recognize it for the haven of rest and orderliness it was as a rule. Things everywhere. The trunk packed, closed, and marked with her new and exciting initials 'G. G.-T.' A half-open suitcase (a lovely hide one from her old friends, the nurses at St. Martha's) and on a hanger outside the wardrobe, the exquisite white satin gown which she was to wear when she became Steven's wife.

One of Daddy's cousins had come forward with that dress—most unexpectedly—for it was her grandmother's own wedding gown. A lovely Victorian thing which Glynis had said, when she first saw it, ought to be in a museum. She never expected to get into it—with that tiny waist—but a little alteration from Miss

Potts and it was perfect. They all said that it would be a sensation. There over the back of a chair hung the lovely Limerick lace veil loaned by Lady Barley. A coronet of orange blossoms intertwined with pearls on the dressing-table, beside long white kid gloves and prayer book. And hanging beside the bridal gown, the most exciting thing of all—Steven's wedding present—a mink coat. The dark silky mink had been 'raved over' by everybody in Glynis' home circle. But to her—glorious though it was—it seemed a symbol of the life she was going to lead in future, far removed from her old status.

What a month it had been, Glynis pondered, since that night she and Steven had made up their minds to get married quickly. She had never regretted it, although it had given her a pang when she had initiated a new receptionist for Steven. But tomorrow she would be with *him*. They would be alone.

Now for the great Tomorrow . . .

Switching off her light, Glynis murmured a sudden prayer:

'Please God, help me to make Steve the right sort of wife, and make him always love me as he does now. Never let him be disappointed!'

This from Glynis on her wedding eve . . .

Steven spent his in a slightly more boisterous masculine fashion at a stag party—toasted and 'ragged' by his friends and colleagues in the world of medicine. But when he returned home, flushed and exhausted, he sat quiet a moment, smoking a last cigarette, looked at the beautiful head and shoulders of the girl in the photograph by his bed, and said aloud:

'God bless you, and may I make you happy always, my love.'

So these two, each with a heart full of great love and desire to please each other, came to their wedding in the Knightsbridge church that cold crisp February day. Snow lay on the ground. A north wind whirled a few stray flakes into the inquisitive faces of the crowd gathered on each side of the striped awning.

Mrs. Thorne, looking quite youthful and pretty in pale blue, had already been ushered to her pew. On the opposite side, Lady Barley was seated beside Paul Barley in state, wearing an ermine jacket over a caramel-coloured *ensemble*. The organ swelled gently. The church was already packed with distinguished guests, including a number of the staff from St. Martha's.

Then a murmur rose from the crowd outside. The bride had arrived. She stepped out, her rich warm mink over her creamy gown, and a huge bunch of pale yellow roses in her gloved hands. The maidenhair fern among the roses trembled. Perhaps the bride's slender fingers were trembling too; but a woman leaned forward and touched her arm and murmured:

158

'Good luck, dear. You look like an angel. God bless you!'

Glynis turned and smiled at her. Somehow that simple blessing from a stranger did a lot to hearten her. For now she felt none of last night's confident composure. She was frankly terrified. And it seemed almost as though it had been arranged that simultaneously a Rolls drew up at the church entrance. And out stepped the beautiful Mrs. Chayney in sable jacket, with hat adorned by sweeping ospreys. Late, of course, and attracting a great deal of attention.

Somehow it annoyed Glynis to be arriving with Rhona at this critical moment of her life. She turned to her bridesmaids. They wore pale yellow dresses that toned with her roses— Alma, of course, was one. They murmured 'Good luck' to her, then fell into their places behind her. A small boy, son of a great friend of the Thornes, who made an adorable page in his pale yellow velvet suit, picked up her train. Mr. Thorne crooked an arm and smiled warmly and encouragingly at his daughter.

Glynis took that arm and moved forward. She was milk-white. She saw nobody. The church was blurred. And then—the tall gravely handsome man waiting for her at the chancel steps in his morning coat and striped trousers, white carnation in his buttonhole, came into focus. He gripped her hand as she reached him. The colour returned to her face and the courage to her heart.

The service began . . . *'Dearly beloved, we are gathered together . . .'*

CHAPTER FOURTEEN

The wedding was over.

Outside St. Paul's Church the Press photographers and .reporters from all sources had gathered to 'take' the bridal pair.

Glynis, her hand in Steven's, smiled her shy sweet smile and looked, as though for confidence, up at her tall husband. He held his silk hat in his free hand and smiled back at his newly-made wife. The crowd pressed forward. The sun broke through the grey snow-clouds for a fleeting gesture of approval of this wedding. Because of the bitter cold Glynis had kept her mink coat over her shoulders. Her veil billowed and fluttered in the wind. There were cries of:

'Just a moment—hold it, please . . .'

'Give us a smile—look this way . . .'

The yellow-clad bridesmaids came into the picture with the tiny page who looked a trifle glum, but cheered up as the bride bent down and whispered to him:

'I know how you feel, Johnny—but give them one of your biggest smiles—it'll soon be over.'

More cameras clicked. Then Mr. and Mrs. Steven Grant-Tally moved over the red strip of carpet out to their waiting car. Glynis sank into her seat. The best man whispered a few words to Steven. Alma tucked a swirl of Glynis' satin skirt around her feet and put the rug over her knees. They had only to drive a few yards, but the north wind was still blowing and that elusive sun had vanished again. Alma said:

'Jolly good luck, Glyn darling—the sun *did* shine on you for a sec—that's a good omen.'

Glynis nodded. She could hardly speak. She felt that she had been in a daze ever since she arrived here for the wedding. She had only a vague memory of particular moments: the one, for instance, when Steve slipped the narrow gold ring on to her finger and looked down into her eyes with all the love and tenderness in the world. And when his voice, very strong and clear, had said those wonderful words, '*Till death us do part* . . .' it had been like rich warm wine, flowing through her body—giving her strength and confidence. And she had repeated those words, hardly recognizing her own small tremulous voice. Then again, how fantastic it had seemed when in the vestry the vicar had said: '*Let me be the first to congratulate you. Mrs. Grant-Tally.*' Mrs. Grant-Tally. So she really was Steve's wife . . . after her brief, tempestuous engagement and all the doubts and set-backs. Wonderful, glorious fact—she was *his wife.*

Coming down the aisle on his arm (so her mother told her at the reception) she had looked her best and not at all worried. A starry-eyed, radiant bride. Nevertheless she had still been too self-conscious to recognize a soul in the packed church. Until her gaze drifted to *one particular little group.* Her sister-in-law, Kitty Barley, and a slim, elegant woman wearing ospreys in her tiny black Paris hat. That woman was Rhona Chayney. She was clinging to Kitty's arm and she was deathly white and held a handkerchief to her lips. Kitty was patting her arm as though in consolation.

Glynis—for one unspeakable moment—felt her tremendous joy and pride shiver into fragments. It was wicked, scandalous, of Rhona, she thought, to 'stage a scene' today in this church. Nobody who knew and saw her (including Glynis) could fail to see that Rhona was upset: *Why?* Because she had been forced to witness the man she had so violently wanted for herself pledged to another woman? Nothing could remove that impression from Glynis, even though she could tell that Steve had not noticed his sister or her friend. Indeed, later on, he made only one allusion to Rhona:

'Rhona was all dolled-up to the nines as usual—doing us proud . . .'

A casual, boyish observation coming from a man who, Glynis was beginning to realize, was too vague and casual to take note of all the little things which a woman might find serious enough to take exception to. But this being her wedding day, and one of her resolutions having been *not* to feel jealous of Rhona, or be irritated by her, Glynis did not open her mouth on the subject. But whenever she recalled that lovely successful wedding, that unpleasant incident was thrown in—a memory of Rhona's white tearful face and the way she hung on to Kitty's arm.

But once in the car there was nothing to spoil a lovely moment of happiness and unity with her husband. He drew the hand bearing his ring up to his lips . . .'

'I think I must have the loveliest wife in the world!' he said. 'Aren't I a lucky chap?'

'Aren't I a lucky *girl* with such a distinguished and handsome husband?' said Glynis, and bit her lower lip excitedly.

'Let's always stay lucky,' he said. 'Lots of weddings end in disaster. Ours never, never will. *"From this day forward . . ."* That's what I said and that's what I mean. Nobody else but you, from now onwards, my darling.'

Glynis' eyes, suddenly smarting, blinked out of the car window at the Knightsbridge traffic which the policeman was holding up as the car turned in front of the Hyde Park Hotel. She remembered the many times she had walked down this very thoroughfare shopping with Mummy, generally during sale time. It just didn't seem possible that she, sitting in this car, was no longer Miss Thorne (or Nurse Thorne of St. Martha's). She was Mrs. Steven Grant-Tally. It would take some living up to. She turned to Steven again. Husband and wife flirted outrageously. Then Steven leaned forward and brushed her fur coat.

'All that darned confetti!'

'But it was fun!' sighed Glynis.

'Old Fenny did his stuff as best man as though born to the job.'

'And don't you think your mother-in-law looks nice?'

'I think she's most attractive and much too young to be my mother-in-law. I'm glad we've agreed that I should call her Sylvia.'

'Oh, Mummy's in the seventh heaven. You're the sort of man she prayed I'd marry,' laughed Glynis.

'And does that go for you, too?'

'Of course . . .'

Glynis meant it. She quite forgot that she used to pray to marry quite a different kind of man, a quiet retiring sort like herself. That was all in the past.

She was deliriously happy and proud. Rhona couldn't spoil it. And, in fact, when it was Rhona's turn, as one of the long line of guests, to shake hands with bride and bridegroom, Glynis received her with all the warmth she could muster.

'She *does* look ill and unhappy,' Glynis reflected, 'and if she was really so much in love

164

with Steve, I ought to be sorry for her instead of annoyed.'

So she thanked Rhona all over again for the wonderful loan of her flat, and said she hoped Rhona would have a marvellous time in America. Rhona gave a theatrical sigh and murmured that America always 'exhausted her', but that she had dear friends in Washington whom she *must* visit. She added:

'Your dress is divine, darling—who made it?'

Then the spirit of mischief bubbled in Glynis.

'Christian Dior,' she said solemnly.

'*Glynis!*' This from her mother, close by, slightly horrified.

But Rhona had swallowed the story. She said:

'I should have known from the exquisite line.'

That childish moment of triumph quite recompensed Glynis, although she firmly decided that she must tell Rhona the truth one day. Now she was busy greeting Lord and Lady Avermouth (Lord Avermouth was an elderly retired surgeon and a St. Martha's man, who had long been a patron and friend of young Grant-Tally). So Glynis did not see the way Rhona clung to Steven's hand for a moment nor hear her murmur:

'Be happy, my dear . . . I am *always* your friend . . .'

Steven remained unmoved. He was in the best of spirits, very happy. He could afford to be generous. Gallantly he lifted Rhona's gloved hand to his lips.

'Always—the very best of friends, too. I promise we'll take great care of the penthouse and we shall look forward to seeing you when you come back.'

Rhona passed on in the queue, the smile dying on her vividly rouged lips.

After that, Glynis was busy with her hundreds of guests. Champagne corks popped. Steven helped her cut the huge three-tiered glittering cake. Then came the speeches; a perfect one from Steven, who, of course, was used to public speaking, and with Glynis' hand in his, said among other things what a 'lucky chap' he was. The usual touch of humour came from the best man, Fenny:

'I hear from the bride's mother that our little Glynis had her tonsils removed when she was a mere child. The great Grant-Tally feels this deeply.' (Laughter.)

And Mrs. Thorne's brother—Glynis' Uncle Harry—responding to the bridegroom and speaking on behalf of the bride's family:

'I can remember the day when the bride was born, and how pleased we all were because there were a lot of boys in our family and we all wanted a little girl, and I remember when I first saw young Glynis in her cot I decided that all the good fairies must have been present at her birth to endow her with beauty, charm and intelligence . . .' (etc., etc.).

Cries of approval—Glynis blushing crimson, beginning to wish that it was all over. She was a trifle suffocated by so many hours of being the focus of attention. One could stand just so much and no more, she told herself wryly, and kept glancing at Steven to give herself courage.

Came the moment when she changed from gleaming bridal gown into the neat grey dress and jacket which had been tailored for her 'going away'. As she powdered her nose and placed a tiny grey and rose velvet pill-box hat on her shining head, she looked at her reflection in the mirror.

'Oh, Mummy!' she exclaimed, turning to Mrs. Thorne, who was busy with the last-moment packing. 'None of this seems true. I think I shall wake up in a moment and find myself back in Rudge Crest.'

'You'll do nothing of the sort,' laughed Sylvia Thorne, who was quite the proudest mother-in-law alive; a very proud, satisfied mother. Glynis had looked ethereally lovely, and now with her new mink coat over the grey suit, a few of the yellow roses from her bouquet pinned to the fur, she was as smart as Sylvia Thorne could ever have wished her daughter to look.

'God bless you, my darling,' she said, hugging Glynis for an instant, 'and don't ever say again that you can't live up to being Mrs.

Grant-Tally—you've proved today that you can.'

'Hear, hear,' seconded the faithful Alma.

It was in Glynis' mind to say that any girl ought to be able to make a success of her wedding day—that the real moments of trial in any marriage come later. But she remained silent. In a funny way she sometimes felt that she was much older than her own mother. Mummy's feet were not planted nearly so firmly on practical ground as her own. But now all that Glynis longed for was peace—to be alone with her husband.

She had a special kiss for her father.

'Thanks for *everything*, Daddy. It's been absolutely *marvellous*.'

Paul Barley, her new brother-in-law, touched her cheek with his lips, when it was his turn to say '*au revoir*'.

'You looked every man's idea of a lovely bride. Steve's a lucky fellow. Be very, *very* happy, my dear.'

Kitty, in her best Society fashion, also embraced the young grey-clad figure and said, '*Lots* of love, darling.'

But later, at home, when Paul started to tell Kitty what a successful wedding it was and how nice the Thornes were—simple, unaffected—very nice people—she had nothing to say. She had, in fact, felt remarkably gloomy all through the affair. Rhona was a menace and Kitty's unpaid debts worse than that. She felt her brother's marriage to be a disaster from her point of view and she alternated from wanting to be fond of Glynis and kind to her, and wondering anxiously what Rhona might or might not do when she returned from America. That she meant to start a subtle campaign of 'infiltration' into the home and lives of the newly-married couple Kitty was certain.

But now at last Glynis' happiness had reached the supreme fulfilment. The wedding was over. They were at the Savoy. She was alone with Steven in their bridal suite overlooking the Thames in that beautiful historic hotel where so many famous people have stayed since the days of Queen Victoria.

It was a wonderful dream to Glynis. The big elegant room was filled with pink roses. Darkness had fallen, soft-shaded lights and a bright fire defied the gloom. The short February day was ending with more snow. But the forecast was for milder weather, and tomorrow they would be flying into the sunshine.

Glynis flung her hat on one of the beds and felt suddenly helplessly shy at the sight of Steven unpacking, cigarette between his lips, looking so at home and composed. *Steven*, her husband. Her fingers trembled with excitement as she ran them through the crisp waves of her hair. He looked up suddenly, took his cigarette out of his mouth, and gave her a boyish grin.

'Come on, Lazy-bones—where's the key of your suitcase? I'll unlock it for you.'

'How nice to have a man about the house to do the odd jobs,' she giggled, trying not to let him see how wildly her heart was beating. It really was the first time they had ever been so completely, intimately, alone with the knowledge that they need not fear interruption or separation.

She took the key from her bag and tossed it to him, then turned back to stare down at the hazy lights along the Embankment, the river craft, the wonderful flood-lit buildings on the other side. She felt choked with sudden breathless poignant emotion. Then she felt Steven's arms around her. He was pulling her round to face him. His kisses were swift and warm against her cheeks and then on her lips with lingering passion. He said in a voice that held no teasing note now but an emotion to match hers:

'Glynis . . . darling . . . *my wife. . . .*'

Now there was no more world for them outside that warm rose-filled room. Only themselves and their eager mutual love and desire for each other.

CHAPTER FIFTEEN

The honeymoon—which ever afterwards Glynis was to remember as being perfect while it lasted—unfortunately came to a speedy end. But, as Glynis thought after the catastrophe, even disaster could not really spoil their happiness. Marriage with Steve was all, and more, that she could have desired. He was an ideal, tender lover, and had chosen a fascinating spot for their honeymoon. The Formentor Hotel in Majorca was a wonderful building on a promontory overlooking an exquisite little bay, fringed by pine trees. From their bedroom balcony they looked down on a cobalt blue sea glittering in warm sunshine by day—silvered by moonlight at night. It was even warm enough to bathe. They were as happy as two children. Steve delighted his young wife by completely casting off the cloak of 'successful surgeon' and becoming a boy with ideas as simple and unadorned as her own. And she grew brown and even more beautiful, he told her, in that radiant sunlight and fresh champagne air. Even when she had to come back to earth every evening and appear in public as the dignified Mrs. Grant-Tally, dining and dancing in the hotel in one of her new smart evening dresses, she was blissfully happy. She lived for Steve, and he for her. He felt as she did—that none of their differences of opinion or environment counted any more. They were close in mind, heart and body during those six rapturous days. If ever Steve did turn his thoughts to the hospital or his private patients, and gave Glynis the slightest idea that he was only a half-satisfied man away from his work—she said that she understood. Now and again perhaps she experienced a twinge of fear as she glimpsed the faint but inevitable shadow of the future— a time she must leave this paradise, shared with him—and give him back to his job, his old fully occupied life.

Then the first accident happened.

It was one of those pieces of bad luck that might happen to anybody.

It was about four o'clock on a brilliant afternoon. The sea looked like dark blue silk. Steve was on one of the hotel tennis-courts, playing a singles with a young Spaniard. Glynis, in shorts, with a pale yellow shirt and a Spanish straw hat on her fair head, sat watching the game for a few moments; her eyes bright with pride behind the dark glasses as she saw Steve beat the younger man—six-love. How young and fit Steve looked in his white shorts and shirt, his legs and arms sunburned, his hair ruffled. Oh, he was a darling and she adored him now!—far, far more than she had loved the busy specialist for whom she had once worked, and who she had so often criticized—adversely at times. She wondered how she could ever have lived without him, or how she could ever have been afraid to marry him.

He waved and called out to her.

'One more set, darling—then tea.'

She nodded and, with a book under her arm, started to walk, enjoying the cool breeze which had suddenly sprung to life. The February weather could still be coldish out of the sun even in Majorca. But today, she reflected, was perfect. She wished she could bottle some of that health-giving sun and send it home to her parents.

She made her way down a zigzag path into the bay, and on to the rocks. There she stood a moment breathing in the salt fresh air. She could not settle down to read. She had just had a *siesta*. Now she wanted exercise. But her tennis was poor—she had never had time to practise—and so she had not offered to play with her husband.

(Every time Glynis thought of those words *My Husband* her heart seemed to turn over and her cheeks flamed with happiness.)

She walked quite a way, nimble-footed, over the glistening black rocks. Then suddenly she slipped—dropped her book—flung out her hands helplessly and fell, twisting an ankle under her. She gave a cry of agony and lay huddled a moment, face grey, undreamed-of pain shooting up her calf.

The seagulls wheeled over her, screaming unsympathetically. The sea lapped gently around the rocks. The sun beat down and from afar came the pleasant sound of a Spanish voice singing. The fishermen were never tired of singing their plaintive, native songs while they mended their nets.

It was one of these men, a big muscular young Majorcan, who found the English 'señora' on the rocks, sobbing, unable to move, and carried her in his arms back to the Formentor Hotel.

Glynis was in great pain and terrified that she had broken her ankle. She was only too right. A fateful but much distressed Steven took her from the smiling gallant rescuer—and up in their room examined her leg and found what he called a 'Potts' fracture. Fortunately only a simple one—but enough to keep the ankle in plaster and irons—and make walking extremely difficult. When he gravely told her the bad news and said that he must drive her at once to the nearest hospital, and get a local *medico* to give him the necessary things in order to set the ankle, Glynis wept bitterly.

Steve, sitting on the bed, kissed her and tried to comfort her.

'There, darling—don't be upset. It's damnable luck—but it just can't be helped.'

'On my h-honeymoon!' She bit hard on her lip, trying to be courageous and philosophical about it because he looked so upset. 'It's the

174

end!'

'I still love you,' he smiled, trying to make her smile back. He succeeded. Glynis sniffed and laughed while he dried her tears with his handkerchief, and rang for tea. She needed it. After a cup he would put the ankle in an improvised splint, he said, then whisk her off to hospital. She flung her arms around his neck and kissed his brown handsome face.

'I love *you*—terribly. I'm so sorry to spoil our honeymoon by such a silly accident.'

'It's you I'm sorry for, darling, as it's such a rotten business for you to be put out of action like this—but nothing can really spoil our honeymoon. We'll stay out in the sun and I shall sit beside my beautiful incapacitated wife and hold her hand and all the Majorcans will come and sing sad Spanish songs in sympathy.'

She stopped crying and laughed with him, despite the ever-increasing discomfort and pain of the broken ankle. But now she could, indeed, be thankful she had a doctor for a husband and one who understood things so well. He had never been more tender or attentive. He did not leave her side until, with the aid of a very charming Spanish doctor, Steve had the ankle X-rayed, then put in plaster and walking-iron. After that she was more comfortable but he insisted that she went to bed. She did not feel too well and looked pale and big-eyed. He was full of admiration.

'You were so brave, sweet—the *medico* said

a lot of girls might have howled. You were marvellous.'

'So are you,' said Glynis—and clung to his hand a moment, and then told him to forget about her and go down to the cocktail bar.

'And don't flirt with some lovely girl,' she ended, teasing him.

He teased back.

'I shall, too. No nagging wife to stop me. I've got you nicely chained. Farewell for ever, my love.'

She was laughing when he left her. But the smile faded as she lay there alone, thinking. She felt more miserable than she would let him know. This first separation—even their dining apart tonight and the knowledge that tomorrow they could be together only if she did in fact chain him to her side, instead of going for the bathing picnics and drives. She would only be able to walk slowly and with great discomfort. And when they first got home she would be unable to rush round and get their new home ready or do any of the things they had planned. Just before the wedding Steve had practically bought the lease of a lovely house in Weymouth Street—only a stone's throw from his consulting rooms. He had meant to settle on it—and get Glynis to see about the decorations and furnishing.

'Oh, how sickening it is . . .' Glynis reflected, and tried desperately not to dissolve into tears again. Above all things she must keep cheerful

176

for Steve. This accident must be a disappointment for *him* and if she was miserable it would only make him feel worse. She was all smiles when Steve came up to have coffee with her. He teased her again about all the beautiful girls he had smiled at in her absence, but later that night, lying beside her, one arm around her slim beautiful body—he told her how good and brave she was, but his lips suddenly found tears on her lashes. Then he was deeply moved, and repeatedly kissed and comforted her.

'I'll stay with you—my darling, lovely wife—I'll never leave you,' he vowed between the long kisses. And he told her she was a marble goddess of love, with the Spanish moonlight silvering her face and hair.

Glynis knew and he, too,' knew, however, that once the old routine claimed him, the busy specialist would find it impossible to stay with her—particularly if she could only go out in the car. And how she would hate having to stay in Rhona's flat most of the day alone . . . for weeks, Glynis thought desolately.

From the hour of that unhappy fall on the rocks, their luck seemed to change. Fate organized another calamity—one that brought the whole honeymoon to a speedy end. For Paul Barley died—suddenly and tragically for so young a man—of a coronary thrombosis. Kitty telephoned the news. He had been out in the Row, riding, and fell suddenly from his horse and was dead by the time they got him to St. George's Hospital.

When Glynis heard this news she was greatly distressed. Of all the members of her husband's family whom she had so far met, she had liked Paul the most. How would Kitty take it—she who had been so hard to him in his lifetime? Steve said that she was almost hysterical in her grief, and after speaking to her he had wondered whether, honeymoon or not, he ought to go home. Kitty ought not to be alone. He, Steve, was her only relative.

Steve sounded Glynis on the subject. Her sympathetic intuition told her that he was shocked by his brother-in-law's sudden death and wanted to go home at once. He, too, had been fond of Paul. He was less aware than Glynis (the woman) of the unkindness Kitty had so often shown her husband. Naturally his sympathies were with his sister. Glynis saw, too, that it would be tactful of her to suggest, herself, that they cut the honeymoon short.

'What with my silly old ankle and everything we might as well go home,' she said.

'How sweet of you, darling, and Kitty will appreciate it,' said Steven gratefully.

As usual the glow of his eyes and pressure of his hand rewarded her.

But a gloom had been cast over both of them, she thought ruefully. It was the first real test for their love. She was sure they would both stand up to all the disappointments and difficulties involved. But it was not the triumphant home-coming they had planned.

Twenty-four hours later Glynis was helped out of the 'plane at London Airport by Steve and the air hostess. Her mother and father were waiting in the lounge. They had watched the 'plane come in and greeted her warmly. Mr. Thorne whispered:

'You're prettier than ever, darling—*such* wretched luck, this, and *poor* Sir Paul, too! . . .'

Glynis hugged them—absurdly pleased to see her parents again, even after seven days. She still did not feel that she was Mrs. Grant-Tally, she said. But back she came with a thud to all the side of it that she most disliked. Reporters and camera-men were there too. '*Hold it—just a moment, Mrs. Grant-Tally—an arm. around Mr. Tally's shoulder—that's it, hold it!*'

Tomorrow in the papers:

Double calamity befalls honeymoon couple. Mrs. Grant-Tally, the beautiful wife of the famous ear, nose and throat specialist, returns from honeymoon with broken ankle; and husband to funeral of his brother-in-law, Sir Paul Barley.

It was all there—and countless telephone calls and telegrams to answer, and then all the intense sadness for Steven at Thurloe Square. He sent Glynis with her mother straight into

179

Rhona's penthouse.

No use her being harrowed unduly at Thurloe Square, he said, and she was fatigued after the air journey and the painful ankle. Mrs. Thorne was delighted to have her now well-known and wealthy daughter to herself and was going to 'desert' Daddy, she said, and stay a couple of nights in the Penthouse. The magnificence of it all there took her breath away. Two Italian maids to receive Glynis; flowers everywhere (most of them from Rhona herself), a dozen evidences of Rhona's generosity. Champagne, fruit, every delicacy left in the larder. Mrs. Thorne exclaimed:

'How sweet Mrs. Chayney must be—I'm sure you've done her an injustice. She must be quite fond of you, dear . . .'

Glynis kept silent. In her bed in the wonderful spare room—the divan drawn up to the window from which she could look down on Park Lane and right over the Park—she felt subdued and really rather wretched. The afternoon was wet and dark. London felt icy after Majorca. Glynis left it to her mother to go into raptures about Rhona's gorgeous off-white carpet and pale blue and silver walls, and blue satin curtains; the wonderful gilt and painted Italian furniture: the whole extravagantly furnished penthouse. But none of it pleased Glynis. She wished passionately that this was two days ago when she had been walking hand in hand with Steve along the beach in the Majorcan sunlight, without a care in the world. Why, *why* could life never stand still when one was so happy? she wondered. All the rest of today he would be away from her—with poor Kitty. He telephoned her at teatime and sounded depressed and unlike himself. Poor Kitty had collapsed, he said, he would have to remain the night with her, then take her down to the country tomorrow to the village where poor Paul would be buried among his ancestors. But from what Kitty had already told him finances were in a somewhat parlous state—and Kitty had confessed herself personally in financial straits. He did not say much on that subject, but told Glynis that he thought it might be a good idea if Kitty stayed with them in the penthouse for a week. Her own house was so gloomy. She seemed broken-hearted and pitiable and needed him.

'She needs her little sister-in-law, too, I'm sure, darling.'

'Of *course*—we must do everything we can for her, Steve darling,' Glynis said at once.

Steven thanked her, apologized, and rang off.

But this did not revive Glynis' already drooping spirits. Much as she liked Kitty—to have her ladyship with them would not be an unmixed blessing. She was so autocratic. She would interfere. She would most certainly want to 'take over' and see to the new house for her brother. Glynis was *hors de combat* for

181

at least six weeks. Yes, Steve had said it would be early April before they could take the ankle out of plaster and irons. She would be forced to sit about the penthouse and 'take it', she thought. And Kitty would seize the opportunity to 'help Glynis get her home ready'.

Much as she loved Mummy, Glynis thought, she longed passionately to be alone with her husband again. It was a sad beginning to their married life. Owing to circumstances over which he had no control, Steve seemed already to have been taken right away from her.

CHAPTER SIXTEEN

Steven had never found himself in a more difficult position. First and foremost he wanted to be with his young newly-made wife—his bride of little more than a week. He was more than ever in love with her. The unfortunate and abrupt end to their honeymoon had upset him more than he had let her see. First of all there was her accident, and then he had his brother-in-law's funeral and affairs to see to. And Kitty was far removed from her ordinary gay, easy-going self. Perhaps because she was suffering more from remorse than grief now that Paul had gone beyond recall—she had given way completely. She could not stop crying—lay in bed in a darkened room and refused to see anybody but her brother. Steven had always been attached to his attractive sister—feckless and, at times, heartless though she was. But she had given him a home for years, so he felt now that he must do all he could for her. But Kitty's tragedy had come at a most inopportune moment in Steven's life. He had a wife to consider as well.

On top of everything else he had his work. True, he had arranged for a full fortnight off for his honeymoon, and he knew that he could rely on Fennymore to stand in for him—but only for six days more, and during those six days there was an enormous amount to be done for Kitty.

Things were made worse the afternoon after the funeral when Kitty, her pale wet face hidden in her hands, gulped out the confession of her indebtedness to Rhona Chayney.

Steven listened, horrified. Only an hour ago he had been reading Paul's Will with the family later, and they had been forced to the unhappy conclusion that, although Paul had not died in debt, his widow would be badly off. Paul's father had died only recently, so in one year there had been two lots of death duties, which meant that the one-time 'fortune' of the Barley family had shrunk to a pathetic size. On top of this their country place was mortgaged to the hilt. There was a second mortgage on

183

the house in Thurloe Square. It looked as though Kitty would have little beyond Paul's life insurance and certain small trust moneys which would amount to only a quarter of the income to which Kitty was used.

As for the money she owed Rhona, that left Steven aghast. He sat silent, smoking, heavy-hearted as he viewed the future. He had his lovely Glynis and his own future to think of—as well as his sister's. He could understand some of her extravagances, but not the wild fashion in which she had been gambling lately—mainly on horses.

'It's because I was so unhappy—Paul and I were not getting on—I had to throw myself into something in order to keep up my spirits,' she sobbed.

Steven remained silent. She seemed so unhappy and was facing ruin (it would be ruin to Kitty to have to cut down her expenses so drastically), he felt she had been sufficiently punished. But it scared him not a little. One never knew what was going to happen in this world, he thought. He must be careful—try to save for Glynis and any children they might bring into the world. After all, a specialist's life was not a long one. At a certain age he would have to retire. And it was so difficult to save with the drain of taxation, and having to keep up appearances. A man in his position must have a biggish house, an expensive car and entertain fairly lavishly. He relied, after all, on

184

wealthy patients.

'I wish to heaven you hadn't taken all that money from Rhona of all women,' he told his sister glumly.

Kitty wiped her streaming eyes.

'I always imagined you would marry her—that she'd be in the family. She has so much—such a fortune in America, as well as over here.'

Steven flushed.

'I am perfectly satisfied with Glynis. I married for love and not money,' he said coldly, and added: 'Of course I must raise money—sell out some shares—and pay Rhona back. It is essential. Such a debt puts us all in a most degrading position.'

Kitty moaned:

'Oh, Steve, don't tell Glynis—she wouldn't think very well of me—don't tell *anybody*—swear it!'

He gave her his word. He had no wish to let Glynis know this side of his sister's character. The one happiness left to him was his Glynis and the memory of her sterling qualities, her idealism. His Glynis would starve before she would borrow a shilling, he told himself.

That next morning after breakfast he had a long talk with Glynis, who was looking her prettiest, in a new blue housecoat, lying on the chaise-longue by the window. Outside it was wet and windy and cold. In this centrally heated bower of flowers it was cosy and attractive. Mrs. Thorne discreetly left them alone and went out to shop. Steven, sitting by the chaise-longue, drew Glynis close to him. His kisses rained hotly on her lips and soft white throat.

'My darling, darling little wife—I do love you so much . . .'

'I love you, too, Steve,' she whispered and closed her eyes while he kissed her long silky lashes.

For a moment they knew no heart-burnings or anxieties, but in each other's arms recaptured some of the perfect bliss of their interrupted honeymoon. Glynis told him that her ankle felt more comfortable, even though she could only hobble on Mummy's arm or with a stick. Steve forbore to tell her a word about Kitty's troubles. But Glynis, herself, was first to bring up her sister-in-law's name.

'She must be so miserable—it must have been such a shock—Paul's sudden death—we must do all we can to cheer her up. Bring her round today and let her stay here with us.'

'I am sure she would love it, but it doesn't seem fair to you, darling,' he said.

Glynis looked at him anxiously. His tan was already fading and he looked, she thought, unwell. There were new little lines criss-crossing under his fine eyes. Was it deep feeling for Paul, she wondered, or just worry about Kitty's future? Full of desire to help and comfort him, she leaned her bright gold head against his shoulder and stroked the hand she was holding.

'I'd *love* to have Kitty here,' she said warmly. 'Of course she must come. I'll ring her up and say so. She'll love being with you. Mummy can't stay, anyhow—she must get back to Barnet. Daddy loathes it without her—don't I know! They're an inseparable pair, really.'

'So are we,' murmured Steven, some of his natural humour returning, and gathered this lovely and much-loved wife of his back into his arms and kept her there until one of the Italian girls came in with coffee and biscuits.

So it was arranged. Kitty—very subdued and wretched—accepted Glynis' invitation. Steven drove her and her luggage round to the penthouse later that afternoon. Glynis was an *angel*, she declared. But of course in a day or two, when she had had a little time to recover from the shock, she said, she would go back to Thurloe Square. It was quite obvious she must at once dispose of the house and organize a sale. She would have to take a much smaller flat.

Glynis was quite perturbed by this news. She had had no idea, she said, that finances were so bad. She tried to console Kitty.

'Lots of money and entertaining is okay in its way but very worrying—everything is so terribly expensive. I'm sure you'll find it less of a strain when you don't have to do so much.'

Kitty gave a feeble smile. She was pleased to have her young sister-in-law's affection and support just now, but the last thing she wanted was to 'cut down', she thought, and give up what Glynis called the 'strain of having money'. And grateful though she was for being allowed to live for the next week or two with the two who should really be alone at the start of their marriage, in her heart Kitty resented Glynis.

It would all have been all right now had Glynis never come into Steven's life. She, Kitty, could have kept house for her brother and eventually he *might* have married Rhona.

Full of envy, Kitty spent the time wandering around the magnificent penthouse—wishing she had Rhona's means. Even the shock of losing Paul so suddenly, and despite her remorse, Kitty Barley could still only live and breathe in terms of what money could buy.

She had upset her brother and knew it. She had caused him a lot of inconvenience by enlisting his aid in settling her debts just now. But she had done it in her careless fashion— thinking first of herself. There might in consequence of her action be less for dear Glynis, she reflected bitterly—but Kitty was not going to fret over that.

Mrs. Thorne went home delighted with everything and confident that Glynis was the luckiest girl in the world. The fractured ankle was a setback, but a very temporary one, she said. As for Lady Barley—she was so pathetic and so *sweet*—Glyn must be glad to feel she could be of use and comfort her for a few days.

'I'm sure you don't mind and that it won't make any difference to you and Steve. You'll soon be alone together,' were Sylvia Thorne's bright parting words.

Glynis thought over them that evening especially when she was trying to hop round the flat on one leg and leaning on the stick Steve had bought for her. The ankle in its plaster cast felt huge and stiff and most unwieldly. It did so impede her progress in all ways. She couldn't get about with Steve—or Kitty. *They* had been out together most of the afternoon. Now she seated herself gingerly in a corner of the yellow satin-cushioned chesterfield by the fire in Rhona's wonderful drawing-room.

A huge jar of pink tulips spilled their beauty on the piano. Beside it stood a large silver-framed photograph of the owner of the penthouse. Rhona in a backless evening gown with a glimpse of the famous sables; her handsome almond-shaped eyes looking at one beguilingly. She was an exotic woman, Glynis thought, grimacing. Everything in this flat was imbued with her personality—her 'exoticness'—even her familiar perfume. She had left huge jars of her perfumed crystals and bottles of essence in the big bathroom that led out of the bedroom Glynis and Steven occupied. Whenever Glynis tried to order a simple meal for Steve and herself, the chef flung up his hands in horror. *Madame* had commanded him to carry on as though she were here. So Glynis had to sit down to three-course exclusive luncheons or a four-course dinner, beginning with the sort of things she had no liking for. Such delicacies as avocado pear with sauce piquante, smoked salmon, or *hors-d'oeuvre* were too rich for Glynis. And followed by rich dishes such as grilled salmon or chicken with mushroom sauce and ending with French pastries and sweets with whipped cream—these were all very well for parties, but one got sick of them. Glynis longed for a good plain dish of eggs and bacon, or one of Mummy's omelettes, and a big cup of milky coffee instead of the tiny china cups of ink-black coffee served up by Rhona's chef.

But Glynis did not complain. Steve seemed happy with the diet (used to it, no doubt, she reflected ruefully), and Kitty was a *gourmet*— she openly adored her food.

That last week which should have been part of poor Glynis' honeymoon was a mixed one for her. The days were the worst. Steve took her out in his car for a drive every morning. But it was, as she said, a 'palaver', what with getting her down in the lift, and into her seat— then out of it and upstairs again when she came back. And Steve seemed so busy with Kitty's affairs. Kitty, too, was often out with him. Perforce, Glynis was often left alone in the borrowed nest of luxury which she would so gladly have exchanged for a primitive cottage alone with her husband. But she was as cheerful as she could be. Friends like Alma came to see her, and of course all were full of admiration for Rhona's wonderful home, and although sympathetic about the poor ankle, took it for granted that Glynis was a very happy girl.

So she was—when she had Steve with her. At night when she was clasped in his arms, feeling his heart beat against hers with passionate love and longing—knowing herself utterly his. That was purest bliss for her. For him, too. He did not spoil the magic by telling her how troubled he was about Kitty's finances. Nor did he breathe a word about the debt to Rhona.

Then the week came to an abrupt end. Steve had to go back to his job. That was when Glynis really began to feel helpless because of the injured ankle and lonely without Steve. From the moment he left the penthouse, she could not hope to see him again except for the odd rushed meal. He became the preoccupied busy surgeon again. Appointments, operations, hospitals, consultations and another girl to look after him in the consulting room. That was the thing Glynis felt most deeply. His new receptionist, Nancy Phillips, was a nice girl and an efficient secretary. How Glynis envied her being so much with Steve. She saw more of him than she, his own wife, at times. Chained to the penthouse, Glynis brooded and pined. Kitty was no kind of companion. Either she was out or giving cocktails to her own personal friends (at Steve's expense) and talking endlessly, so it seemed to Glynis, about nothing that mattered; on the telephone for hours.

'I could never be like that,' Glynis reflected. 'I must have something concrete and useful to do. I should go mad if I had to hand things over to staff. When I *do* get my own home I shall work in it—whatever *anyone* says Mrs. Grant-Tally ought, or ought not, to do!'

CHAPTER SEVENTEEN

Things continued in this way for two more weeks. Each day that passed Glynis did, at least, feel pleased that her ankle was mending and the time drawing nearer when she could have the horrid plaster and iron taken off. But she was not very elated when Steve came home one evening and announced that he had signed the contract for their new house.

It wasn't that she did not like the house. It was one of the smaller and more modern types in Weymouth Street with attractive square-paned windows. But by Glynis' home standards it was very large and needed a lot of keeping up. She had been over it several times recently with Steve and agreed, however, that it was the ideal house for a doctor. There were three big rooms on the ground floor—one with parquet floor and a big bay window, most suitable for Steve's consulting room. A lovely double drawing-room on the first floor, and a large bedroom over that for Steve and Glynis.

Steve was delighted that the house problem was now settled although he had had to put down quite a bit of capital, and borrow the rest. He was in a hurry to move and, rather surprising to Glynis, anxious not to remain any longer than he had to in Rhona's flat. It was exactly as Glynis had felt from the start, but knowing nothing about Kitty's affairs, she was puzzled by Steve's new strange attitude towards Rhona. He seemed to become silent and moody when Glynis mentioned her name. And when Glynis told Kitty about it, Lady Barley reddened but merely gave one of her theatrical laughs and said, 'I really don't know what's wrong with our Steve—he's just a bit moody these days.'

Nobody wanted to get into her own home more than Glynis. But the broken ankle made it most difficult for her to go shopping. And Kitty showed no signs of leaving the penthouse, but was taking more and more on her own shoulders. She would sweep into the room (looking most effective these days in black and white), and fling dozens of patterns of curtains and carpets in front of Glynis.

'Steve adores *this* . . .' she would say, or 'I think *that* just right for your drawing-room,' or 'You must choose *this* one . . . it's *perfect* taste . . .'

And so on until Glynis felt confused and uncertain of what she did, in fact, really want for her home. Kitty was so domineering. Glynis' own mother was not allowed to come into it.

'Do rely on me, darling. I *do* know about these things and I'm so conversant with Steve's taste—*do* let me advise you,' Kitty would beg. Then at night over dinner Kitty would attack her brother, giving Glynis little chance to protest.

'You *adored* the room I did up for you at Thurloe Square—the white and red—rather Victorian—didn't you? You'd like it for the dining-room at Weymouth Street, wouldn't you, Steve darling?'

Steve, vague and wrapped in his own thoughts, would answer:

'Oh yes—*quite*—anything—I rely on you.'

'There!' Kitty would say triumphantly, turning to Glynis.

The young girl sat quiet, biting her lip.

Alone with Steve, Glynis questioned him.

'*Do* you prefer the red and white, or shall I make the dining-room pale grey and chestnut—*I* rather like *that* combination?'

Steve seemed to have little interest.

'Work it out with Kits, my angel—I'm no real judge. Kits has marvellous taste.'

'What about mine! It's my house and I've got to live in it,' muttered Glynis darkly.

But Steven was not listening. He had begun to concentrate on some papers he had brought home concerning the Barley estate. He had so much to do these days he had little time for worrying about interior decoration. And so far as he could see Glynis and Kitty were getting on well. Kitty had almost recovered her good spirits and Glynis seemed quite happy. He had not heard her muttered remark. Only when he had finished reading the lawyer's documents, he glanced up and suddenly saw his wife's face—pale and tearful. Yes, there were actually tears on those wonderful lashes. At once Steven was stricken. He threw down the papers and gathered Glynis on to his knee, ruffling the beautiful satin gold hair.

'My angel—what is it? Is the old ankle hurting?'

She hid her face against his shoulder, pressing her cheek to his.

'No, it isn't—it has nothing to do with my ankle.'

Then what is it, my darling? My *darling*—why are you crying?'

'I'm not!'

'Then you're giving a very good imitation of it,' he laughed and tenderly kissed her. She clung to him, her throat aching, although she echoed his laugh.

'I'm very silly sometimes, I expect, but oh, Steve—I wish I could choose everything for our home *alone*—or with Mummy.'

Now he saw suddenly that it was Kitty's help that she resented. He was sympathetic but not entirely so.

'Sweetie,' he said, caressing the lovely lissom form he always found so enchanting and exciting. 'You needn't upset yourself. What does it matter *who* helps—your mother or my sister?'

Glynis remained silent. There was a logic in this against which she could hardly argue. She only knew she would rather it had been her mother than Steve's sister. The house, when finished, would be all Kitty's taste—little of hers—she thought bitterly.

In his lazy masculine fashion Steve had no wish to be drawn into female differences of opinion. But he tried to take his wife's part.

'Look, darling—if you don't want this or that, just *tell* Kitty. It is your right.'

'She talks me down,' said Glynis a trifle sulkily.

'Well, shall I talk her down for you?' asked Steve with humour.

'No, I don't want to make trouble,' said Glynis, and sat up, frowning, and decided to fight her own battles. She would stand up to Kitty. She would tell her tomorrow that she

196

had decided on the grey and chestnut décor for the new dining-room.

All this seemed a bit childish and unimportant, but Glynis was aware that it is the little seemingly unimportant things that can go wrong and mar a marriage. She was fully determined not to allow them to do so— for Steve's sake. But she did wish she had a less busy and important husband. Even when the week-end came and Kitty went away to friends, Glynis did not have Steve to herself. They had to entertain a German surgeon and his wife who had come over to a Medical Conference in London. And Glynis was still hampered by the wretched ankle.

Then—at the beginning of the next week— Kitty electrified Glynis by coming into the penthouse one evening, about six o'clock, and bringing a visitor with her. The visitor, much to Glynis' dismay, was the famous Mrs. Chayney herself. Rhona, looking wonderful in a new *ensemble* from New York and a Hattie Carnegie hat on her sleek dark head, walked into the drawing-room arm in arm with her friend. They seemed to be on the best of terms, bubbling over. Kitty at once rushed to show Glynis a fascinating piece of 'costume jewellery' that Rhona had brought her as a present. A pair of chunky gilt and amethyst clips.

'Aren't they *wonderful*, Glynis?'

'Wonderful,' echoed the astonished Glynis

from her sofa. And she was further astonished and embarrassed when Rhona opened her big crocodile travelling-bag and drew out a small box and gave it to her.

'For you, darling,' she said glibly, 'and a little piece of New York for dear Steve, too—in my case.'

Glynis took the box—it was thrust into her hand. Her face was pink and her pulses fluttered. She stammered:

'B—but I thought you were s-staying in America till May.'

Rhona glanced towards Kitty, then gave Glynis a sweet sad smile.

'My dear, when I heard the dreadful news I had to come back—after all, Kitty is my dearest friend.'

'Wasn't it marvellous of her!' exclaimed Kitty. 'And she has been so upset—she adored my poor Paul.'

Glynis was dumbfounded. As far as she knew Rhona had always spoken rather disparagingly of Paul Barley as a dull, stodgy man, decried his amateur paintings as 'ghastly' and encouraged Kitty to criticize him. Glynis had never before come in contact with such shallowness or affectation. It seemed to her nauseating in its hypocrisy.

She sat there fingering the unwanted present and wishing Steve were here to champion her. The two older women were standing by the fire, divesting themselves of furs and hats, talking like magpies. Suddenly, gulping, Glynis said:

'Of course, Rhona, we must move out of your flat at once.'

Immediately Rhona pounced, waiting like a beautiful cat, Glynis thought uncharitably, claws hidden under velvet paws; purring:

'Under *no* circumstances. I said you could have the penthouse till you get into your own home and I shall stand by it. I came back to be with darling Kitty—nothing else. I shall stay with her at Thurloe Square. It's all settled, isn't it, Kits?'

'It is,' echoed Lady Barley, more gaily than she had spoken for some time. She was feeling very elevated since Rhona had rushed home to be at her side and was showing such friendliness and desire to help. (The help was urgently needed just now.) Rhona had told her when they met that she wished Kitty had said nothing to Steve about the debt, as she *quite* intended to forget it, and would tell Steve so.

Rhona had turned up at Thurloe Square thinking Sir Paul's widow would be there, and found Kitty sorting and packing up. The fabulous Rhona appeared to Kitty in excellent form—more than ever anxious to 'keep in' with her *and* Steve, of course. And this was where Rhona's cunning came in, Kitty had decided somewhat grimly. Rhona's eyes had glinted when she heard about Glynis' broken ankle. What could be better—little Glynis incapacitated. She, Rhona, could rush round with Kitty and do so much for darling Steve.

Now Glynis was arguing with them both, cheeks fiery red and heart pumping nervously. But she was not going to be bullied.

'I absolutely refuse to stay here now you are back, R-Rhona,' she stammered. 'Steve will insist we go to an hotel.'

'Nonsense!' exclaimed Rhona. 'It would be absurd. It'll just stay empty. Kits needs me at Thurloe Square. I might take my own personal maid, Maria, if you could spare her—but that's all. Kitty still has her married couple there.'

The argument continued. Eventually Rhona and Kitty won. (Rhona, of course, had to be asked to return for dinner.) Later Glynis sat alone, reviewing the situation. She could hear laughter, and high-pitched voices from the kitchen. The *Signora* Chayney was exchanging greetings with her staff. The drawing-room reeked of that familiar expensive scent Glynis always connected with Rhona. Glynis pictured the party this evening; no peace, no quiet; Rhona's theatrical personality dominating them all. Glynis' spirits sank to zero. How frustrating it all was! If only she could get out of this gilded cage. But if Rhona really did mean to help Kitty pack up and dispose of her house—and if it meant that she, Glynis, was to be left alone with Steve, well—the idea had its compensations. But Glynis had grown cynical and wondered what the snag was—what

Rhona had at the back of her scheming mind. Somehow Glynis felt she could never trust either of those two women—after that faked illness on Rhona's part on the night of the party.

Mechanically Glynis opened her parcel. Ordinarily speaking, she or any girl would have been delighted with the expensive toy from Fifth Avenue. A beautiful jewelled vanity case for evening wear with Glynis' own initials in diamante 'G. G.-T.' across one corner. Yet Rhona's very generosity troubled Glynis. It never seemed to her *genuine.*

When Steven came back from a late consultation, about eight o'clock that evening, he was amazed to find a small impromptu champagne party in progress, and one of the three women waiting for him—the *châtelaine* of the penthouse herself.

Rhona, wearing one of her smart housecoats, was exquisitely made-up as usual, and full of gaiety. Having greeted him effusively, explained her presence, and whispered, *'I'm trying to forget about poor Paul and help Kits to forget her sorrow, too . . .'* she handed Steven the present she had brought back for *him.* She chatted about her lug-gage being 'over-weight' on the Skymaster that had brought her home; the severe cold in New York; how delighted she was to be back; how *dreadful* it was that this honeymoon was cut so short by darling little Glynis' accident in

Majorca, and a stream of chatter to which Steven listened, slightly bewildered. He, like Glynis, was forced to appear grateful for his present, but was not. He, too, protested that they must at once leave the penthouse and was talked down by both Rhona and Kitty.

Only later, when he was alone with Glynis in their own room, did Steve feel able to say that he really wanted—and draw breath. He flung himself on to one of the elegant beds in the softly lit room, lit a cigarette and raised an eyebrow at his wife.

'Well—what do you know about that?' he exclaimed.

She hobbled over to him, slim and alluring in a white lace and chiffon slip, and twined bare arms about his neck.

'Oh, my darling, this is peace after a tornado—getting away from Rhona and being quiet and alone with you.'

He held her close, his lips moving over her rich hair.

'You look exhausted, my poor pet.'

'I am,' she confessed with a laugh. 'With all due respect to Kitty and Rhona—they are exhausting women.'

'Yet Rhona is essentially kind—she seems to have dashed back to England especially to stand by Kits.'

'M'm,' said Glynis, holding her counsel.

'Let's stay on here, anyhow, if it means we can be by ourselves,' said Steven cheerfully.

'I quite agree,' she nodded.

But she wondered how much they would be left alone . . . and what chance those two would give her of arranging her own home in the way she wanted. Rhona had horrified her during dinner by saying that she had brought back some 'marvellous curtain material from New York', especially for Steve's consulting room. The fantastic pattern which might be very smart but was not at all what Glynis would have chosen. The worst of Rhona, thought Glynis, was that she would deluge one with these presents and make it so hard for one to reject them without appearing rude or churlish.

Unknown to Glynis, however, Steven was harbouring his own anxious reflections about Rhona and Kitty. He had come to the sad conclusion that Rhona exercised a bad influence on his sister and living with her would only influence Kitty to spend money she could ill afford. Kitty had even let drop the hint that she might permanently share the penthouse with Rhona. Ridiculous, thought Steven quite angrily, with all those bills banging over her head, and the quite ghastly debt to Rhona herself. However, he was determined to pay that back even though it strained his own resources.

Glynis, in his arms, was drowsy and content now—wishing as always that life could always be like this, with *him*. She murmured:

'What's up, darling? You're scowling.'

He had sworn to Kitty never to tell Glynis about the debts. So he laughed and hugged the delicious fragrant form in his arms and became her gay, boyish lover again.

'Who's got a huge ugly thick ankle? Who's an ugly wife?'

'Me,' giggled Glynis.

He had reached out a hand and switched off the rosy table-lamp. The room was dark and quiet now. Laughter died softly in their throats as their lips met and clung passionately.

During the next two weeks Steven had a few difficult cases on hand and one sudden call to operate at a small hospital in the West Country which kept him away all night. In fact, Glynis saw little of him and he had no time at all in which to remember Rhona—or his sister's affairs, which had been handed over to the Barley solicitors.

But Glynis was subjected to a fortnight of petty aggravations which tried her temper sorely. It was as she had feared. Rhona, under the cloak of generous friend, tried to put a finger in every pie (backed by the satellite Kitty, of course). It seemed to poor Glynis that never did she enter the Weymouth Street house which was her home of the future without having to admit one or the other of those two women, who made endless suggestions and often tried to persuade her to cancel the things Glynis had ordered. She *knew* that she was inexperienced. She *knew* that although she adored beauty, she had no training in expensive, exclusive interior decoration or furnishing. She *knew* that she could quite well have accepted Rhona's and Kitty's help and benefited by it. But she had begun to resent them both so much and to dread so much the increasing shadow they were flinging across her daily life, she rejected many ideas which she might otherwise have liked. In her quiet moments she thought it over and was unhappy, wondering if *she* was at fault, if she was being silly and over-possessive of Steve. Yet—heaven knew—she hardly ever saw him. They had been married a month now, and the had so far only spent seven whole days alone with her husband.

Quite naturally Glynis dreamed of that other life she had so much wanted—the quiet domestic life with a husband, who, once his job was over, had no other interests and was happy to be sequestered with her in their small home from the rest of the world. Steven loved her—she knew that, but he *belonged* to that world which so often scared and at times depressed Glynis.

There was bound to come a moment of reckoning with Rhona. It came one evening a few weeks later. It had been a happy day earlier on for Glynis. She had been taken by her mother to St. Martha's where the walking-iron and plaster had been removed from the injured foot. Now the ankle was slim and whole again. Glynis walked on her mother's arm down the hospital steps in fine spirits. It was so exciting, she said. She could wear her two shoes and be normal again.

Mrs. Thorne kissed her and caught her Green Line bus. It was just before four. Glynis had a sudden wish to see how things were going at Weymouth Street and took a taxi there. With any luck she and Steve would be able to move in by the end of April. Kitty was selling a lot of her lovely furniture at a low price to her brother and they had decided to start with little and buy more once they were in—and knew exactly what they wanted.

The painters were putting the last coat on the dining-room (the grey that Glynis had insisted on despite Kitty). The hall and consulting-room carpets had already been laid—a beautiful pale mushroom-coloured Wilton. Glynis was thrilled with the whole house now—even ready to admit that some of the advice thrust on her had been worth taking. The drawing-room curtains were the kind she had always admired; glorious Regency red and white striped satin. The furniture was for the most part in the same period.

But when Glynis entered Steve's consulting room—that beautiful oak-panelled room where they had been most extravagant about building special glass cupboards and bookshelves for the surgeon—the radiance left Glynis' eyes. They grew a cold, hard green. Curtains had been hung. Not the curtains *she* had ordered, which were dark olive green velvet, but the showy patterned ones Rhona had brought back from New York and which Glynis had politely refused.

'How dare she!' an angry, crimson-cheeked Glynis exclaimed under her breath. 'I shall have them taken down.'

Swinging round she saw Rhona standing behind her. Smart and smiling, violets pinned to her fur jacket, she had found the front door ajar and stolen in.

'*Well*, hello, Glynis darling!' she said gaily. 'Now you see them up—don't you like them? I did it as a surprise for you while you were at the hospital. How lovely it must be for you to have the plaster off and—'

But Glynis cut her short. She had never felt more furious.

'I'm sorry, Rhona, but I think what you did is an impertinence. I have bought the curtains for this room and Steve and I decided on them.'

Rhona waved an arm at the windows.

'But, my *dear*, don't you agree these look *gorgeous!*'

'No, I don't,' said Glynis bluntly. But as she afterwards described it to her friend Alma, she felt as though there were butterflies in her stomach.

Then the good humour died from Rhona's face. A frozen expression replaced it.

'I think you are being rather stubborn and ungrateful, aren't you, Glynis?' she asked icily.

Glynis rarely lost her temper, but she lost it it now.

'I'm a little *tired* of having to be so grateful to you, Rhona. You *will* do all these things without being asked. I think it's time you—and Kitty—left me alone. This is going to be my home—and Steve's—not yours!'

Silence. In the empty room—smelling of fresh paint and newly polished wood, with the glare of a still unshaded centre light on them— the two women who loved Steven in such different fashion faced one another, open antagonists at last.

CHAPTER EIGHTEEN

Rhona walked to the window-sill, drew back the offending curtains, pulled a cigarette-case from her bag and lit a cigarette. She looked cool, but inwardly she was raging. She felt that she had never hated anybody in her life as much as she hated this slim fair girl who had all that she, Rhona, had ever wanted—all that money could not buy. She was beginning to realize with a vengeance how utterly wrong she had been to presuppose that Steve had married a 'little thing' from the suburbs with no spirit of her own. Somehow Rhona managed to laugh.

'This is becoming rather childish, don't you think?'

Glynis had no cigarettes in her bag. She felt the urgent need of one but would have died rather than ask Rhona for it. She was determined not to be browbeaten by this woman, no matter how rich or glamorous or powerful she was in her own way. No matter whether she was Steve's friend or not, Glynis had come to the end of her patience.

At length she said:

'It may seem childish to you, but it isn't to me. It's very important. Thank you very much for your—*generosity*'—that word stuck in her throat—'but I must refuse your very kind present. The curtains I chose for this room are being made.'

Rhona said:

'You're not giving mine a fair chance—you haven't even looked at them properly. In New York they're all the rage—it's a heavenly pattern.'

'Most original,' cut in Glynis, 'but Steve and I have already chosen the curtains for this room.'

Those last few words hit Rhona between the eyes. She felt positively sick with anger and chagrin. Only by a great effort she managed not to snarl like a tiger cat at this young girl whose stubbornness she found madly irritating.

Glynis added:

'Of course, I'll get the men to take these down and return them very carefully to your flat, thank you again for the thought. I wish you'd warned me.'

Then Rhona, shivering with rage, spoke between closed teeth.

;Is Steve to have no say in this?'

'Steve has already approved the curtains I chose.'

'This is absurd!' Rhona was breathing quickly, 'and I won't allow you to insult me like this.'

Now Glynis stared at Rhona, genuinely astonished.

'I don't mean to insult you. You make it all sound *awful* and you've been been so kind, lending us your beautiful flat and all that . . . it's only that I want to do up my own house in my own way—can't you understand? Would you have wanted *me* to *i*nterfere in your house, while you were furnishing it?'

Rhona took one or two rapid puffs of her cigarette, her face changing from red to white under the make-up.

'I would never behave in such an atrociously ungrateful fashion. It can only mean that you positively dislike me.'

Now the glove was flung at Glynis' feet. The shy half of her made her long to turn and run out of this room. This was turning into a most undignified and embarrassing combat of words, and Glynis was terrified that very soon she would do something silly like bursting into tears and letting Rhona see how upset she was. So she made a final attempt to put an end to it.

'Please, Rhona . . . I'm so terribly sorry if you think I'm ungrateful. I'm not—it's just that I want to be left alone. Please *do* leave both Steve and me *alone.*'

Then Rhona turned on her.

'You've been trying for a long time to take Steve away from me, break up our friendship, and you *know* it's one I treasure. Until you came, Steve was my dearest friend.'

'Please!' broke in Glynis, hot and dismayed.

'Have it your own way,' continued Rhona on a high-pitched note, 'make mischief between Steve and myself. Behave as though I'd put those curtains up with a vile purpose instead of wanting to give you a lovely surprise. You look as though butter wouldn't melt in your mouth but you're wicked and cruel!' She broke off, turned, and ran past Glynis and out of the house.

Glynis heard the front door slam. She stood as though rooted to the spot. Her lips trembled. She had never felt more upset; and her mind was confused. Rhona had so cleverly turned the tables on her that she had made her feel it was she, Glynis, who was to blame for all the trouble. *Had* she been ungrateful? *Was* Rhona Chayney a true friend and not the snake in the grass that Glynis feared? Oh, the whole thing was horrid, and left a nasty taste in her mouth. One thing was certain. It was no good going on pretending that she and Rhona could ever be friends. On her wedding day she had vowed to accept Rhona as 'one of the family' because Steve had wished it—but this was the end. Rhona was spoiling everything and had tried to do so from the start.

Glynis turned and walked slowly out of the house and stood on the steps in the dusk. Her beautiful new home, she thought. She had come here today in such a happy mood. What had possessed Rhona to have those curtains hung unless it was out of the spiteful desire to make things awkward?

Meanwhile, Rhona had told her chauffeur to drive the Rolls down Weymouth Street to Steve's consulting rooms. She was in a black mood and determined to carry on with the mischief she had begun.

She was lucky enough to find Steve in. The new receptionist, Miss Phillips, told her that Mr. Grant-Tally was just seeing his last patient. Rhona waited. She waited with that hatred of Steve's wife fermenting inside her. By the time she was shown into Steve's presence she was mistress of herself again, although there was a look of strain in her eyes.

Steven was sitting at his desk writing something on a pad, on which an Anglepoise lamp shed a powerful light. He looked tired.

212

He had had a heavy day in the operating theatre but he welcomed Rhona with a smile as he rose to his feet.

'This is unexpected. How are you, my dear? Sit down. I presume this isn't a professional visit?'

'No,' said Rhona in a low voice.

Steven reseated himself, toyed with a fountain-pen and continued to smile. But she had no answering smile for him and after a second he became aware of her tenseness. As she loosened her fur, he pushed a box of cigarettes towards her. She shook her head.

'No, thanks.'

'Is anything wrong?'

He spoke in his most charming, friendly fashion. Looking at the handsome, vital face and figure, she was fully conscious of what she had lost when he fell in love with Glynis. She experienced suddenly a genuine gnawing misery, a regret that robbed her of her composure. She ceased to be the subtle woman of the world. She suddenly put her face in her hands. Steven looked appalled. Was she *crying*? It was the last attitude he had expected from Rhona, gay, amusing Rhona. The woman with the fortune who seemed to have everything she wanted. His professional instincts overcame any other feelings. Hastily he rose, found a small bottle and medicine-glass from one of the cabinets, and poured out a restorative which he handed to her.

'Here, drink this down,' he said gently.

She drank it, grimacing, and dried her tears. But she thanked him and smiled in the most pathetic manner. Steven sat down again.

'Now, what's this all about, tell me?' he said with the sympathy he would have shown any patient.

But what Rhona had to say, when she said it, was far from welcome to him. There poured from her lips a garbled version of what had just happened at the other house in Weymouth Street, ending up with: 'And, of course, I realize now it was tactless of me to have had those curtains hung, but I thought they were so *cute* (as they said in New York) and meant to give Glynis a wonderful surprise. She seemed to take it so badly and she was so—if you forgive me saying so—so *unkind* to me. Oh, Steve! You know how deeply fond I've always been of you and Kitty, and how I value your friendship. Why does Glynis hate me? What have I ever done to deserve it?'

Steven was seldom at a loss for words, but he remained tongue-tied now. He was embarrassed by the way Rhona's dark tearful eyes stared at him. The whole episode caused him deep embarrassment. The poor man did not really know what line to take; he was on a spot, he thought grimly. Whose side *could* he take? One ought, of course, always to defend one's wife. He knew that Glynis had been jealous of Rhona from the start, and Rhona's story had certainly made it sound as though Glynis had been unnecessarily disagreeable about the damned curtains. But, of course, Rhona (and Kitty) interfered far too much—they always did, the pair of them. That was the trouble. Naturally Glynis resented it.

Steve got up and began to walk up and down his room, hands in pockets. At the end of a hard day's operating the last thing he wanted was *this*. He had looked forward to getting home and having a quiet drink alone with his adorable young wife. He knew that her mother had taken her to St. Martha's this afternoon to have the plaster off. He was longing to see the result. To the devil with Rhona and her 'dramas'! It was all so devilishly difficult because she would keep showering presents on one.

Suddenly he returned to his desk, pulled a cheque book from the middle drawer and opened it.

'Rhona, my dear,' he said, 'I think the time has come for you and me to have a reckoning. I don't want to hurt you—it's the last thing—but Glynis is my wife and my happiness with her is of tremendous importance. You and I have known each other for a long time. You're Kitty's greatest friend—but it doesn't seem as though it's going to be any good trying to pretend that you and Glynis get on. You don't!' he ended bluntly.

Rhona's eyes widened with sudden fear.

'Steve!' she gasped. 'You're not going to turn on me just because Glynis doesn't like me—you're not going to be such a poor friend as *that.*'

Steven flushed but held firm.

'Rhona, my dear, please believe that it's the last thing I want, but Glynis must come first. And the truth is that she would rather you *didn't* spend your money on us and shower us with generosity. You must try and see her point of view. She has been brought up in a very different *milieu* and she just doesn't understand the world that you move in.'

'That's nonsense. What you mean is that she is jealous of me!' broke out Rhona in a choked voice.

Steven coughed and, frowning, bent over his cheque book.

'Don't let us go into all that, Rhona—it won't get us anywhere.'

She stood up. Laying a hand on the desk, she bent over his blotter.

'Steve—what are you doing?'

'Writing you a cheque, my dear,' he said quietly.

'*Steve . . .*'

He signed his name, tore off the cheque and handed her the blue slip of paper.

She looked at the amount and now her heart gave a horrid twist. That cheque was for four figures. She raised her eyes to him again, dumbfounded. He said:

'Rhona, my dear—here it is, and all my thanks for your kindness to Kitty and to us generally. But I cannot allow my sister to be in your debt for such an amount. I hope this covers what she owes you. It has been oustanding far too long. I feel that Paul would have wished me to repay it.'

Rhona sank into her chair—trembling from head to foot. Her face was ashen.

'You can't do this—you can't,' she whispered.

'My dear—one must repay debts of honour.'

Now Rhona, her eyes glittering, tore the cheque in half.

'You're doing this to upset me—I don't want to be repaid,' she stammered. 'I told Kitty I had *given* her the money.'

Steve sighed and pulled the cheque book towards him again.

'Silly girl—you've cost me twopence,' he said, trying to be humorous. 'Please don't tear this one up—if you do I shall merely be put to the trouble of paying the money into your bank direct, and you know how busy I am.'

She sank back into her chair. She felt deflated. She was crying in earnest now. Steven walked round to her and opened her bag and placed the cheque in it. Then he picked up one of her hands and gently patted it.

'Rhona—you've been so sweet to us— please be reasonable now and try to see things from our point of view—as well as your own. We can't go on like this. Glynis and I are newly married—we don't want these misunderstandings. Above all we feel we *must* be independent. If you don't mind—we will return your beautiful flat to you at the end of this week—whether our house is ready or not.'

Now suddenly Rhona looked up at him—her face streaming with tears which made her look strangely young and pitiful to him. It was such a humiliation for the spoiled, domineering Rhona. He was about to say something friendly and kind, when she seized his hand with both of hers and put her lips to it.

'You know what this means to me,' she said huskily. 'How I adore you—you must always have known.'

Steven pulled the hand away rather sharply, his face hot.

'Rhona, don't say anything you'll regret—please, my dear. It's more than charming of you to care about me—but—'

'But you're married—yes—and to a girl who loathes me,' Rhona broke in bitterly. 'We might all have been good friends—and happy—but this is what she has done. If I'm to be separated from you and Kitty and all the old ties are to be broken, I shall be the loneliest and unhappiest woman alive. That's how much you mean to me.'

He felt exhausted—depleted by this

emotional scene. He could not even feel flattered by Rhona's unashamed declaration of her love. It was all too complicated. A busy doctor wanted none of this sort of thing in his life. Steve felt anxious to end the interview and get home to Glynis. At the same time he felt vaguely irritated—knowing nothing of the situation as *she* saw it, he rather wished that Glynis had not so openly shown her dislike of Rhona and brought things to such a pass. It had never been his wish to end his friendship with Rhona. But now she, herself, by what she had just said, made future association with her impossible.

Rhona Chayney, herself, knew it. But she was not long to remain dejected and submissive to fate. She felt only a burning wish to defeat Glynis—even if she could never have Steven. She made a final effort to control herself. She powdered her face and rearranged hair and hat. Then she looked up at Steven, smiling very sadly.

'I apologize, my dear,' she whispered. 'I've made a fool of myself.'

At once Steven, with his frank happy nature, was quick to accept this and be glad of it. He did not like to be enemies with anybody and—after all—this beautiful woman had paid him a great compliment. That he could not deny. He spoke to her warmly.

'Let's forget it all. I'm quite prepared to if you are. There can be no question of breaking the old ties—Kitty would never want such a thing—she is devoted to you. Please just pay that cheque into your bank and let me feel that the debt is paid, and don't let us mention it again.'

Rhona stood up. In a very low voice she said: 'I don't want the beastly money. I shall send it to St. Martha's if you insist on me taking this cheque.'

That was a clever move. Nothing could have appealed more to Steve than an act of charity towards his hospital. He was delighted.

'You're wonderful, Rhona. And I don't want you to be miserable about all this and I know Glynis wouldn't want it either. Just give her a chance to settle down—I *know* how welcome you'll always be in our house later on.'

'Welcome to you—never to her,' Rhona said in a low voice.

Steven mumbled something about *'giving it time'*. Then he said that he really must go and would she mind if he said good-bye as he wanted to dictate a last letter to Miss Phillips.

Rhona held out her hand and gave Steven her sweetest and saddest smile.

'I'm ashamed of myself—I'll never be so silly again. Just go on being my friend,' she said.

They shook hands, and she left, feeling that she had gained only a small victory, and with the bitter knowledge that Glynis still had him. But she, Rhona, still had Kitty under control and she was going to make quite sure that Kitty shared the penthouse with her, once Steven left it.

CHAPTER NINETEEN

Glynis emerged from the house in Weymouth Street. As she stood on the steps she noticed two familiar cars parked outside Steve's consulting rooms: Steve's—and Rhona's Rolls-Royce. She knew the Rolls only too well—and the chauffeur. Already upset, it did not help Glynis to realize that Rhona had had the effrontery to pay a call on Steve. She was surprised, too, that Steve was still there. He must be working late this evening. She felt a sudden longing to contact him. They could drive home together. She went back into the empty house and stood at the window watching and waiting until Rhona departed. Rhona was there so long that Glynis' spirits fell and her ankle, fresh from the plaster, began to feel stiff from standing. She was conscious of a mutinous feeling—she was not going home without Steve now. At length, with considerable relief, Glynis saw the elegantly dressed Rhona step into her car and drive away. Then Glynis emerged from her own retreat and rang Steven's bell. She sighed as she looked at the plate that bore Steven's name and initials. How different everything had been in the old days when she used to come here to work for him, she thought. Now Nancy let her in and greeted her smilingly.

'Mr. Grant-Tally is just going, Mrs. Grant-Tally—do wait in his room—he's in my office looking at some X-rays.'

'Right—don't hurry him—I can wait,' said Glynis, and walked into the room which was, as it had always been, warm and imposing—full of Steve's own personality.

Suddenly Glynis wrinkled her small nose, and thought: '*She* has been here all right—I can smell her perfume.'

Then she seated herself in 'the Chief's' chair, loosened her coat and took off her hat. Her features relaxed into a smile as she saw her photograph on Steven's desk, and remembered the day she had gone (so much against her will) to have it done. It was signed, '*Your Glynis*'. Yes, she thought tenderly, she was all his and she loved him more than anything in the world.

'I quite envy Nancy in working with him,' she said aloud, and laughed at her own stupidity. Why bother about being his secretary when she was his wife? Then her gaze lit on the open cheque book on the blotter—a brand-new one. Without meaning to pry she saw her husband's neat concise writing on the first counterfoil. For an instant the sight of the name on the page and the amount shook her. '*R. Chayney—£1,250.*' Some of the healthy colour left Glynis' cheeks. She felt cold. *Pay Rhona twelve hundred and fifty pounds.* But why, *why*?

Why should Steve write such a huge cheque for Rhona? There could be only one explanation, of course—that it was a repayment of a debt. Now Glynis remembered a conversation she had had with Kitty when they were together in the penthouse, before Rhona came back from America—a hint Kitty had dropped about 'how much money she and Steve owed Rhona'. After all, Glynis reflected, although she was Steve's wife, *she* knew little about his finances. He seemed to have plenty of money, but so did most successful specialists. As far as the knew, Steven had also inherited something from his uncle, Sir Campion. On the other hand, whenever Steven *had* discussed money with her it was to the effect that he was spending up to the hilt; that these were days when it was impossible to save, and he had told her that poor Paul Barley had left nothing much for Kitty.

Perhaps Rhona had loaned Steve money to start his career? Whatever it was, Glynis felt upset. She just *couldn't bear* the thought that Steve had taken money from Rhona. Then she heard his footsteps, quickly stood up and walked to the mantelpiece trying to control her agitation. It had always been her principle in life not to be 'a busybody' and, as a wife, not to criticize her husband's actions nor demand confidences that were not voluntarily given. So she would not dream of telling Steven that the had seen this counterfoil nor question him about it. If he wanted to tell her, he would do so. If he loved her as she loved him he would keep no secrets from her. Besides, the had always had his assurance that Rhona Chayney, as a woman, meant nothing to him. Glynis told herself that it would be insulting of her to be suspicious.

When Steven walked into the room and opened his arms, she deliberately put away the unpleasant memory of the money he had just paid Rhona, and ran into those beloved arms. He gathered the slim figure, kissing her like the lover he still was.

'How incredibly nice to see you, my darling, and what a drink for a thirsty man after a long and difficult day . . . He kissed her lips again, then pressed his cheek against hers with a deep sigh. 'I'm very much in love with my wife,' he whispered.

All her heart went out to him. A thousand Rhonas did not seem to matter. 'And I'm in love with my husband, and look'—she laughed gaily and pointed to her ankle, then held out a well-shod foot—'don't I look nice again? Look how I walk . . .' and she began to move around the consulting room with the exaggerated grace of a model-girl.

Steven laughed. He, too, was beginning to

feel gay and content again.

'Let's go home and have some champagne—I feel like it tonight,' he said.

She put on her hat.

'Wonderful, darling. And must we dine in the flat? Couldn't you take me in the car out of London somewhere where we can be quite quiet and alone?'

He was on the verge of agreeing, then frowned and shook his head.

'I wish we could, but something's cropped up, angel. I've got to dash out and leave you for an hour after dinner. You remember those Marradines—that baby we took to the clinic on . . . *the* night,' he added, smiling, 'when I first told you that I loved you?'

'Yes.' Her limpid green eyes looked up into his and he bent to kiss her again. The breathtaking beauty of those wonderful eyes never failed to move him. He added:

'They aren't having much luck with that poor kid. I'm afraid he's seriously ill this time. Marradine is due back from Paris tonight and the mother has begged me to go round to Park Lane and talk to them and their G.P. A sort of conference. We've got to take a vital decision. So it can't be the country for us tonight, my darling.'

She nodded. Her pleasure in the love they shared was somewhat blunted when she remembered how often he had to leave her; how hopeless it was to try and live in a

225

charmed circle with a man who must always move and breathe outside it at the request of others. Oh for that other mythical existence in a tiny cottage or flat where they were *alone*!

Now Steve picked up the cheque book and tossed it into a drawer. She saw the action and her pulses stirred with disagreeable memories. Then she said quietly:

'Rhona was here just now, wasn't she?'

Steven hesitated. He would have liked to have made a clean breast of the whole show to his young wife but he was held back by two reasons. One that he could not explain about the money because he had given Kitty his sacred word that he would never divulge the matter of her debt to Rhona. The other was his masculine unwillingness to precipitate any further 'scenes'. He felt he had had enough for one day, with that half hour of Rhona. The Rhona affair had ended up quite well, and it would be a pity to start up anything fresh by so much as a single reproach to Glynis for treating Rhona in an unfriendly fashion. So, clearing his throat, he said:

'Yes, she dropped in for a talk.'

That was a masterly understatement and Glynis knew it, but did not comment. Her heart sank a little, however. It was obvious that Steven was not going to take her into his confidence. She said:

'I saw Rhona, too. She put some curtains up in your consulting room without telling me, and I thought it rather interfering of her. We'd already chosen what we wanted for your room. Don't you agree?'

'Oh yes, certainly—it's your home, my angel, and you must have exactly what you want,' said Steven promptly.

Her eyes looked gravely up into his.

'Are you sure you agree?'

'Absolutely, darling'; he bent and kissed the tip of her nose. 'Let's go, shall we?'

She thought: 'He doesn't want to say any more.'

She was silent and subdued for the rest of the drive home. Steven, too, was preoccupied. And each was conscious of a slight hesitancy and 'withdrawness' in the other. Only when they reached the penthouse did Steven bring up Rhona's name of his own accord. Then he said:

'By the way, darling, I think, taking it by and large, we'll let Rhona have her flat back at once. We can move into a hotel for a week or two until you've got the house arranged. I think you'd like your own home now, wouldn't you?'

That cheered Glynis enormously. She flung her arms around his neck.

'Darling, I'd adore it, and honestly I think we could move in some of the stuff and get one or two of the rooms arranged so that we needn't go to a hotel at all.'

Steve threw himself into a chair. He had

poured out a sherry. As he sipped it, he said:

'I scarcely think so, darling. You've got no staff and—'

'Oh, but I don't need a staff to begin with,' she broke in eagerly, and knelt by his chair and tucked both her arms around one of his. 'Now my foot's all right, and I can get about, I'd simply *adore* to show you what a good cook I am as well as Mummy. And I can get a daily— that nice Mrs. Wickens who cleans your consulting rooms would come, I'm sure. She *adores* you. If you'd put up with picnicking until the rest of the house is ready, I could soon get our bedroom and kitchen ready, and we could eat out, if you prefer it. Oh, I think it would be marvellous—such terrific fun—oh, *do* let's . . .' she broke off breathlessly.

He was touched by her childish enthusiasm, and she looked lovely enough with her flushed cheeks and sparkling eyes to make any man feel glad to be alive, he thought. He, too, yearned for some peace and quiet with this enchanting young wife of his. But he was not quite so sure as Glynis that picnicking in a half-empty house would be ideal. Men, he reflected, are selfish brutes and like their creature-comforts. And what Glynis didn't quite understand, perhaps, was that he had absolutely no time or place for the ultra-domestic life for which she seemed to crave. On the other hand, he wanted her to be happy.

'We'll do *whatever* you like, sweet,' he said.

'I'll leave it all to you. You arrange things, and let me know and I'll fall in.'

'Then I'll get on to the removals place tomorrow and have some of the things we've bought sent straight to the house. I know the bedroom curtains are ready—they told me so yesterday.'

'Then at least we shall be hidden from the world while we sit up and drink our early morning tea,' laughed Steve.

'You won't mind picnicking with me?' the asked anxiously.

'Far from it—it will be great fun,' he said lightly.

'When will you tell Rhona that we're leaving?'

'I've already told her,' he said and drained his glass.

'What did she say?' Glynis found her pulse-rate quickening slightly. Somehow she could not bear to look at that dazzling photograph of Rhona standing in its usual place on the piano. Without there being any real reason for it the woman's personality seemed always to infiltrate its way between her and Steve.

But Steve seemed disinclined to give Glynis further details of any conversation he had had with Rhona.

'I'm going to have a bath,' he said abruptly.

Glynis went to her bedroom to change her own dress. She did not feel particularly gay. She felt that she could never hope to know what was going on in Steven's mind. Passionately though they were in love, she could not reach that state of mental unity with him that she had always thought essential to marriage. She wished that he had not got to go out to the consultation after dinner and leave her alone with her own thoughts. She tried to cheer herself with the reminder that he had at least consented to move into their half-empty house with her—it would be *her* home and his—wonderful thought!

She drew the curtains and opened the windows. Rhona's staff would keep the penthouse at a temperature that nearly stifled Glynis. The April night was not cold. Glynis drew in a breath of the soft air, looked reflectively across the Park and thought: '*Soon it will be spring and all the trees will be out. I must make Steve so happy* in *our home that he won't ever want to leave it.*' And the sparkle returned to her eyes as she put on a dressing-gown and began to brush her crisp gold hair into sleek waves and to dream about the things she would do.

But not yet was she to be allowed to forget Rhona Chayney. After dinner, when Steven had gone, and she was alone, her sister-in-law telephoned her. Kitty spoke coldly.

'I really do think, Glynis, that you might try not to be so churlish to somebody who has been exceedingly good to all of us,' she began.

If this reproach flung Glynis into a shy

panic, she hid the fact. She answered with equal coolness.

'I'm sorry. I didn't mean to be churlish to Rhona. Perhaps you don't quite understand.'

'Oh, I understand, and you were rude just because she had those glorious curtains hung in Steve's room. If you want a word of advice, my dear, you won't annoy Steve by being so blatantly jealous and possessive.'

Glynis thought: *She's trying to get me down and cause trouble. I won't let her.*

Kitty continued to speak more sharply than she intended to Glynis, but she was in a poor humour. It had been a shock to her to learn that her brother had paid up the huge debt that she owed Rhona, and although grateful, she did not want anything—even repayment of the debt—to come between her and the one person who seemed able to give her the things she craved. She did not blame Steven. It was the fault of that stupid little wife of his, she thought. So she continued to reproach and advise, and was, perhaps, a little nettled when Glynis answered with the most admirable restraint:

'Believe me, Kitty, I have no wish to hurt Rhona. I *told* her how grateful I am for the loan of this flat—and everything. Please tell her so again. But Steve and I are moving into our own home on Monday. It is all for the best. I'll see that everything is in order before we go.'

'But your house isn't ready—' began Kitty.

'We can manage in the rooms that *are* ready,' broke in Glynis, and flung back her bright head with a defiance that Kitty felt even though she did not see it.

Later, Kitty repeated this conversation somewhat gloomily to Rhona. Rhona, drinking coffee with her at Claridges, where they had dined, twisted her lips. She was still smarting from the recent scene with both Glynis and Steve. She said:

'Never mind, Kits darling. You and I will move into the penthouse. We'll entertain and I shall find you a rich, charming husband and you shall be as happy as you deserve. I can't forgive Glynis. She has not only ruined your life but Steve's. Let her try this bread and cheese and kisses in the basement on him, and see how he reacts. I know Steve. He'll soon get sick of it.'

CHAPTER TWENTY

Rhona might have been right in what she said that night to her friend Kitty, but she overlooked one important factor in the case— *Steven did not have time* to get sick of the 'picnic'.

The move duly took place. Glynis had never been more thankful in her life to leave a place than she was when she said good-bye to Rhona's penthouse. She had no use for Rhona—for the expensive staff who looked boldly for farewell tips—or for the life she had been forced to lead in all that magnificence. Even in the years to come she was able to look back on the first hectic week in her new home as being the happiest of her life. Happier than her golden honeymoon in Majorca. For now she knew Steven so much better and he knew her and they were living in a practical everyday world, and not that dizzy rapture of the first few days during which all things good or bad are so much magnified.

A hectic week it certainly was! But there was no question of Glynis having to see people she hardly knew and entertain them, or change her dress several times a day, or live, as she described to the faithful Alma, 'like a duchess'. It was heaven to be busy all day long in the ordinary domestic work, with only Mummy to help. Kitty did not pay unwelcome visits. Steven had had a few short sharp words with his sister and suggested that she might be responsible for a lot of trouble if she insisted on interfering with Glynis' arrangements. And when Kitty protested that she had only 'tried to be helpful' and that 'dear little Glynis should not be so touchy', Steven had retorted:

'Never you mind—I'm sure you mean well, Kits—*but please let her alone.*'

Kitty had rung off in a huff. Neither Steven

nor Glynis had been particularly sorry to learn that she had left town. She had even left Rhona, and gone to Paris to stay with old friends of Paul's. Rhona was back in the penthouse; Thurloe Square closed down. But Kitty, when she returned from Paris, intended to share the penthouse with her friend.

There might be trouble in the future, Glynis told herself, but for the moment she was gloriously free from unwanted advice and dangerous subversive influences. She literally thrived on the discomforts of living in a house that was only partially furnished. *It was hers and Steve's.* She and Mummy had the time of their lives. (Sylvia Thorne found it delightful to participate in the move and, for once, to feel that she need not worry about the bills.) Steven was generosity itself and gave Glynis *carte blanche.* Glynis, brought up to be economical, was determined, however, not to be unduly extravagant. During the few short weeks she had lived as Steve's wife she had learned quite a lot about 'décor' and she had the surplus furniture from Thurloe Square; the entire contents of the rooms Steven had once occupied there; all lovely things.

But for a few days Glynis and Steven lived in the kitchen and one double bedroom, with the smell of fresh paint, with men wandering in and out, with Glynis rushing round, with the faithful Mrs. Wickens—mop, duster and broom constantly in use. Paper spread over polished parquet and new carpets; grumbles at the workmen's footmarks; new central heating being tested; cold bath water for three or four days, and Glynis heating up kettles and pans of water. Impromptu meals—at night a healthily tired Glynis, but still full of joy in the domain where she reigned, at last, supreme.

Unforgettable and sweet, that first night there when they had to use their trunks as a dressing-table because the van did not turn up until the next morning. When Glynis unpacked some of the new linen which had been embroidered with her initials and Steve's. When she made her first omelette for Steve, and he sat opposite her at the kitchen table, coat off—the golden strip-light making the big basement kitchen look quite sunny. When Glynis proudly listened to Steve praising the humble repast and he, himself, made the salad. Steve prided himself on his French salads. When, at last, one of her innermost ambitions was realized and she and Steve together washed up the dishes. (Not that wonderful dinner service which the Barleys had given them, but *kitchen* china.) And not Rhona's expensive glass—but good solid cheap tumblers which Glynis had found in Marylebone High Street. And lastly, the coffee that Glynis knew how to make hot and strong, and which Steve pronounced to be every bit as good as that made by Rhona's French chef.

'Oh, isn't it absolutely thrilling?' Glynis

235

exclaimed when at last she and Steve settled down to a last cigarette.

They were still at the kitchen table. Steve looked at his wife's lovely young figure (in slacks and jersey tonight), her hair a golden tangle, her face pink and hot from her labours. He said:

'You really are a remarkable girl. I honestly believe you *do* find this more thrilling than if we were having a meal at the Ritz Grill in Paris.'

'Absolutely right,' said Glynis promptly. 'This, to me, is *super.* We're absolutely alone in our own home. I'm sorry we've got to have any staff at all, *ever.*'

He laughed, but held out a hand and drew her into the circle of his arm. He touched her long lashes with his lips, lazily, lingeringly.

'You're sweeter than honey and I could eat you,' he said, 'but you'd get sick of running this big house single-handed, my love. The novelty would soon wear off.'

'I'm prepared to argue, but I know it wouldn't suit you,' she sighed and ran her fingers through his thick hair till he caught the fingers, imprisoned and kissed them.

'By the way, poppet, I shan't be able to picnic with you tomorrow night, alas. I forgot to tell you, but I've got to dine with a professor of medicine who is flying over from Holland to see me. I must take him out to dinner. Would you like to come, or would it bore you?'

'I wouldn't dream of coming—you two will want to talk. Besides, I've got masses to do here. I'm going to start on your consulting room tomorrow. It'll be *marvellous* when you can move all your things over. Then we'll be complete.'

'We must give a House-Warming. I'm afraid I've got rather a formidable list for you, but we *must* ask all the high-ups.'

Glynis stuck her hands in the pockets of her slacks, feet apart like a boy's, and wrinkled her nose at him.

'What you say goes, darling, but it won't be as much fun as *this*.'

'You're an enchanting person,' he said seriously, then, with her hand in his, walked with her out of the kitchen and up to their half-empty bedroom.

All this for Glynis was sheer delight. She was almost too busy that next fortnight to think of anything but getting the house straight.

It was a particularly wonderful day, of course, when Steven's consulting room was made ready (Rhona's offending curtains had been taken down and returned) and the new brass plate was put up by the front door bell. *Mr. S. Grant-Tally, M.D., F.R.C.S.* Then there was another lovely day when the workmen finally left, when the last van was unloaded and the whole house could be called complete except for the finishing touches.

237

Busy though Glynis was, she could not help but notice that Steven took little part in it all. Not because he did not wish to, but because he could not. His engagements were too many and work too pressing. He was away from her all day, except when he was in his consulting room; then it was Miss Phillips who saw and worked with him. Glynis did not dream of going down to join them and interrupt. She knew her old job too well. But she felt absurdly lonely when separated from him. Odd glimpses of him—quick kisses—then off again; to a conference, to a consultation, to St. Martha's.

But oh, those wealthy patients . . . how Glynis hated them! The people who *imagined* they were ill; who were sure they had something wrong with their throats or noses or ears and hadn't; the doctors who sent them to Mr Grant-Tally because they insisted on seeing him. Strangely enough, Glynis felt really satisfied about Steve's work only when she knew that he was at St. Martha's operating on the really sick.

After three weeks of this life in her new home, she faced up to the fact that she had only had Steve to herself two or three times in all. She had had to go out to two public dinner-parties with him, and ask four lots of doctors and their wives to dinner at Weymouth Street. And *then* there was the House-Warming—a cocktail party to celebrate the move.

That had been a day of disaster. There had been a tremendous crush in the lovely drawing-room of which Glynis could be rightly proud. Everybody in Harley Street was here. But trouble started when the married couple (Mr. and Mrs. Garlott) whom Glynis engaged as cook and houseman proved their dishonesty. Mrs. Wickens came every day 'to clean' and they had a special waiter for the party. Glynis had ordered all kinds of lovely cocktail-pieces, and Steven had found time to order the drinks.

But this time poor Glynis was the victim of her own inexperience. The Garlotts, who had seemed so nice and had had excellent written references, were only in the house a week. They vanished on the morning of the party, taking with them (in a car, so Steven and Glynis afterwards learned from a neighbour) many bottles and quite a number of Glynis' beautiful wedding presents—mainly table silver.

Horror-stricken Glynis found herself having to interview police and detectives on the very day when she should have been free to make the preparations for her party. Then, of course, Kitty heard, and being, in her way, not unkind, rushed around 'to help'. Inevitably Rhona Chayney also 'heard' and at once sent her two Italian maids to Weymouth Street.

'You *must* have help, you poor dear!' she

239

said down the telephone to Glynis. 'I *insist.*'

There was nothing Glynis could do about it. It was too late. So her first big party in her own home was run chiefly by her sister-in-law and Rhona's servants.

Glynis received her guests with every appearance of calm, and looking smart and smiling in one of her trousseau cocktail dresses. But, of course, everybody eventually heard about the horrible Garlotts and knew who had helped the hostess out (Rhona saw to that). So when it was all over and Rhona and Kitty stayed on, Glynis felt that she wanted to scream. But she had to thank them and go on smiling and sit listening to Steven talk to them both—just as though they were all the best of friends.

Her cup of bitterness overflowed when Kitty said in front of Steven:

'Glynis, my treasure, you *never* want to accept written references. You must get personal ones. Now I know a splendid agency. We'll go tomorrow and see if we can find you the right couple, dear.'

When at last the two women left, Glynis' nerves had reached breaking point. She was tired out and burst into tears.

Steven petted and soothed her.

'Never mind, darling—the party was quite a success—don't take it to heart. And the C.I.D. think they may get back some of the silver.'

'But it was my first party—I didn't want

240

anybody to run it but me,' she wept.

'Don't take it to heart,' he repeated and hugged her. Then he left her, to go down to his consulting room. He had that Marradine child on his mind. The little thing still lived, but it was 'touch and go'; one of Steven's most exacting and worrying cases. He was too busy and concerned to worry about the cocktail party, or the robbery—or even to see how deeply Glynis felt her humiliation. That night when Glynis asked him if she *must* have Kitty's help in finding new staff, Steven yawned sleepily and told her to do exactly what she liked; he didn't mind.

'But I *do* mind,' said Glynis in a low voice, 'you know I do.'

'Okay, sweet,' he said drowsily, 'I'll leave it to you.'

She was sitting at her new beautiful dressing-table, brushing her hair. In front of her stood a tall, gilt-stoppered and expensive bottle of scent from Paris, alongside many pots of creams and lotions, all that any woman's heart could desire. The bedroom, too, was lovely, with its powder-blue silky curtains, and off-white carpet; its white and gilt painted French furniture. There was a crystal vase full of roses from Steve in front of the mirror; in Glynis' wardrobe, plenty of clothes; tonight she wore a new grey chiffon nightdress and satin dressing-gown. She was Mrs. Grant-Tally, the beautiful, pampered wife of a successful surgeon. Why wasn't she absolutely happy and satisfied? she asked herself. What in heaven's name had she to grumble at? It was only this temperament of hers that she had to fight all the time—this longing to be quiet and to lead that simple life with Steve. She felt a sudden passionate desire to feel his arms around her, and to be reassured. She knew how busy he was—she wouldn't worry him with petty domestic details, she told herself. She would just be patient and hope that in time to come things would be different. Now she would give him all her love and her heart.

'Steve,' she began and turned to him, a tender smile on her lips.

There was no answer. The tired surgeon was asleep.

Suddenly Glynis started to laugh helplessly.

But she had never felt more alone.

CHAPTER TWENTY-ONE

One morning in August—one of those close grey days when the summer sun was hidden behind clouds and the atmosphere was close and sticky—Glynis sat at her bureau in the drawing-room packing up a parcel. It was a wedding present for Robin and Moira. Her one-time boy-friend and the faithful little red-haired nurse were being married in a fortnight's time. Robin was continuing to work at St. Martha's but Moira meant to give up her nursing career and devote herself to her husband. They had found a tiny flat not far from the hospital, which they had managed to furnish with the help of Robin's mother. It would be a struggle, but Moira was blissful and Robin seemed a new man—happy and confident and going steadily up in his profession.

'You wait—one day my Robin will be as famous as your Steve,' Moira had said when they both came to dinner with Glynis on a night when Steve was out. That had brought an answer from little Mrs. Grant-Tally that Moira thought rather curious.

'I hope not for *your* sake.'

Back in St. Martha's, Moira had repeated this to Robin. When he had thought it over, he said:

'Tally is a pretty busy chap, of course, and I expect Glyn doesn't see as much of him as she wants.'

Moira added:

'She's terribly in love with him and everybody says he is with her. But you always said she had funny ideas about not liking a lot of money and fame. It may upset her.'

'Well, she's just the same as ever—no side, just because she's married to the Chief,' was Robin's next remark.

That was the trouble with Glynis—she had

not changed and could not—just because she was Steve's wife. But this morning while she packed the beautiful silver teaspoons that she and Steve were giving Robin and Moira, she surveyed the future with some trepidation. She even envied Moira that tiny flat and the life she would share so completely with Robin. The trouble with a famous specialist was that he could never really give much time and attention to his wife—even when he was at home. Glynis was growing used—yet never really used—to the fact that Steve's thoughts and energies were but rarely turned in her direction.

He had promised to take her away in the late autumn—but he had had two holidays already this year, and should not really take any more.

At times Glynis would arrange a theatre or cinema but they were not always able to use the tickets because he would be called away to an emergency. She never quite knew whether he could keep any date she made for him or not. It was often very disappointing.

The happiest three days had been about a month ago when Nancy Phillips had gone down with 'flu, and she, Glynis, stepped into Nancy's shoes and once more became Steve's secretary and receptionist. She seemed to see quite a lot of him then, even if in a professional capacity. She was so happy. She wished that Nancy need not come back and that she could go on working for her husband, but knew that it would not be 'correct'. She was childishly delighted when Steven said:

'You're a lot quicker on the uptake than Miss Phillips and I must say it's been great having you to work for me again, Goldilocks.'

How she had laughed over that name which used, once, to irritate her. It brought back the memory of the hospital days, of her short career as a nurse and all the old dear associations.

Rhona Chayney continued to be a chip on Glynis' shoulder. With the utmost tactlessness, she insisted on flooding the Grant-Tallys with invitations to the penthouse and, of course, as Kitty was there, Glynis could not say 'no' to them all. She did not want to feel responsible for coming between Steve and his sister. But she never felt at ease in the presence of those two women. If she had gained any more self-confidence and poise since she married Steve seven months ago, she lost it in front of *them.* And she still could not forget that cheque and the fact that Steve had never told her about it. Once or twice she had been on the verge of asking him outright, then half afraid of what the answer might be, said nothing. But the very fact that he *had* paid so much money to Rhona and did not tell his own wife about it made Glynis unhappy.

She had been forced to accept Kitty's help over the staff problem, and had to admit that

Kitty found quite a good couple for her—a well-trained English houseman with an Austrian wife who cooked delicious food which Steve thoroughly enjoyed. There were very few occasions on which Glynis could make her own omelettes for her husband now, or enjoy her kitchen. On the cook's night out Steven seemed to prefer Glynis to accept one of the dinner invitations they perpetually received. He seemed to grow more busy instead of less so.

Recently there had been quite a bit about Steven in the Press because he had saved the life of the Marradine heir and successfully operated on a member of the Royal Household. After the final visit Steve had returned to Glynis announcing quite bashfully that he might find himself one day attached as Physician in Ordinary to the Royal Household.

The very idea held nameless terrors for Glynis; though she was proud for him; the terror increased when Steven added:

'We must get you presented. Lady Marradine will present you, I'm quite sure.'

Glynis began to imagine all that such an honour would mean to them and how young Steven was to have reached such a peak, like his uncle before him; Sir Campion had rushed early up the ladder of fame and glory. Wonderful surgeons, both. At St. Martha's they always said that 'Steve was a wizard'. And he had such a flair for the social side . . . he had been so clever with his life, and yet . . . he was hard up. He had astonished and dismayed Glynis by telling her so only this morning. He had given her a new cheque book with which to pay some of those household bills and the others which were accumulating. She was staggered by them. It seemed that the life they were leading forbade that she should economize. Expenses kept piling up. In Barnet, the house at Rudge Crest, the bills seemed so small in comparison. But her parents never bought anything they could not immediately pay for. This new casual way of life with Steven (which appeared normal to a woman like Kitty) persistently troubled Steven's young wife.

But she had to go on—especially with the entertaining. It was for 'business' as well as pleasure. For instance, they were dining tomorrow night at Park Lane with the Marradines and Lady Marradine had said to her on the 'phone: 'We want your husband to meet a friend of ours from America. He's a multi-millionaire. He was so impressed by what Mr. Grant-Tally did for our son—I think he'll ask him to operate on one of his own boys who has very serious ear trouble.'

The Marradines' millionaire friend had a yacht. It had been hinted that if Steven could get away in September they might all take a Mediterranean cruise. If Steven could get off he would enjoy it, Glynis knew, although the thought of the French Riviera did not attract her. Not unless she could go alone wish her husband. She had little with to spend a precious holiday on a yacht with all those Society people. *Oh, to have him to herself again!* Or would it not be true to say that she had never *really* had him to herself. Even when she was clasped close in his arms it seemed only for a brief moment of passionate happiness. Then . . . he was gone again.

She realized that to give Steven what he wanted out of life she must sacrifice all personal desires. If she had believed the existence he now led was for his ultimate happiness, she would not mind, but sometimes Glynis had a vague fear that he was living on the crest of a wave *which* might break in the wrong direction. Life was too feverish for him. Young and strong though he was, he often seemed tired to death—and good-humoured though he was, he was growing irritable when things did not turn out as he wanted. Sometimes she felt that he hardly noticed whether *she* was there or not. That even when his lips were on hers, that brilliant restless mind of his, full of thoughts and plans and ideas (ephemeral as the darting swallow), escaped her. As for the financial side—a royal command job and all that it would involve might only prove an added worry and expense.

'He's such a good doctor—such a good

surgeon!' Glynis cried one, day to her friend, Alma, when they were alone. 'Too much social success *can't* be good for him or for any man. It doesn't seem to me half as worthwhile as the life, for instance, led by a humble G.P. with a poor practice.'

Alma sighed and shook her head.

'Being married to Steve doesn't seem to have altered you. That's what Robin and Moira were saying.'

'More's the pity, perhaps,' said Glynis sombrely. 'It doesn't pay to be so idealistic— one gets too disappointed.'

'But you are happy with Steve.'

'I adore him.'

'I rather agree with you,' said Alma, 'that I wish he'd let up a bit in the work and find more time for you, but—'

'But he can't—it's in his blood. It's second nature for him to enjoy the limelight, just as it is for me to want to avoid it.'

'Good old Glynis,' laughed the young nurse who had been her greatest friend.

'*Idiotic* Glynis, perhaps,' observed the other girl and joined rather ruefully in the laughter.

But this morning she felt subdued. She wished that Mummy and Daddy were not away. They were taking their annual summer holiday at Frinton. The darlings, Glynis thought tenderly; they had been to Frinton for the last twenty years; taken her there when she was a child. Daddy was so conservative and

249

insular—he never wanted to go abroad. He liked the little hotel where he was well known, and to sit on the sands wearing his old blazer that he had worn long before Glynis was born. Poor Mummy would have preferred something more exciting. Glynis had quite made up her mind to take her to France one day—to Paris—for which her heart hungered—and give her the time of her life.

What a pity it was that she, Glynis, had not inherited more of Mummy's passion for excitement, or the social whirl which had always been denied *her.*

'I'm the square peg in the round hole,' mused Glynis sadly.

Yet she could not contemplate leading a life that did not include Steve. She could not bear even the minor separations from him. So it must have been 'meant' that she should marry him. But she was only human, her reflections continued. *Why, if Steven was so hard up, had he paid that cheque to Rhona Chayney?*

'I'm going to ask him about it tonight,' she said aloud, and then set to work to concentrate on a list of the things she must do today. Her nursing and secretarial training had made her methodical and her memory was good.

First she must go down to the kitchen and find out what Mitza wanted in the way of food. Then she had promised Steven to collect some shirts he had just had made from his shirt-makers in Dover Street. She was lunching with an old school friend. Afterwards a detective from Scotland Yard was coming to see her here. A bit of the silver stolen by the abominable Garlotts had been traced and she must identify it.

Tonight threatened to be just the sort of thing she dreaded: a dinner for six which included a professor of surgery from Edinburgh, a wealthy bachelor patient of Steve's, *and* Kitty and Rhona. It had been Steve's suggestion that his sister and her friend should be invited 'to make up the party'. They hadn't seen Rhona for some time, or much of Kitty, who was busy these days seeing a great deal of a Belgian diplomat, a widower, whom Rhona felt quite sure Kitty would eventually marry. Lady Barley would then exchange her title for that of a Belgian 'Comtesse'—and live in Brussels.

Sometimes when she thought about Kitty, who seemed to be in the seventh heaven living in the penthouse and rushing around London with her distinguished-looking Count, Glynis felt a little sad and cynical. Poor Paul! With his widow remarrying only a year after his death. He had been already forgotten. But Glynis, soft-hearted and always sorry for the gentle worried-looking Paul, often remembered him with regret. He had been so nice to her, and tried so hard to put her at her ease that very first night they met. Kitty seemed to her a hard woman. Thank God, Steve was different. But

if anything ever happened to him . . . Glynis'
heart failed at the thought; she wouldn't want
to live, or if the did she would never, *never*
look at another man. Nobody could replace
her adored Steven.

'I'm getting morbid,' Glynis admonished
herself and went forth to do her shopping,
trying to forget the bills—only a quarter of
which the could afford to pay (according to
Steven's reckoning). When he came in that
night to change for dinner she remembered
her resolve to face him squarely and ask about
Rhona's cheque. But Steven was in such good
spirits this evening that she felt loth to destroy
them, or start the evening off on the wrong
foot. He had apparently had a good day. A
tricky operation which had harassed him had
turned out a great success. He came out of the
bathroom, struggling with his tie, and grinned
cheerfully at his wife who was rolling on a pair
of gossamer nylons—still wearing a black lacy
slip.

'Duckie—don't forget I want Rhona to sit
next to Professor McKillick. He is one of these
handsome gentlemen with a young face, white
hair, and fierce eyebrows. I'd like to see
Rhona twining herself around him and putting
the old boy right off his food.'

Glynis giggled. She loved Steve in this sort
of mood.

'I should love to see it, too, but I think it's
rather hard on the Professor.'

'He can take care of himself, and by the way,' added Steven, 'don't forget we've got to ask Kit's new boyfriend to dinner one night next week. I'll give you his address.'

Glynis stood up.

'*What* we spend on food and drink in this house!' she exclaimed.

'My economical little angel—how I love you!' he said and gave a ravished look at her small feet in the high-heeled satin sandals, then dropped a kiss on one bare shoulder, adding:

'What are you wearing tonight?'

She indicated the dress which hung outside the wardrobe—ballet-length, off-the-shoulder, caramel-coloured chiffon with an accordion-pleated full skirt and chestnut-brown velvet sash.

'Good,' said Steven, 'you look wickedly attractive in that.'

It had been on her lips to mention Rhona's cheque—and all the financial problems, but Steve in this boyish lover-like mood put it right out of her thoughts. She found him irresistible. She reached up her arms and kissed him for a moment, murmuring:

'I do so love my husband.'

'A very right and proper remark,' said Steven and kissed her lingeringly on her upturned mouth.

When she broke away from him, she was flushed and breathless.

'Now look what you've done! I'll have to make up my face all over again.'

He laughed and returned to the bathroom.

'Jolly good. When's the Gellow wedding?' he sang out.

'Saturday week. We're all asked afterwards to St. Martha's—the hospital is going to give them a party because Moira's home is in Ireland and she has no relations over here.'

'I'm afraid you'll have to go alone,' he called back. 'I was rather afraid that was the day. I shall be in Scotland. McKillick's fixed something up for me at Edinburgh Infirmary and I can't get out of it. I shall be going up on the night train.'

That was disappointing in the extreme for Glynis but she said nothing, reminding herself that she must be a good doctor's wife and not grumble when these contingencies arose.

Anyhow, the dinner-party was successful. Rhona flung some of her 'sad sweet glances' in Steve's direction, but having practically decided that it was no use, and that she would have to abandon all hope where he was concerned, she turned eventually to the Professor. Watching her *mondaine* efforts to attract the staid solid Scot, who unsmilingly received this feminine attack, was a matter later on for private laughter between Steve and Glynis. Kitty was in good form and behaved well—complimented Glynis on the dinner and talked continuously and significantly about her '*cher Jean-Phillipe*'.

So, after all, Glynis' resolve to open her heart on the subject of money never materialized and there followed a hectic fortnight followed by the Gellow-Thomas wedding.

After the ceremony, back at St. Martha's, Glynis found herself between the Matron and one of the senior sisters. Both chatted to her in mellow tones, regretting the absence of their dear Mr. Grant-Tally.

'What a *lovely* coat you've got, Mrs. Grant-Tally,' the sister gushed, fingering Glynis' mink.

'And hasn't our little Nurse Thorne-that-was been a success,' added Matron in a benign tone.

Glynis thanked them both demurely. '*What's in a name?*' she thought, and giggled at the memory of how these two women had terrified her when she was a probationer. Neither would have deigned to address her except to say 'Good morning' or 'Good night'.

It was quite fun being Mrs. Grant-Tally, she decided, and yet . . . when at Matron's request Glynis walked through the wards and stopped particularly to speak to some of the sick children, she looked quite longingly at a couple of new probationers who were making a leg-case more comfortable. Glynis had loved nursing with a deep and real love. Even now— as wife of one of the most important doctors at

St. Martha's—she could still feel regretful and nostalgic. She gave a special smile to the two probationers who shyly bade her 'good afternoon'. She said a friendly *'Hullo you two,'* and they rushed over to tell one of their colleagues that Mr. Grant-Tally's wife was 'terribly glamorous-looking' and 'absolutely adorable'.

All through Robin and Moira's wedding, Glynis had felt a warm glad feeling that she had helped to bring those two together. She could hardly believe that the happy-looking bridegroom was one and the same man as the desperate creature who had rushed away from London and nearly ruined his career—for love of *her.* Thank God she had gone down to Brighton, and that dear Steve had followed and done so much for Robin, too.

Robin's mother had embraced Glynis when they came out of church, and said:

'You're the best friend Robin ever had, and I shall always be grateful to you and your wonderful husband. This is a happy day for me.'

But as Glynis stood now on the hospital steps and watched the bride and bridegroom move off in a hired car, under a shower of confetti (they were going to Cornwall on the night Riviera train), she thought:

'I suppose I'm a bit silly but I still wish Steve was as unknown as Robin. I wouldn't mind doing what *they* are going to do—just a honeymoon in a Cornish farmhouse, with no one in the world to worry them, then back to their humble little flat. *Steve, Steve, if only you were more mine,* and could give up this life that you lead!'

Someone touched her on the shoulder. She turned and saw old Popham Gray who had in his charming courtly fashion given the bride away. Now he said, just as he had done on that night of the Hospital Ball when the had still been Miss Thorne:

'You're looking depressed, my dear, what's wrong?'

History was repeating itself. She made the very same answer:

'Nothing,' she said and laughed.

'And how is our Steve when he's at home?'

'Oh, fine, Pop, but terribly tired. He falls asleep as soon as his head touches the pillow, and in spite of all his tremendous vitality, I can see he's doing far too much.'

Popham chewed his lips and searched in his pocket for a pipe, then said *'damn'* under his breath, remembering that he was wearing his festive suit. He had a shrewd suspicion that little Glynis Grant-Tally was just as worried about Steve as she could be, but wasn't going to admit it. He turned from the laughing crowd of wedding guests still thronging the steps of the hospital.

'Come in and have a chat,' he said, but Glynis could not wait, much as she wanted to talk to the elderly doctor.

Her parents had returned from Frinton. She was driving straight down to Barnet for the week-end. As she waited for her car, she heard the *clang-clang* of an ambulance bell. She watched the white vehicle drive up to the steps. Two stretcher-bearers made ready. Glynis thought: This is *life. Births, Marriages and Deaths. In the middle of wedding festivities, some poor soul has had an accident . . . one never knows what lies in front of one!*

She spent a quiet peaceful week-end in her old home, missing none of the luxuries of Weymouth Street. It was so good to sit in the old familiar garden with her parents, under her favourite walnut tree. Robin and Moira had chosen a perfect summer's day for their wedding. If Glynis had any worries on her mind she did not let either her mother or father know it. Mrs. Thorne, as usual, wanted to know all about the important people her daughter had seen, and the exciting things she had lately been doing. But there was only one thing that Glynis really wanted—to have her husband here to make the family circle complete—and a charmed one at that.

She did not feel really happy until a trunk call came through from Edinburgh and she heard his voice for six brief minutes. Then he was gone. She would have to wait till Monday before they met again.

When she saw him it was in their own home.

He did not go straight to St. Martha's, as she had supposed, but came direct to his own home from the station. One look at him and Glynis felt positively stricken. Her heart seemed to go down like a plummet and her pulses thrilled with fear.

'*Steve!* What on earth is the matter?'

He had changed from the cheerful healthy-looking, if tired, Steven she knew, to a man who was obviously very ill. His face was grey. There were dark circles under his eyes. He held his right arm stiffly. He sat down rather heavily and said:

'Sweet, I wonder if you'd call Martha's and ask if Benson is on duty yet? If so I want a word with him urgently.'

At once her heart gave another thrill of fear. Benson was the Senior House Physician.

'Steve—what *is* it? Have you had an accident?'

He nursed his right arm, grimacing.

'Of all the damnable things to have happened,' he muttered, and she saw the sweat pearl on his forehead. She dropped on one knee beside him, her own face white.

'Steve, what's happened?'

He told her, briefly, while she jumped up and got that call through to the hospital. It was 'just one of those things,' he said which had happened to many a surgeon before him. Twenty-four hours ago he had been operating at the Infirmary in front of a lot of students, showing them at Professor McKillick's request a special type of throat operation which had been Sir Campion's initial triumph.

Steven had pricked his finger during the operation. The patient's throat had been particularly septic. Steven had taken due precautions, but not in time. He knew that he was over-tired and his resistance low. Septicaemia of this kind could be a menace in the speed with which it spread. Already the poison was above the elbow. His temperature was high. He had realized that during these hours of pain and wakefulness in his sleeper coming down from Scotland.

Glynis listened, sick with dread. But she tried to comfort him.

'It'll be all right, dearest. But you should have gone straight to St. Martha's. Silly old thing—why didn't you?'

'Wanted to see you,' he mumbled. 'Afraid you would be in a panic if they 'phoned you from the hospital. I reckon if they get me there they'll keep me.'

'Oh, Steve—*darling!*'

He tried to smile up into the green beautiful eyes that were wide with dismay. But the smile was feeble. He had a cracking headache and his arm throbbed. He knew—so much better than Glynis—the danger of the thing. One of his best friends had died this way—during his last year of training. For a moment Steve leaned his head against his wife's shoulder and felt her strong young arm go round him.

'Sweetheart—I'm so tired,' he whispered.

She fought not to let him see her tears and fears.

'Hold on, darling. It'll be okay. Dr. Benson is going to speak to you—they said in two minutes—they're fetching him from his room.'

After that for Glynis it was sheer nightmare. Dr. Benson spoke to his friend and colleague. When Steve hung up, sweat trickling down his cheeks, he muttered:

'Put fresh pyjamas in case, darling . . . Collins can drive me . . . I won't let them send an ambulance.'

But he had no choice. While Glynis was putting clean silk pyjamas and some handkerchiefs into the night-case he had taken up to Edinburgh—Steven fainted. It was by one of the familiar St. Martha's ambulances that he finally left the house in Weymouth Street—flushed, in a high fever, and muttering incoherently. Glynis, tight-lipped, sat beside him, clutching his left hand. Dr. Benson had come, personally, to inspect the Chief. He admitted to Glynis that it was a 'bad show'. He, too, was in the ambulance with them, having given Steven an injection. He shook his head at Glynis.

'All the big men are the same—they work themselves to a frazzle, then go down at a scratch.'

'And what for?' Glynis had asked herself.

'Not just for the hospital, and out-patients, but all those "important people" for whom Steve has always worked so hard. Now he is seriously ill.'

She had had no need to ask Dr. Benson his opinion. Her short spell of nursing had taught her the full gravity of a condition like this. She knew it, while she sat there, face haggard, eyes fixed on Steve's beloved form under the hospital blanket, and listened to the clang of the bell that she had heard so many many times before. Always it had been a sinister sound. Today it seemed to her far worse than sinister. It clanged through her very being. *Steven's life was in danger.* He had let things get too far. It would be touch-and-go.

CHAPTER TWENTY-TWO

By the time the ambulance reached St. Martha's, Glynis was almost too numbed by shock and the terror of this thing that had happened to Steven to feel further emotion. She had to fight to keep a stiff upper lip. She tried to be cool and cheerful in case Steven should know what was going on around him. She must not alarm him. But as she sat there holding his burning fingers in hers—her gaze fixed on the beloved face that seemed to her the face of a stranger—flushed with fever, changed—she knew that he did not recognize her.

Then at last they were in the familiar hospital, and this time it was not Nurse Thorne, but Mrs. Grant-Tally, walking beside a wheeled stretcher, and this time under the blanket lay her own husband's form. Many who passed by seemed to know about Steven. The rumour had spread around the hospital. Matron, herself, had been there on the steps to greet the surgeon who for so many years had come here to operate. Sister Yardley, a kind and clever woman who had always been good to the little probationer, Nurse Thorne, was here, too. Mr. Grant-Tally was being placed in her particular care. Old 'Pop' rushed up to whisper a quick, *'Bad luck, my dear, but don't worry . .'* And Alma appeared from one of the wards, looking scared and troubled for her friend, but clutched Glynis by the arm and also whispered, *'Don't worry too much, he'll be all right.'*

Now some feeling returned to Glynis' stricken heart. She felt warmer—more comforted. They were all here—their friends—and in Steve's own hospital, renowned for its medical school and fine staff. Steve would be in the care of the best physicians in England.

They wheeled him into the big lift, up to the second floor, then into a private room, in what they called the *'Campion Wing'*. It had been inaugurated by Steven's own uncle.

It seemed quite unreal—even absurd to Glynis when eventually she had to leave him in the care of Sister Yardley and a young nurse. *She,* his wife, was not allowed in his room. Sister Yardley, however, looked into the agonized eyes of the lovely girl who was Steven's wife and spoke gently in that voice which held a rich Scots burr:

'Dinna fash yourself—he'll be a' richt, Mrs. Grant-Tally.' And she added that Glynis could come back later on after Dr. Fiennes-Carr had examined Steven.

Now Glynis sat in the Nurses' Common Room with Alma holding her hand, and one or two of the other fourth-year nurses all talking and trying to comfort her. Fiennes-Carr was brilliant . . . he would pull Steven through . . . there wasn't a finer nurse in the world than Sister Yardley . . . etc.

And Alma said as cheerfully as she could:

'Don't be too worried by the high temperature, Glyn darling. You remember when you were here, don't you, how these septicaemia cases shoot up. It terrifies people who don't understand—but *you* do.'

'Yes, I do,' she said dully. But her face was pale and she made no movement to take off her hat or look in her mirror to see if her lipstick was smudged, or do any of the little things a woman generally does. She just sat still, trying to smoke the cigarette Alma had pressed into her fingers. Many of the nursing staff came in and spoke to her, trying to cheer her up. She thanked them all with a swift charming smile, but in a flash the smile vanished again and her face grew grave. She *did* understand . . . all too well. She knew what could happen when a surgeon developed blood poisoning after being in contact with a particularly septic case.

It seemed a whole day instead of an hour before Sister Yardley appeared and told Glynis that Mr. Grant-Tally was in bed, and that she could pop in for a moment to see him.

'Just for a wee moment. He'll no' be knowing you just now.'

Glynis stayed only that brief moment at Steven's side. He was delirious and moaning. Fiennes-Carr came in and gave him an injection, then took Glynis out into the corridor to talk.

She looked up at him piteously. He was a short grey-haired man wearing horn-rims. She remembered that when she had worked in the hospital she used to be terrified of him. They all were—he was so short-tempered, especially during exams; and a noted misogynist. But today his eyes behind the strong lenses were full of kindliness. He even patted little Mrs. Grant-Tally on the shoulder. She looked distracted, he thought, poor child!

'Better for you not to see Tally any more just now. Leave him to us. Go home. We'll ring you, the moment we think necessary.'

Her heart gave a frightful jerk. *Necessary,* she thought, *oh, dear God!*

'Dr. Fiennes-Carr . . . is he . . . in danger?'

'You know the answer to that, my dear. You've had some experience,' he said. 'That clever husband of yours has been a damned fool, if you don't mind my saying so. He ought to have had his hand seen to twenty-four hours ago.'

Glynis preserved a helpless silence. She, too, knew that Steven had been foolhardy to come home and that he should really have stayed up in Edinburgh Infirmary. They'd given him a penicillin injection but it just hadn't worked—he one of those people who do not react to penicillin. Therein lay the initial misfortune.

'Leave him to us,' repeated Fiennes-Carr.

With all her heart she longed to go back into Steven's room, crouch beside his bed, and stay there until Steven opened his eyes and looked at her with the old smile. Oh, God, oh *God,* her heart cried out, *must it take a thing like this to show you how much a human being means to you?* Glynis felt sick with fear. Yet there was nothing that she could do about it. And with the eyes of the whole hospital watching Steven's wife, she must behave with courage.

So finally she drove away in Steve's car, back to the lovely house in Weymouth Street.

She telephoned to her mother who immediately came to London and joined her.

'Darling, what atrocious luck—what do they say?' were her first words.

'They expect he'll be all right,' said Glynis with difficulty, 'but this sort of blood poisoning rushes through the body at such an alarming rate. His temperature is 105 degrees. Oh, Mummy, he doesn't even *know* me!'

Mrs. Thorne's eyes filled with tears. Glynis was dry-eyed. But the lovely face that her mother had last seen radiant with happiness had a pinched grey look that went to her heart.

'Come back to Barnet with me, darling . . .' she said.

But nothing would induce Glynis to leave town. She must be within a moment's call from St. Martha's, she said, and spoke the words that she could hardly bear to say:

'It's bound to be touch and go, Mum. I've got to face up to it. Things have gone a long way. His whole arm is affected. Fiennes-Carr, himself, said that the infection is right through the blood stream now. General septicaemia. They'll be giving him aureomycin or streptomycin. That ought to help.'

Mrs. Thorne blew her nose vigorously.

'Yes, there are all sorts of wonderful drugs these days. We mustn't despair, darling.'

Mitza, the cook, with her husband, came in to enquire about the doctor, and express their sympathies. The telephone began to ring.

267

Glynis refused to speak to anybody except Steve's sister. She left Nancy Phillips to cancel Steve's engagements and answer all calls. By that evening there were hundreds. Photographs of Steve—with Glynis—appeared in the evening papers.

FAMOUS YOUNG SURGEON SERIOUSLY ILL

When the papers were brought to Glynis she tossed them aside. She had never cared for publicity and in *this* crisis she positively hated it.

Kitty came round and sat with her for an hour. She was sweeter and nicer than Glynis had ever known her. She brought magnificent flowers from Rhona.

The card had a few words scribbled on it:

These are not for Steve but for you. I know how you must be feeling.

'She really is upset for you,' Kitty told Glynis.

'I'm sure she is,' said Glynis in a low voice. 'Please thank her *very* much.'

'As for me—well, you know I've been a bit of a witch at times but I adore my brother,' added Kitty. 'I'm frightfully upset.'

'I know,' repeated Glynis.

But it was Kitty who wept and still not

Glynis. She was resolved to be brave. But suddenly as Kitty left her, something deep down in Glynis that had been repressed for a long time, made her say:

'Kitty, I want to ask you—do you still think that Steven oughtn't to have married me—and that I haven't been much use to him?'

All that was best in Kitty Barley rose to meet that question. She hugged her young sister-in-law and kissed the white set face with genuine warmth.

'Little idiot—of course I don't. To begin with I admit I didn't think it would work, but I was wrong. It's been a roaring success. Steve adores you and he's—oh, *I'm* the one who hasn't been any use to him,' the added and gulped and began to weep again. And it wasn't long before she was blurting out the secret she had asked Steven to keep . . . feeling, perhaps, that she was salving her own conscience by humiliating herself in front of the young girl she had once tried to humiliate.

'I'm going to be quite frank with you, Glynis darling—it was really because of the *money* that I wanted Steve to marry Rhona. I was a swine, darling. I got into frightful debt, you know, and I had borrowed it from Rhona.'

A light suddenly sprang into Glynis' green sad eyes. For a second she felt that a burden was lifted from her. She gasped:

'Oh, Kitty—did *Steve* pay back that money to Rhona for you?'

269

Kitty turned to the mirror and adjusted her smart new hat.

'I'm afraid he did, sweetie. Aren't I a pig to have let him? But he didn't want anyone in the family to owe Rhona so much. It was all rather awkward, because she was so attached to him, you see. However—if I marry Jean-Phillipe at the end of the year, I can let Steve have the money back again. Jean's got plenty.'

Just how useful that repayment of the debt was going to be in the future, Glynis was not then to know; nor the repentant Kitty. For the moment all that mattered to Glynis was that she knew the truth about the cheque. She *understood* at last. She thought with added love and pride of her husband. Dear generous blessed Steven! *He* had never borrowed that money from Rhona Chayney. He had paid back a debt that his extravagant sister had incurred.

Somehow it seemed to upset as well as please Glynis to learn all this. For, if possible, Steven rose higher in her estimation. That night of anxiety was a truly terrible one—full of an anguish which did not allow her to close an eye in sleep. Her mother, ever devoted, slept the night in the house with her, but the two women found it impossible to turn the light out for long. Twice during those long anxious hours, Sylvia Thorne went downstairs and made tea and brought it up to her daughter. Glynis was a heart-breaking sight to the mother. She looked so young, so defenceless, sitting on her bed fully dressed, arms around hunched knees, eyes fixed stonily on the telephone as though waiting for it to ring.

Now and again she rang the hospital and spoke to the night sister. For twenty-four hours, Steven was a very dangerously sick man with a temperature that would not go down, and the infection was spreading.

Just before dawn Glynis was sent for. That was the hour of crisis and one that she would never forget. She felt frozen with terror when Matron spoke to her over the telephone:

'We think you might like to come, my dear . . . .'

That was all she would say. For Glynis it was enough.

It was a hot sticky August dawn. The rest of London was still sleeping as Glynis and her mother drove to St. Martha's. Glynis had not even bothered to make up her face. Hatless, flinging a short white coat over a cotton frock—she rushed up the steps of St. Martha's.

Then she was in Steven's room; sitting by his bed. Fiennes-Carr and Sister Yardley were there beside him too. One quick scared look showed Glynis the cylinder of oxygen standing in a corner of the room. That alone struck terror in her. Fiennes-Carr had come— obviously in a hurry—with grey flannel bags over his pyjama suit. He was unshaven and tousled. His stethoscope hung from his neck. He had a finger on Steven's pulse. Glynis looked horrified at her husband's changed face. Changed in so brief a time, she thought. Leaden-coloured, with sunken cheeks.

'Just a slight heart attack,' Sister Yardley had murmured before Glynis entered the room. 'We've given him an injection and the pulse is steadying. But if only we could get this temperature down . . . !'

Glynis slipped on to her knees beside the bed. She laid a cheek against Steven's hand. She felt bemused and sent up a prayer that had no sound.

'God, don't let him die. Please, please, God, don't let him die!'

Over the bowed gold head, the eyes of the physician met those of the sister in charge. A poignant look. Then frowning, Fiennes-Carr looked at his patient. Sister Yardley said:

'It might be better if you didn't stay here too long, Mrs. Grant-Tally, dear. I don't think his condition will change for a bit.'

'I can't leave him . . .' began Glynis wildly.

'There's an empty ward next door. You shall stay in there as long as you like, and I'll call you, if I want you—or if he does—I promise.'

Outside in the corridor, shivering from head to foot, teeth chattering, Glynis clung on to the older woman as though on to a rock in the midst of a surging sea.

'Tell me he isn't going to die, *tell me.*'

272

'I don't think he is, myself. He's holding on and he's young and strong,' said Sister Yardley.

'But there's a doubt?'

'He's very sick,' admitted the sister unwillingly, and she thought she had never seen anything more pathetic than Glynis' face with all the youth and beauty wiped from it as by a sponge. She looked positively old in that early morning light. Left alone in the next room Glynis stumbled to the bed and lay on it, face downwards. Still she could not shed a single tear, but she bit through her lower lip until the blood came. Her whole being was concentrated on that man who was fighting for his life on the other side of the wall. She sent out a cry to him:

'Hold on, my darling . . . hold on for my sake . . . don't leave me now!'

After a moment somebody came in and shut the door quietly. She felt a hand take hers. She knew that it was her mother's. Neither of the women spoke. The tears were running silently down Sylvia Thorne's cheeks.

It was not for another hour that a knock on the door roused Glynis who had fallen into a kind of stupor, with her mother nodding besides her. Both of them were exhausted. This time it was Fiennes-Carr who walked in.

Glynis sprang off the bed, pushing back a tangle of hair. She looked at the famous physician wildly, speechlessly. Then a flood of relief poured through her whole body. *For he was smiling.* Smiling—and yawning.

'A nice sleepless night your husband has cost me,' he said briskly and the humour in his voice raised the spirits of the two women yet higher. He added: 'It's all right—Tally's going to get better. Heart much stronger and temperature down *at last.* If I know anything about *anything,* he'll pull through this, and he won't lose his arm either.'

It was then for the first time that Glynis burst into tears.

Fiennes-Carr shrugged his shoulders at Mrs. Thorne.

'Don't ask me to understand women. I thought your daughter was going to give me one of her best smiles.'

Mrs. Thorne gave a shaky laugh.

But Fiennes-Carr got his smile, and he got a kiss, too—Glynis recovered herself, sprang up and actually touched his cheek with her fresh lips. She was afterwards overcome with embarrassment when she remembered it. It became 'a story' at St. Martha's that Mrs. Grant-Tally had actually *kissed* the surly Fiennes-Carr. Glynis felt in this moment that she loved him with all her heart.

'You've saved Steve—you've saved him!' she kept saying.

'Nonsense, he's got a damned fine nurse in Yardley,' was the modest reply.

'When may I go up to him?'

'When he wakes up—Yardley will tell you.'

And Yardley did tell her. And there came the ineffable happiness of the moment when Glynis sat at Steve's bedside later that summer's day and realized that she was not going to lose her husband after all. He was weak and still a bad colour, but his temperature was right down and the arm less painful. And he knew his Glynis at last. His eyes were sunken in his head, but they looked at her with the old devotion. Somehow he managed one of the familiar grins that heartened her greatly.

'I've been a so-and-so . . . a damned nuisance to everybody . . . so sorry, sweet,' he whispered.

She picked up his hand and kissed it again and again. She gulped.

'Don't apologize to me or I'll beat you.'

'Listen to my cruel wife,' he grumbled. She slid on her knees beside the bed and was blissfully happy to feel his fingers threading through her hair. *If she had lost him . . . if he had died . . . how could she have borne it?* she wondered.

'I'll never, never grumble about anything in this life again,' she added to herself.

But there was a time of further test waiting for Glynis and of tribulation for Steven which she had necessarily to share with him—to suffer for him—because it hit him harder than it did her.

CHAPTER TWENTY-THREE

During the next fortnight Steven gained strength. Now it would only mean getting his blood condition right again. But hardly had Glynis recovered from the initial shock than Steven developed trouble of a different kind. This time it was more aggravating than dangerous. It was a skin condition. The drugs he had been given did not agree with him, and his nerves were bad. He awoke one morning to the fact that he had generalized dermatitis. His hands were the most affected. He could not use them, nor would he be able to walk.

He suffered almost unbearable irritation and there was nothing much that could be done about it quickly. The treatment for such a condition would be long and slow. He might not be cured for six months. Both he and Glynis had to face up to that fact.

Nearly three months after Steven had been taken ill he was still at St. Martha's. He and Glynis sat discussing the situation one grey, chill winter's morning.

Glynis, from an armchair, surveyed a room that was virtually a garden—it was so full of flowers. Nobody in the Campion Ward had ever received so many floral offerings, Sister Yardley had said. All the nurses chaffed Mr. Grant-Tally. He had beaten the record of a most important film star who had once come here as a patient. More than half the flowers that still came almost daily for the popular young surgeon had to be distributed through the general wards.

Rhona, of course, sent extravagant bouquets from a Park Lane florist, and as soon as one withered, another replaced it.

'She's determined to go on being attentive,' Glynis had observed one day when a fresh consignment arrived, bearing Mrs. Chayney's card. But Glynis said those words without rancour. She had been cured of her last possible feeling of jealousy of Rhona—or of anyone else.

Steven's illness had brought her much nearer to him spiritually.

Since this last tragedy of the skin complaint, he had grown morose and depressed, but he relied utterly on his wife—her visits—her tenderness—her almost maternal care of him. Her devotion was touching. Everybody at St. Martha's commented on it. Even Fiennes-Carr had congratulated Steven on having such a wife.

'Young pretty creature like that—you'd think she'd want to get out and play. But not her—we can't keep her away from the hospital,' he said.

Steven knew it. He knew, too, from his mother-in-law, the state that his poor little Glynis had been in when she thought he was

277

dying. He loved her just as much as she loved him. He lived for the moments when she walked through the door wearing one of her pretty dresses for him to see and admire. He was a tired sick man after his long ordeal. He feasted his gaze on Glynis' golden beauty. She was, he often told her, more lovely than any of the flowers that filled his white room with colour.

For Glynis it was a terrible deprivation. The beautiful new home in Weymouth Street had ceased to be home, because Steve was no longer in it. It had become just an office wherein Nancy Phillips came daily to attend to letters and telephone calls. Mr. Grant-Tally's patients had been diverted to other ear, nose and throat specialists. Steven was losing touch, which was serious for any doctor.

At first Glynis invited various girl-friends to stay with her, to keep her company. Her mother could no longer leave Barnet and her own domestic duties. Glynis was often left alone except for Mitza and her husband. She was not naturally nervous, but a burglary in the house opposite affected her, and after it Steve forbade her to stay in the big house by herself. She just must go home to Barnet, he said, until he left hospital. Now it seemed to Glynis that she was leading another life. No more dashing round town as Mrs. Grant-Tally; no more entertaining or being entertained; just the long hours spent at the hospital at Steve's bedside.

Endless discussions of what they would do when he was well again.

But on this November morning they talked about money and faced up to the fact that things were serious. There were hundreds of pounds going out and nothing coming in. Steven's hands, and particularly his right one, were the most affected parts. It would be many long months before he could operate again. Inevitably his practice must dwindle. There were too many other good E.N.T. specialists, and old favourites are soon forgotten in this fickle world. Steven's finances had not been good for some time before the accident—*this* had put the final touch to it.

'We can't go on piling up debts, darling,' he said gloomily. 'I think the best thing we can do is to cut our losses.'

And he felt even more gloomy as he surveyed his young wife and saw that she had grown very thin, and was not ' looking as well as she used to.

'You *are* well, aren't you, sweet?' he asked anxiously.

She did not answer for a moment. Then she said:

'Steve, I saw Marian Critchley yesterday.'

He stared. Marian Critchley was a woman gynaecologist on the staff at St. Martha's.

'What on earth did you have to see old Marian about?'

Glynis' face went suddenly pink.

279

'I haven't been feeling too fit,' she mumbled, 'and Mummy thought I *ought* to go and be examined.'

Steven scowled. His hands were worrying him at the moment He loathed this prolonged session in bed. And most of all he loathed being away from his work; the terrible waste of time; the lost energy; the futility of the whole thing.

'What did Marian say to you?' he asked a bit stupidly.

No answer.

Then suddenly the light broke over Steven. Glynis came and sat on the edge of his bed and burrowed her head against his knees that were hunched under the white coverlet.

'What a time to make an important announcement,' she said in a muffled voice, 'just when you don't want any fresh worries.'

'Darling,' he said, and his throat felt tight, 'darling, *darling.*'

She looked up at him and nodded.

'That's it. I'm going to have a little Steven— or, at least, I hope so!'

'But how absolutely *tremendous!*' he said in a hushed voice.

'You aren't sorry?'

'I couldn't possibly be. I couldn't want anything more.'

'In spite of all our money troubles and your dermatitis . . .'

'In spite of everything,' he said, 'except that

I want you to be all right.'

'There's a fine thing for a doctor to say,' she jeered, 'you ought to know how *very* all right I'll be.'

But he was anguished because he could neither touch nor kiss her and so it had been for months.

The warm mellow autumn had drifted into winter. London, this morning, was washed by a cold rain. It beat persistently against the hospital windows, The forecast was bad. But now these two in the flower-filled private ward sat staring into each other's eyes, feeling so close that it did not seem to matter that they could not embrace each other. Steven said:

'I know you'll have a healthy, lovely baby, my darling, but I just want you to have every comfort and luxury beforehand.'

'You know how I hate luxury,' she giggled.

'But, my darling, this is no laughing matter. When do you expect this baby?'

'At the end of April.'

'Good heavens, that's not very far!'

'Silly, it's another five months.'

'But I've got to get you settled by then and I've got to be all right myself and earn some more money. I've got to *support* my family.'

'So you will be able to,' she soothed him. 'I didn't want to tell you before while you were so ill, but now I thought you'd better know.'

Steven's face, thinned and refined by his long illness, wore a grim expression.

'How right you are. *I had* better know, and make some plans.'

'The skin's much better, darling, Yardley said so.'

'Yes, and they think I'll be out of here next week. And after that I've got to learn to use my feet and walk, and above all use my *hands.*' He spread out the famous fingers. They looked to her pitifully thin and white, still covered in the powder he was using.

'What shall we do?' she asked in a low voice.

'What do you *want* to do, Glynis?'

'It's not much good asking, Steve darling.'

But his eyes held a new look, almost one of humble entreaty.

'Will you forgive me if I've tried ever since we married to make you lead the sort of life that you hated?'

'Oh, Steve, why do you say that?'

'Because I've done a lot of thinking while I've been lying here, Glynis. I don't think I ever used to allow myself time in which to think before—except about my work, and where it was leading me.'

'Well?'

'Well, now I see that I did nothing much but make a name for myself and spend money on a lot of people who didn't really matter.'

'Your patients always mattered.'

'But not some of my friends—not even some of the said patients.'

'Never mind all that now. What you really want is to get back to your operating again.'

'Yes, darling, but not in the way I did before,' said Steve quietly. 'I have a new outlook altogether. I shall not go back to the old mad rush and so much entertaining.'

'*Steve!*' exclaimed Glynis amazed and held her breath. He folded his arms and leaned back on his pillows.

'Yes, when I thought I might die, you were always in my mind and you'll never know what it meant. You gave me the *will* to live. With that will has come the wish to concentrate on research work, I shall also limit my practice and wash out Mayfair patients.'

Glynis' eyes looked huge and bright. Her lower lip trembled.

'Oh, *darling!*'

He half-closed his eyes as though ruminating.

'Of course, I shall never chuck St. Martha's, and the work I do here, but I shall do more at the lab. in a quiet way. And I think we'll give up the big house, too. Mind you, I'd thought about all this long before you told me the wonderful news about our child.'

'Then what will you do?' she asked breathlessly, her heart hammering.

'Convert the house—let the top part at a huge price, and make a flat for ourselves of the lower half. I'll use the proceeds to buy you a tiny week-end cottage somewhere just out of

283

town. What about Sussex?'

She gulped.

He went on regarding that sweet excited face with tremendous love in his eyes and in his heart. He continued, she would want to be in the cottage when she first had the baby and they could have a good maid—(a Spanish girl, perhaps) as several of their friends had done— but of course Glynis would want to look after her own baby, he knew that. She wouldn't approve of Nannies. He and she could be in town when pressure of work demanded it, or drive down to the cottage when they were slack.

'No rock-like routine or rigid time-tables. No more *just do this* and *can't do that* for us,' he ended. 'You and I and our child must be together as much as we can.'

This was a promise so magical that Glynis could hardly believe her ears. Only last night she and Mummy had been talking about the future. They were all so thrilled in Barnet— Mummy and Daddy fancying themselves as grandparents—but Glynis had secretly worried about having to lead the old life with Steven. Now she gasped:

'But, *darling,* will you be happy leading a quieter sort of life without all your smart patients and parties?'

'Yes,' he said, 'I think I shall. It would obviously be silly for me to give up the whole show. You wouldn't want me to. What I

284

suggest is a compromise.'

'Darling, I absolutely agree. I should loathe you to abandon ambition because of me. But what you suggest seems perfect.'

'Well, I certainly wouldn't be much of a father if I remained the old Steven. You were always complaining you never saw enough of me. My child must get to know its father. Yes—my New Year's resolution when the New Year comes will be to develop a liking for domesticity.'

Now they laughed together, but Glynis shook her head.

'You'll never really be domesticated. And I won't let you. I won't be responsible for you feeling bored. But it's a simply gorgeous idea—making ourselves a flat in town, and having that cottage for the week-ends for our child, *and*,' added Glynis, 'you can bet your life little Glyn won't want a Nannie.'

'Children are fine in London up to a point, but I think they need the country,' announced this new Steven.

'Listen to Daddy!' said Glynis and added, choking, 'I'm going to cry.'

'I forbid you to, angel. There's no time. I want you to take down some letters—just for a bit you can become my secretary again. Miss Phillips is too expensive and Grant-Tally has got to cut his cloth according to his means now.'

'I'll go and borrow a pad from one of the

girls in the office,' said Glynis excitedly.

'There's a lot to do,' Steven warned her. 'I want to make an appointment with the chap who did up our house, and find out about the conversion. We should make a handsome profit with a modern flat in that position. There's plenty of room—four bathrooms, too—so it should be easy.'

'Are you going to be fit for all this?' she asked anxiously.

'Fiennes-Garr says I shall be able to start work in the New Year. I'm going to see old Professor Jensen about giving me the research work which I know he will do—he's been trying for a long time to get hold of me, but I've been too busy for him up to now. And, by the way . . .' Steve called Glynis back just as she reached the door.

'Yes, darling?'

'I had a cheque from an unexpected source this morning which will help. A repayment of a debt.'

She gave a little secret smile. She knew when to keep her counsel. Nothing would have induced her to let Steve know that *she* knew about Kitty; and knew, too, that Kitty had sent that cheque. For tomorrow, very quietly, Lady Barley was becoming the Comtesse de Viernot. She was marrying her Jean-Phillipe, and she was going to have all the money in the future that she wanted. But her conscience had dictated that she should repay her brother while he was still in the hospital worrying, as she well knew, about his finances. All that Glynis said to Steve was:

'Jolly good, darling. Now I'll go and get ready to take those letters.'

'Glynis . . .' he called her back again.

'Yes, darling?'

'I'm frightfully thrilled about this child, you know.'

Her heart went out to him. She answered, eyes shining:

'Oh, *darling*, so am I!'

And as she went along the corridor towards the Bursar's office she felt her heart beating with slow strong throbs at the memory of those other words he had just spoken.

'Children are fine in London up to a point, but I think they need the country.'

They had meant more to her than if Steve had told her he had just come into a fortune.

She brushed past Robin Gellow in the corridor. Tall and lanky, wearing a short white coat, he waved his stethoscope at her with a cheerful greeting.

"Morning, Glyn.'

'How's Moira?' she asked.

'Fine. When are you coming to eat with us?'

'As soon as I can.'

'As soon as you can tear yourself away from that husband of yours,' he chaffed her.

That, she thought, as she walked on—*will be never!*

CHAPTER TWENTY-FOUR

If, indeed, variety is the spice of life then it was given to Glynis and Steven in full measure, for innumerable changes were wrought in their particular lives during the next six months.

Just before Christmas a gaunt but a cheerful Steven left the hospital wherein he had once trained—then worked—and later spent so many months as a patient. For the first time since his illness he was able to drive his own car. Glynis sat beside him looking and feeling extremely happy. Half the medical and nursing staff were present to wave good-bye to them and wish them luck.

'It's just as though it's another wedding,' Glynis remarked.

'So it is, my darling,' said Steve, 'and I'm taking you off for another honeymoon.'

It was exactly what Steve's doctors had ordered for him. Rest, change and sea air. And if it were possible—sunshine. This time Glynis could be grateful to one of the wealthy patients who owed much to Steve, and in turn repaid him handsomely. Having learned of the throat specialist's illness, he had offered the Grant-Tallys his villa in the South of France for as long as they wanted it. He himself was away in South Africa. So Glynis had what she called her *real* honeymoon—uninterrupted bliss without subsequent disaster, and no feeling that Steve had to face heavy bills.

There in golden sunshine, wandering like two happy children around an enchanted garden or sitting on the white terrace looking down to a brilliant blue sea, they lazed and laughed and loved through that whole month in Monte Carlo. Steven grew brown and well again, but not quite as strong as he had been before. The long and serious illness had left its mark.

He and Glynis were more in love than ever. They were passionate lovers and excellent comrades. Glynis felt that her whole outlook was changing. She had gained poise and lost much of her timidity—that sense of gaucheness that used to make her wonder in the first place whether or not she should marry the great Mr. Grant-Tally.

Now she knew that he wanted nobody but her. Their compromise was going to be a great success. With him it would merely be a sublimation, Glynis had decided, of his previous ambitions. It was not notoriety he wanted now, or adulation and the fat cheques of the rich. He would work for the love of it, and for what he could give mankind. After that—for enough money to live on comfortably, and ensure the future of his son (for, of course, it was going to be a boy!).

At the end of the second honeymoon, the Grant-Tallys returned to quite a lot of hard work and worry. But Steven, on the advice of his doctors, went slowly and quietly. He had already established himself at regular intervals in the laboratory at St. Martha's. And he had limited the number of patients that he would see at Weymouth Street.

By February, their house had been converted. A regular income ensued from the letting of that top maisonette. Glynis was perfectly satisfied with her new flat. The ex-pensive Austrian cook and her husband had been replaced by an ex-soldier with a slight disability which did not prevent him from working hard. He was to become the joy of Steven's life; both caretaker for the flats at Weymouth Street and general factotum for Steve and Glynis.

Then there was the cottage—oh, that wonderful cottage! Glynis and her mother found it—Steve bought it—and in a very short time it was ready for its owners. Glynis' dream-come-true. A short drive from town, with a view of the rolling Sussex downs, a tiny garden, oak beams and latticed windows. A home that Glynis could run herself, although as the time drew nearer for the baby's birth she had to accept help. But she had entire charge of her little kitchen and there was many a night now when Steven enjoyed food cooked by his own wife, both in the London flat and the cottage. At first it wasn't easy refusing all the invitations that poured in, but Steve was determined not to waste so much time or money on entertaining. He clamped down on it remorselessly. There had to be the odd dinners and lunches that a man in his position must attend or give—but only on occasions.

Steven began to realize that this new, more peaceful and simple existence brought him a contentment he had never known before. He even thrived on it. Particularly at the weekends when he was in that tiny cottage quite alone with Glynis, he found an extraordinary peace of mind as well as body. For the first time in his life he was able to mow his own small lawn and grow his own flowers, and be all the better for the fresh air and exercise.

'What you've taught me to do, my darling, is to relax,' he told Glynis. 'In consequence, I'm sure I shall live twice as long.'

This new quiet joy was crowned by the birth of their son. He arrived quite easily and normally one spring morning in the maternity ward of St. Martha's.

The matter for rejoicing seemed general. When Glynis was able to receive visitors, she chaffed Steven about her flowers. She had as many as *he* had had, she declared, and the whole staff, medical and nursing, popped in frequently to have a look at that wonderful baby.

Steven affirmed that his wife had never looked more beautiful than when she was sitting up in bed with her baby in her arms. She blushed and shook her head, and said:

'No—look at our son—*he's* the beautiful one.'

He had his mother's bright gold hair and his father's handsome features. They were going to call him Charles, which was Mr. Thorne's second name, and, of course, Campion. And there could be no baby in the world quite so wonderful as Charles Campion Grant-Tally.

'Nobody shall look after him but me,' announced his proud young mother.

And she stuck to that, in spite of all the work and washing. She only gave way to Steve sufficiently to accept a 'daily' who took the rough work and the midday cooking off her shoulders.

During that first month after Charles Campion's birth, Mrs. Thorne stayed at the cottage to help, and Glynis' aunt temporarily 'took over' the house at Barnet. Very glad Glynis was to have her mother with her. There was more work than she imagined there could be with a baby in the place (although she would have died rather than admit it to Steven!).

Sylvia Thorne thought the cottage charming and had never seen her daughter look so radiant. But in secret Mrs. Thorne regretted all that Steven had given up.

'Don't you ever miss that old life—it was so wonderful?' she asked Glynis, who promptly answered:

'I certainly don't. If it had been this time a year ago I'd have been wondering where Steve was and when on earth I'd ever get him to myself again. Now I know he'll drive down tonight and we'll have the whole week-end together, and when I'm fit after you've gone, he and I will go up to the flat regularly on Steven's busy days and spend the night there.'

'All this moving about with a baby!' said Mrs. Thorne doubtfully.

But Glynis' eyes danced. She was ironing, while she talked, one of the tiny warm white nightgowns that Charles wore at night.

'I'm a gypsy at heart and I shall enjoy moving about with my baby on my hip,' she giggled, 'and I think it's *good* to get him accustomed to change and noises, and Steve says it won't do him any harm.'

'Well, of course, anything that *Steve* says must be right,' said her mother, and giggled almost as youthfully as her daughter.

Glynis glanced round the room. The May sun slanted through the casements and lit up rosy chintzes and Bristol glass and some of the lovely hand-painted china which they had brought down from town. Even Rhona Chayney would have approved of this lovely little place, Glynis thought proudly; although she mightn't have liked all the bits of sewing and mending hanging around, the domestic touches which, oddly enough, had become quite precious to Steve. Suddenly she said:

293

'If our dear Comtesse and Rhona Chayney could walk in here now wouldn't they look out of place?'

'What has happened to those two?' asked Mrs. Thorne.

'Oh, Kitty writes occasional letters saying what fun it is in Brussels and how she's met the ex-King of the Belgians and never stops having parties and so on and so on—it all sounds *ghastly* to me.'

'And Mrs. Chayney?'

Glynis began to bubble with laughter at the thought of Rhona. She told her mother that Rhona, true to type, had written from New York (she happened to be there when Charles was born) announcing that she intended to be the godmother and was going to bring a magnificent present for the baby back from America.

'Well, now, I think that's very magnanimous of her considering you got the man *she* wanted,' said Mrs. Thorne.

'Dear old Mum!' giggled Glynis again. 'You do fall for it, don't you? *I know* Rhona. She just wants to dip one of her highly manicured fingers into my pie, and she's going to be disappointed, because there will only be one godmother and that will be Alma. Charles doesn't want a wealthy fairy godmother. He wants a good Christian who'll take some interest in his Confirmation!'

'I suppose you're right,' said Mrs Thorne

meekly. But being herself she regretted a little all that Rhona Chayney might have done for Charles with pounds, shillings and pence. She never *had* been able to understand her idealistic Glynis. She had little else to regret, however. She had never seen a happier couple in her life than Glynis and Steven were these days.

She was upstairs with the adored grandson when Steve came back from town.

He came straight into the sitting-room, put an arm round Glynis, and walked with her to the french windows. The sky was blue and the sunshine still quite warm.

'I must cut the grass tomorrow,' said Steven meditatively.

Glynis rubbed her cheek against his arm.

'If you want to see Charles before he goes to sleep, you'd better come up with me now, darling. You remember Mum's going up to town on the seven-five. She wants the week-end with Daddy. You must drive her to the station.'

'Just a moment, sweet, I want to tell you something. You know I have a friend who is the head of one of the big Regional Hospital Boards?' He stopped, and Glynis looked at him enquiringly.

'Yes?'

'Well, he rang me up today and said that a recent death had left a vacancy for one of the most fashionable and highly paid practices in

Belgravia. He thinks I've got the bedside manner and the name and that I might like to chuck what I'm doing and—' But he broke off again. He had seen a look of sheer horror cross Glynis' face.

'*Steve!*' she exclaimed, and put a hand over her mouth.

An imp of mischief entered Steven, who was looking and feeling remarkably well these days.

'Would you like it? Back to a nice big house in a place like Harley Street, and you could have a lot more new dresses, and of course we'd have to get a nurse to take Charles right off your hands.'

'*Steve!*' she interrupted him again and flung herself into his arms. He felt that loyal passionate young heart pounding against his, and stroked the thick fair hair.

'Just like a frightened bird,' he murmured.

Then said Glynis in a small faint voice:

'If it's what you want—*of course*—but Steve—'

He cut her short with a kiss.

'Angel, *never!*' he said. 'I was only pulling your leg. I turned it down. I didn't want the job. I like this quiet two or three days a week in my consulting room and the rest of the time in St. Martha's. The Professor and I are doing some very good work and I think we've hit on something that's going to revolutionize the treatment of mastoid.'

Glynis hugged him, crazy with relief. The happiness had returned to her eyes. She said:

'You *brute* for frightening me! I'm so happy as we are now and I do so want to go on minding Charles myself.'

'So you shall, sweetheart.'

'And are you absolutely sure *you* are happy, too?'

'What do you think?' he whispered, and she was satisfied.

By mutual consent they kissed each other, then walked together up the shining oak stairs to say good night to their son.